THE TRUTH, THE LIE & THE DARE

SINMISOLA OGÚNYINKA

PWG PUBLISHING

Dedicated to
All my Destiny Helpers. Thank you.

Words written on a poster hung against the wall in Chico's office, beside a complicated attendance chart.

ODE ABATTOIR.

OPENS 4.00A.M. CLOSES 4P.M.

OWNER: USMANI V.

HIERARCHY OF OPERATORS:

MASTERS – 100 (RESPONSIBLE FOR CONVEYING THE COWS TO THE ABATTOIR)

BUTCHERS – 300 (KILLING AND SLAUGHTERING THE COW INTO DIFFERENT PARTS)

INSTRUMENTS USED:

BUTCHERING – CUTLASS, ROPES

SLAUGHTERING – CUTLASS, BIG AND SMALL KNIVES

RESIDENT VET DOCTORS:

2 – DR. GODWIN AJAYI DR. NIKE EJI

VISITING VET DOCTORS:

4 – DR. ABAS DR. USHI DR. PEPPLE DR. ISABELLA

PROLOGUE

U SMANI SAW RED! HE sprang up from his rocking seat in spontaneous action, his hand connected with the metal in his belt. The sun set to the east, casting a growing shadow on the tropical climate of cool harmattan evening. His mother screamed at him to stop and he did, just in time. He stole a glance at the knife in his hand, raised above his head, and clenched in his fist till his skin seemed like it would burst along the veins. His breathing, uneven and despite his attempts to calm down, soughed.

His father stopped short when Usmani charged from the seat, the long belt Papa held against his fleeing mother, dropped on impulse.

"You'll leave my house. Now you'll leave my house," Papa mumbled in rigid control.

"Ha, Papa Usmani. Please I beg you. Don't, please." Mama slid to her knees at the corner of the backyard where she had run in from their one-room accommodation a few seconds earlier, disturbing his oft solitude.

His breathing slowed and he lowered the knife. A gust of wind blew in his direction carrying with it the familiar smell of cow dung. He inhaled, involuntarily.

Nothing more needed to be said.

He walked toward the house, tucking his knife in his belt. He was going to leave anyway. It would happen sometime. If not now, when? When his control slipped and he stabbed his abusive father to death?

His mother sobbed his name and he stopped just at the entrance of their trashy dwelling. He turned to look at her.

"Come with me." He heard himself say. It did not make any sense. He did not have a place to go—oh, of course, there was the one place but he couldn't cater for more than himself there.

"Go with him," Papa said. "You won't last long here anyway."

Mama wept. Papa snarled. Usmani left.

News of his Mama's death reached him a week later.

CHAPTER ONE

CHRISTINE'S EXPERIENCE OF ODE Abattoir began on what seemed to be a typical day but the weather diverged when it was too late to turn back, for the better though. More vehicles became available to transport people. The wet weather debarred many from heading toward the abattoir. She'd heard on a dry day, the whole town headed west to the same place she now had the pleasure, or otherwise to visit. She'd told herself it was an exaggeration but with the crowd, she met on this rainy day, it couldn't have been truer.

The abattoir was situated outside of town, a good five kilometres from the first sign of civilization. But it had become a city on its own. Approaching it were small shops by the roadside with food sellers, provisions stores, juice and drinks stores displayed wares on both sides of the road. The slaughterhouse itself spanned over a large expanse of land ten hectares the records stated, with at least two small settlements on the premises, and lots of unclaimed land over and yonder.

The hustle and bustle around the grounds impressed Christine. She took note of everything. People moved like they'd lived all their lives in this environment and Christine looked to see faces of newcomers like her. There seemed to be none. One or two familiar faces bumped into her and exchanged pleasantries.

At the taxi stop, where several other taxis were arriving and leaving, shuttle tricycles waited to convey passengers to other locations.

Christine walked up to one of the drivers and asked for directions to the main abattoir. The driver told her to take a seat. The near-free ride surprised Christine. Was there a place you could still get such a cheap ride in this life? Cool. Well, niceties were not meant to move her here.

At yet another stop just about half a kilometre from the entrance, the tricycle stopped and offloaded its five passengers in a hurry.

Right before the terminus, were giant slabs with more than ten cows laid on their sides. It was the beginning of lots of lessons for Christine. Initially, there was no one on the slabs with the cows. The crowd pressed around each and Christine noticed there were four others at a close distance. Each of them had people surrounding them like the one she stood close to. There were cows laid on the clean massive concretes but no men. Christine fought the urge to ask where the butchers were. It was quite early and though she'd been told to get here very early—earlier than she believed was necessary, she was glad she heeded this piece of advice.

At about ten minutes to six, the butchers trooped in and, began to climb with their knives. More than ten strong-looking men on each slab. Within minutes, blood was flowing all over the blocks.

Christine stepped back a little as the lookers pressed against her. She brought out her pen and notepad and took some notes. Boys ranging between the ages five and fifteen walked bare-footed along the narrow aisles created by the dying cows, with small kegs which they tilted toward the knife wounds on the animals. To Christine's dismay, they collected the blood.

She also noticed the speed and accuracy of the butchers. They worked as though being conducted and within minutes, were all straightening or dismantling the cows.

With profound interest, Christine noticed the haggling women. They had tremendous strength on their muscled arms and legs, and climbed on to the bloody slabs, picking dissected cow in bits, the hunchback, and other parts, dripping and delicately slung. Younger men climbed on as well, heaving heavy portions on their backs like the thighs and arms, the back side, removing them to the different shops. Everything was done like clockwork with speed, concentration and aptitude.

Gradually, the slabs cleared, and the shops filled. The offal was removed. Then the cow tail and cow legs. And then there were just the heads and three butchers cutting them apart.

The blood had been left to flow through a gutter to a covered tank. Christine made some notes and when she looked up, a weather-beaten woman in her mid-twenties or early thirties—hard to tell, stared at her. Her stocky build stood just a couple of inches taller than Christine's 5'5. Her fair complexioned skin was firm and fresh despite the sort of job she obviously did. The sleeveless dress shirt she wore exposed part of her full bosom. She wore black leggings and carried a pouch over what Christine realised was a half-apron.

"You go buy meat?" she said.

"Yes. Small sha." Christine said, tucking her pen and paper back in her bag.

"Which part you go like? I get liver and kidney and shaki," she said, enthusiastic about making sales.

"I'll just buy small liver and maybe lungs. Do you have lungs?" The way she asked made the lady smile. Christine got the joke and laughed.

"My lungs fine well well," the lady said and headed into one of the already packed full stable-like shops.

The women sold in retail while the men sold wholesale. One or two women crossed the wholesale boundary while most of them bought and resold special parts like the hunchback, offal, cow tail, and skin. Above the quibbling crowd, Christine and the lady pushed to the end of the shop where offal was scattered by parts close to the edge of a big table.

She brought up a big chunk of liver and another of lungs. Christine laughed.

"That would be too much for me." She smiled. "I live alone." The lady stared at her as though she did not understand. Christine shrugged. "Cut it into four and give me a part each."

"I no dey sell like that. I sell big big. You go get small from another person o." She dropped the lungs.

"I want to be your customer now," Christine said, wooing. "Sell for me, abeg."

"Na wa o, madam." She put her knife, which she produced from within the clutter of offal where Christine had not noticed, and slashed the flesh in one swipe. She threw it aside narrowly avoiding the other. She did the same for the other offal and called some cheap price. Christine gasped before smiling.

"Less it small for me," she said, not sure the bargain would pull through.

To her surprise, the lady reduced the price by a fraction. She packed it with alacrity, already looking to another woman walking toward her. Christine thanked her and collected the pack after paying.

"Please I want to ask you—"

"Madam, check here," the meat lady cut her off so, she stepped aside.

Before she knew it, another customer, an elderly woman, picked up the parts she left. She stood aside and watched as the old woman bargained and bought the larger chunk at just about the price Christine had just bought hers. "A man is not cheated if he is satisfied with the price" the saying dropped in her mind and she consoled herself.

"Who is the owner of this place, please?" she asked as the meat lady moved out toward the open where buyers still loitered.

"Why you want see am?" she counter-asked.

Christine pushed through the crowd to the open space in a bid to catch up with her. "I'm a student doing research and I want to ask him questions."

"He no dey. Go ask Bala over there." She pointed at a stumpy, rugged-looking, dark-skinned man who was surprisingly well-dressed in a flowing white caftan and cap. Christine nodded her thanks and walked over to the man.

Bala was not as educated as he looked, and he spoke with a deep, accented voice. But he was quite knowledgeable about the workings of the abattoir. Christine scribbled till her fingers were tired and she had to flex them several times. After what seemed like an age, Bala shrugged and told her this was all he knew.

"If you want more, only Chico can tell you. And he doesn't talk much."

"That's the owner of the abattoir, right?" Christine wondered what else was there to know. She had filled four pages.

Bala sneered. "I am the owner. You may call him the manager."

Christine took a deep breath, conscious of her environment. "Of course. Where is he?"

He shrugged and sniffed. "Killing somewhere I believe."

"Would you take me to him?"

"Of course," he said but made no move.

"Well?"

"I need to make sure this place is all cleared up before I leave here," he said, waving his fat hands through the air in front of her.

Christine wondered at his change of mood and body language. Just before she asked about the Chico's position, he had been cooperative. Now he shrugged, sniffed, and shoved his hands in his pockets. She looked around. Five slabs cleared but not nearly for her. This place could mean anything. Clearing up this place could be more time than she had to spare.

"Do you think you can describe where he is to me?" Christine pressed.

"What more do you want to know anyway?" he snapped. "I have told you everything except the man's salary." He chuckled at what he must think a joke.

Christine shrank back at his charge. "Well, you have tried. Thank you. You made it look like there was more to tell."

"Bye bye. Student." He walked away with a scowl on his face.

He yelled at the top of his voice to a young boy and the latter ran off to do his bidding. One of the butchers shouted a question at him and he got angry with the man after glancing to see if Christine was looking his way.

Who couldn't pose? She wondered with a smile. Leaving Bala's authoritative voice behind, she walked around the abattoir, making notes and ticking off facts she'd collected from him. He was accurate on most.

The slabs on which the cows were slaughtered had narrow gutters channelled to the septic tanks and these were drained daily to prevent decomposition of blood and faeces. Christine made a note to invite the services of the waste management board and the naval waste disposal tanks in disposal of pollutants, if they were not already involved. Bala did say they had people come to flush the gutters once a week. Once a week? Not often enough to make more inquiries about waste disposal, she wrote in front of the detail.

For most of the rest of the time, she bothered no one. She wasn't sure she could take pictures, but she moved toward the septic tank. It wasn't properly covered, and some stench came from it. She moved away, careful not to sink her feet in the mushy sand around it.

This butchery stank if ever there was a better way to describe it. She scribbled more on her notepad and walked back to the exit. She would need to come back and see the owner of this abattoir. Not Bala.

⚬❧⚬

Chico Ode stood at the entrance of his shop and followed the little lady with an eagle eye. He missed nothing in this place. It's what made him and kept him the owner of Ode Abattoir. She stood out as a sore thumb anyway. Dressed like she was off to the beach in jeans and t-shirt, and sneakers. Though of course, several women dressed the same.

On weekdays like this, many women came to the slaughter early enough to buy their meat before going to work. And Chico saw most of them. Many were regular people. They dashed in once a month, or bi-monthly bought large chunks, and rushed off. Some called to place their orders and then drove in or sent their drivers to pick them up. And many were new. He noticed almost all the new ones almost all the time.

But this was a first. A little lady with a pen and pad, walking to the edge of the septic tank and scribbling furiously? He sent for Bala as the latter paddled away from her to continue his inspection.

"What does she want?" he said. He didn't need to say who. Bala knew him well.

"Na student wey dey do research," Bala said in broken English.

"I see," Chico said, without taking his eyes off her.

He hated anyone snooping around his territory. He sent Bala away with a curt nod and continued to watch the student till she entered a tricycle and rode away from his land. He didn't think he'd seen the last of her, though.

CHAPTER TWO

C HRISTINE WAS BURIED IN her research work when her phone rang. Since the beginning of the week, she had worked on her findings at the abattoir. She realised to her dismay no organised body discharged waste at the place. The urban development agency was not even involved in any way. Which was so strange. How could this be? The local government authorities had no records either. Though it had been a month since she visited, she had just reached the concluding stages of her report and would then have to formulate her plans to correct all the wrongdoing at the abattoir.

"Hello, good morning?" She spoke in clipped tones. "Research department, Christine Bello speaking."

"Hello, Ms. Bello. I'm calling from the naval force headquarters with regards to your query about waste disposal?" the deep voice said.

"Yes, please. My specific inquiry is on Ode Abattoir," Christine said, her pencil poised to take notes.

"We did get a request from them to assist with their waste, but we referred them to the ministry of environment since the abattoir does not host any of the military concerns," the man said. "You know naval presence here is base."

Christine gasped. "Oh."

She thought Bala mentioned naval intervention. She'd been checking up on his facts and figures anyway, and they led her to the naval headquarters. The Navy was not so visible in Ode town. They only had a small camp because of the Ode River, which somewhere went into the Atlantic Ocean.

"Yeah," the man said softly. "Christine?"

"Yes, please." She wondered why the man switched to her first name.

"You don't seem to remember me?" he said, then paused. "Lt. Cdr. Ayo Lawrence."

"Oh, of course. How are you?" Christine said with a genuine, apologetic smile translated to her voice. "I'm very poor with voices, I'm sorry."

"You don't need to apologise." There was laughter in his voice also. "Ode Abattoir requested for our services from the onset, and they were promptly referred." He switched back to business. "I believe you can have access to the files."

"Okay. I'll let you know if I need more details."

"You still have my card?"

"Yes, I do. And I'll just store your number right away."

"I'll appreciate that," he said. "And a call with your mobile too." His call came through her office number, which was the only number she gave on official duty.

Christine liked to maintain official protocols.

"Well, Lt—"

He chuckled. "You can call me Ayo—off duty of course."

"Sure. Thanks for your kindness," she said.

"Thank you."

"Bye." She hung up after his soft reply.

She didn't realise the pencil she held still dangled in her hand long after the call ended. An officer and a gentleman. He would eventually speak what she had coming.

When she'd met him at the naval base, he had glared at her, and made intermittent easy but silent insinuations. Now she could call him 'Ayo' off duty. He was a good-looking guy anyway, which wasn't bad at all, considering being an officer as well. Christine laughed.

Her love life had had its adventures until recently she found herself alone. Not that she didn't want a relationship, but the right person had not come along yet. With her recent promotion at work, she hoped she could start to date again.

Christine searched out Ayo Lawrence's card from her cardholder and stared at it with a lazy smile. He wasn't bad at all. Public relations officer in the navy. Courteous, respectful, and handsome. Her heart thudded and she tucked the card away. She could see herself with this man.

"We'll see how that goes," she mumbled and turned back to her work.

Her colleague and friend, Tolani, peeped through the door and walked in. Christine's face lit up.

"Hey girlfriend! Didn't know you were back."

Christine arched her eyebrow. "Back from?"

Tolani folded her arms across her chest. "The slaughters."

"I stopped going since last month—though I've been roaming. Girl, this country is messy."

"That's why we're here to clean it," Tolani said, referring to the ministry of environment, their workplace.

"Yeah, right." Christine smiled. "I've just been looking through my research and putting the reports together. Ode slaughter is in deep shit."

"Literally." Tolani laughed. "What did you find?" She sat on the edge of her friend's table and considered the documents in front of Christine.

Tolani worked in internal audit but had been friends with Christine ever since they both first got employed in the ministry. Over the years, they'd both grown. Christine went on to get her master's degree, while Tolani got her ICAN, and both rose in their ranks. Tolani, two years older than Christine, had gotten married shortly after getting the job, to her high school sweetheart, Abbey Okueko, who worked as a construction engineer and was often out of town.

"Ode does not have records at all in urban development. Neither do they have here in waste department. They just are non-existent."

"How is that possible?" Tolani said. "Where do they keep all the cow dung?"

"Beats me. I may have to organise a raid. But I'll have to go there again and meet the owner."

"You haven't met him? How did you get your figures?"

Christine remembered Bala and smiled. "I met one egomaniacal fellow. I'm sure all his facts are wrong, but he had a good command of the knowledge he passed on. According to him, even the navy helps them to clean up."

"Really?"

"No evidence. No one seems to know about Ode Abattoir's waste management." Christine closed her file with a sigh. "You know, when these new files came to me, I just had this feeling I needed to check things out on my own." She sighed. "I hate to admit it but the guy who did this job before me should be fired."

"He was promoted and transferred to the federal capital."

Christine grunted. "Hmm."

Her new position as senior research officer had placed all the major factories, markets, and large business premises in the local government under her supervision. She had drawn up a schedule and gone to visit them one by one, sometimes undercover as she did with the abattoir, her last port of call.

"Well, you're the new senior research officer. All the dirt in Ode is on your shoulder."

Christine rolled her eyes. "Not if I can help it. Everyone waits on me. Even my director."

"Especially your director. He knows you're the best fit for the job. Are you doing the undercover thing you considered?"

"I think it would work. Before everyone in Ode town hear my story."

"Ode is a small town. I don't know how you plan to pull off fooling these people. Most of them know you."

"As my father's daughter but nothing more at best."

Tolani snickered. "It would be funny if the abattoir man knew you from Adam."

Christine shrugged. "I'll ensure I meet him tomorrow and then I can finalise my report and know the next line of action. And if he happens to know me by some chance, I'll tell him Bala was hallucinating."

They both laughed.

"I wish you luck. So, what's with you, girl?" Tolani chuckled. "Saffron is grouchy about your promotion."

Christine groaned. "Saffron is grouchy about everything where I'm concerned. How did you know?"

"I met her at the mall. She was heavy-shopping."

"She's always heavy-shopping when she's at the mall. And what was her grouch?"

"Your working hours."

"Really?" They laughed again.

Tolani stood. "I was just passing by. Let me get back to the pile on my table."

Christine rested back. "Thanks for popping in."

At the door, Tolani turned. "Freebies for adults at Toke's birthday. Sure you don't wanna come?"

"Oh." Christine laughed. "Don't tell me you're scouting for adult audience."

Tolani gasped in fake surprise. "Well, just nice adults."

Her five-year-old daughter, Toke, was going to have a big birthday party just a month away and she had tried without success to drag Christine to come along.

"That reminds me, meat at Ode abattoir is sold for pittance. You won't believe the bargain," Christine said.

"We'll go shopping together close to the time," Tolani said.

"That would make me want to come for the party—not so?" Christine winked. "I'll bring Saffron along."

"Wouldn't you love to?" Her friend closed the door behind her, her soft chuckles carried along the corridor.

Tolani knew Christine was squeaky around children's parties, and Saffron would never attend with her.

Christine had a smile on her face when she turned back to look at the abattoir file. She decided to pay a visit. It was just about ten in the morning. The abattoir should be clearing by now from the morning rush. She could meet the owner there. Better get this done with. She picked her handbag and locked up her office. At the reception, she left the message she'd gone for field inspections.

As a newly promoted senior officer, she was entitled to a utility vehicle. But though it had been approved, she was yet to get the truck and driver, so she took the same alternative she'd taken previously, public transportation. She wasn't ready to risk driving her small car uphill on bad road.

The weather was good, and the journey went smoothly. Ode abattoir was winding down as she'd thought when Christine got there fifty minutes later. Most of the shops now had retail meat. The slabs were being cleared of the residue of slaughtering, scrubbed with strong scouring brushes.

Christine walked around a bit, noting workmen and butchers who simply focused on what they do. She walked to the drains and followed it to the end where the septic tank was located. Bala came up behind her, startling her.

"Student! You have come back?"

"Yes, I was hoping to—"

"Chico wants to see you in his office now."

"The owner of the abattoir?" she said impulsively and then shook her head at Bala's expression. "Oh yes, sorry. I forgot you are the owner."

"No one told you that," Bala murmured, and snapped, "Come with me."

Christine followed without comment. No use rubbing his ego.

Chico's office sat at the centre of the abattoir, an odd edifice amid grits. She had noticed the bungalow in passing, wondering what it was. A rectangular building painted a dirty brown with reflexive windows, she'd had a strange feeling it was someone's residence, as ridiculous as this sounded.

Christine stood stock still inside the office, amazed by the unexpected size of the room and classy furnishing. A cross between living room and office, to the left were two couches, a TV set, and a small refrigerator. Colours didn't seem much of a conceptual thing for the Ode Abattoir owner. There were browns and greys and blacks. The air conditioner must have been turned to the coolest. She shuddered.

To the immediate right was an impressively large chopping board on four legs with an extensive washbasin and an assortment of knives, kitchen gadgets and cleaning agents and then a surprising work desk at the extreme opposite corner. A large orange dart board with a knife sticking in the centre hung on half of the wall facing the work desk. Beside the dartboard, just by the door, was a blackboard with a complicated attendance chart. Beside that was a poster with information on the abattoir.

ODE ABATTOIR.
OPENS 4.00A.M. CLOSES 4P.M.
OWNER: USMANI V.
HIERARCHY OF OPERATORS:
MASTERS – 100 (RESPONSIBLE FOR CONVEYING THE COWS TO THE ABATTOIR)

BUTCHERS – 300 (KILLING AND SLAUGHTERING THE COW INTO DIFFERENT PARTS)
INSTRUMENTS USED:
BUTCHERING – CUTLASS, ROPES
SLAUGHTERING – CUTLASS, BIG AND SMALL KNIVES
RESIDENT VET DOCTORS:
2 – DR. GODWIN AJAYI DR. NIKE EJI
VISITING VET DOCTORS:
4 – DR. ABAS DR. USHI DR. PEPPLE DR. ISABELLA

For a moment, Christine glared at the poster, taking in the information given with preciseness. Chico stood at the work desk holding three thin knives, much like the one sticking in the dart board. When Bala closed the door behind him, Chico walked to the wash basin, dropped the knives on the chopping board and ran water over his hands. He took a dishcloth close by, and moved forward to welcome his visitors, his face bland.

Christine was shocked at the slight but muscled frame of the abattoir owner. He was a calloused man, with lines on his face like someone who had seen a lot in life. It was difficult to place his age between thirty and forty. He could be older, Christine thought. His unsmiling eyes glanced her, making her feel small.

Though she was used to facing off men in her profession, Ode Abattoir owner was notably imposing. An arched eyebrow sent Bala scuttling off, mumbling he had to get back to work. Christine shrank inward intimidated by his levelled gaze. He was tall, not for a man though, maybe four or five inches taller than her, and to her surprise, good-looking.

For a moment, they just stared at each other. He was assessing her. And she wondered what he may have heard about her.

He did not keep her in suspense much longer.

"They tell me you are a student of abattoirs?" he said in a questioning manner.

"Yes—sir." Christine was supposed to be commanding and demanding as an environmental officer, but she was undercover, and she had to be the part. "I'm doing my project on waste management in Ode Abattoir."

Three chairs faced the work desk but Chico didn't invite her to sit.

"And nothing told you you ought to take permission before you start on your fact-researching about Ode?" he said.

She was petit, he was close to a head taller than her, maybe more, yet after the once-over he gave her, he didn't look at her again. Instead, he gazed above her head. Christine, on the other hand had the opportunity to assess him. She couldn't ponder on her initial shock just yet.

"I'm sorry," she said.

He walked toward her menacingly and she stepped back in fear just before he brushed past and walked out of the office without taking an excuse. Christine blinked in astonishment. She followed him out through the door and watched him stride toward one of the slabs—and that's when her mouth fell open.

A man tied with ropes around his neck, hands and feet, was pulled to one of the not-yet-cleared slabs. Three men on the slab dragged their meat aside as the bound man was made to step on it. Chico got to the slab in easy strides. Christine walked out to the open space to see what this was about. She didn't hear anything said but in a swift movement, Chico slapped the bound man, once and the man fell flat on his back. Christine had never seen anything so menacing.

When Chico had stood in front of him, it had been obvious the stocky man was taller but the impact of the slap made Christine shudder and the bound man, fall. Just as calmly as he'd left her in his office, Chico walked back. When he got close to her, she shivered and gawked.

There wasn't indifference on his face he had a scowl, though a subtle one. His eyes were remarkable, dark and deep. He didn't have a single strand of hair on his head, or face except for the thick dark eyebrows and long silky lids. The baldness suited him well. His nose, slightly flared to show his displeasure had a subtle crook. His mouth was—well. Full, delicious-looking dark lips, which was now pressed grimly.

The attractive features sat on an oblong face, firm jaws, hard chin with a cleft, and medium-shaped ear now seemed flattened. He had wide, stiff shoulders, and lean but well-toned muscles, which his white shirt and black trousers hugged as though tailored to fit him. He wore black boots. His dressing for a butcher spoke volumes about his taste.

The muscles on his face twitched as he got closer to her and feeling juvenile, she ran back into his office, shaking.

"Do you have a letter from your school?" he said coolly, walking over to the sink to wash his hands, generous with the water.

"Yes?" He turned to look at her, drying his hands for the second time since she met him.

Her face must have paled to a great extent. He arched his eyebrow, which she noticed was not only thick, but well-shaped.

"You killed the man," she said, her voice hoarse.

CHAPTER THREE

HE DID NOT PAUSE for a breath before he broke into a slow grin, which made him more handsome if this was possible. The smile relaxed the muscles of his face, and his eyes softened.

"What business is it of yours?" he said with laughter in his voice.

Christine looked back toward the slab, the bound man lay still where he'd fallen from the one slap. Men milled around but no one took any notice of him. His accusers had deserted him and the butchers on the slab resumed their work. Buyers haggled as though the man was part of the concrete.

To her dismay, tears fell from her eyes. She wanted to say something, but words failed her coupled with the embarrassment of the moment. He mocked her.

"I can't believe this," he muttered. "What's your name, and where's your authorisation?"

Christine fumbled in her bag and brought out a letter from a hoax private university somewhere in the north. No such school existed but then she didn't expect a butcher would know much about it. She was surprised though at his polished accent-less pronunciation, and the mere fact that he'd asked for the letter. She handed it to him and cleaned her face, smearing her makeup. She didn't care. She hoped to be out of the abattoir within minutes. Reflexively she turned to look at the man on the slab again. Could just that slap have killed such a hunky man?

"Christine," he said so softly she almost didn't hear, and the softness hit her harder than if he'd shouted at her. "Who are you? And what do you want?"

"I'm a student." She sucked in her breath. "That's my letter."

He narrowed his eyes. "Can I see your I.D?"

"Yes sir," she said and opened her bag.

The only I.D she carried had the name and emblem of the Federal Ministry of Environment. It was newly done and her new post as a senior research officer written on it in gold. She didn't think it a good idea to let him see it. She rummaged through the bag and as she thought of doing something else to distract herself and the man glaring at her, a disturbance was heard outside.

A big pig with terrible knife wounds ran wild despite its bleeding. The sight of blood, plus her fragile emotions triggered an attack she just thought of faking. Chico left the side of his work desk, where he had stood and headed for the door, only to turn in time to see her wheezing, and fumbling for something in her bag.

He squeezed his face and stopped his advance, as she grabbed her inhaler and puffed three times in quick succession. She found a seat then and lowered herself into it. She felt weak. Recently, her ailment had been controlled but still unusual emotions and excitements triggered her asthma attacks.

⇜⇝

Chico left her and walked out to see to the unrest. He pushed away thoughts of her, having an attack in his office, the look in her eyes—the eyes. They were the most beautiful he had ever seen. A bit watery perhaps from her asthma attack but it only added to the appeal. And her lips, and her throat where the pulse throbbed. He focused his mind on the crisis at hand.

The pig butchers managed to wrestle and finished it off on the slab just next to the near-dead man. Chico stole a quick glance back toward his office and the 'little' girl inside. Thankfully, her back was to the drama with her head bowed.

How many things would happen today, he wondered? The day had started for him quite uneventfully. Now he had an idiot faking death and a sickly emotionally unbalanced student on his hand. He didn't talk but the rigidity of his stance got the pig butchers scuttling off, mumbling their apology and excusing a first-timer. Chico let it pass.

He leaped on to the slab and stood beside the bound man. Without saying a word to him, the man sat up. One side of his face was a tad swollen, the eye bloodshot, and his lip cut. Clumsily, he dragged himself to his feet and jumped down the slab. His jailers came and pulled him away by the neck, much as they dragged the cows they slaughtered.

One of the resident vets, Godwin Ajayi, a handsome, haughty-looking fresh graduate who had done his youth service at the abattoir and decided to stay back and work a little more with the animals, walked up to him.

"New stock. I haven't had time to see to them, mad pigs," the vet said.

Chico scowled. "It must never happen again. A pig has no business running around my abattoir with a knife wound."

"Yessir!" He gave a mock salute. Chico turned away from him to return to the office and he followed. "I see you have a guest—"

"Go back to work, doc. I don't want to fire you."

The doctor stopped following him.

His eyes flared. "And do whatever you want, but I'm not selling a pig not checked. You pass it on."

Christine was bent over on her seat with beads of sweat on her forehead. She dragged in a breath, filling her lungs.

Chico returned to his office, looking miffed. "What triggered it?"

She shook her head. "Fear, I think."

He blinked. "Are you alright now?"

She nodded. There was a tilt to his lips like he would laugh but had it under control.

He stretched his hand toward her. "So, let me have your I.D."

"I don't have it I'm sorry—" She wasn't just a senior research officer, she was trained. Trained to research, undercover and otherwise. Trained to act. Trained to lie. Trained to take advantage. She looked straight into his eyes. "It must be in my folder. I'm sorry. I have been moving around a lot—"

He perched on his worktable and stared right back into her eyes. "Doing what?"

"Preparing for my project, getting permission here and there."

He sat for a bit without looking at the letter in his hand, just staring at her, studying her. Her gaze faltered and she looked away. She mustn't be too confident since she posed as a student who was close to being frustrated. She was impressed and surprised to find him so educated, and so young. She had expected to see a complete illiterate only good with his figures. And someone much older.

This was far from it. He had a good command of English. His speech was polished. And he dressed like a professional.

"I want to see it," he said quietly, and flung the letter on to his desk. "I need some identification. National I.D.? Drivers' license, or passport? And I would want to see your student I.D."

She stood. "I spoke with Bala the last time I came, and he helped me. I was just tidying up on my notes," she said. "I'll take my leave now." She headed for the door.

"Not so fast," he called to her and she halted. "Your letter needs to be confirmed. I'm going to call your school now, while you're still here."

She turned to him fully and shrugged. He read the letter and picked his phone. Her director's number was on the letterhead. He would pick the phone and tell him what he wanted to hear. After a few minutes on the call, he hung up.

"What information do you want?" He squinted his eyes. She noticed how remarkable they were.

"I have all the information I need. I was just trying to tidy up," she said again.

"Who gave you the right to gather information on my property?"

"Bala," she snapped but more softly added, "Mr. Bala."

"I want to see your project before you submit it," he said.

She turned to leave. "Okay, sir."

"And for your info, the man didn't die," he said to her back with some laughter in his voice.

She swirled around and glared at him. His laughter preceded her as she rushed out of his office.

Christine didn't know any other way out of the slaughter, or she would not have passed by the dreaded slab but she was glad the fallen man was no longer there. She felt he must have ordered them to remove his 'remains'. She hesitated by the slab but what could she do?

Men washing the slab ignored her. What had she come here to do? To meet the owner of Ode Abattoir and try and get more information? Well, she did not need any more information. The brute was not worthy of any other form of treatment than the one her 'raid crew' carried out.

She stumbled on a lose pebble and yelped in anticipation of a fall but caught herself before she hit the ground. Her humiliation was profound. She felt as though she had been stripped. Well, her raid was no longer an official task. She took his rudeness and deliberate pursuit of her disgrace personally. She couldn't wait till he got to know who she really was. Her revenge would be sweet.

Christine was still fuming when she got to her office well after noon. She picked her files and marched to her director's office. He would be expecting an update anyway. She had hoped to get some justification from the rude Chico on why there were no records of their environmental protection and waste management with any of the approved environmental agencies, or the department itself.

Many business owners preferred to make private arrangements which were not up to the standard of the department which cost much less and were not as stringent. But the government had propagated the law for all waste management issues to pass through the department and approved agencies and companies. The streets were cleaner and safer from pollutants ever since government clamped down on the laws. If Chico Ode wanted to be devious, then he had another think coming. Again, she wondered what her predecessor had been doing.

The director of waste and environmental management was a veteran in waste management business. A career civil servant of the old stock, one of the few and rare leaders in the business, after graduating with a first-class degree in environmental protection and management, he had gone ahead to run a small business in his field before joining the civil service after which he went back to get a Masters' degree and then a doctorate. After putting in over twenty years and mentoring hundreds of men and women, he was the most respected public servant in his area of specialisation and had become an oracle in waste management. After receiving a chieftaincy title in his village a couple of years earlier, every one switched to calling him 'chief' even in the office.

Chief sat behind his desk, talking to two of the schools' inspection officers when Christine all but barged in. He waved her to a seat but finished with the middle-aged women first.

"Yes, my research student." He turned to her as the ladies left. "I got a call from the abattoir," he said, tongue-in-cheek.

"Yes sir. He said he wanted to call to verify I was a student." She breathed in, trying to calm down. "We're closing down the slaughter." She thrust the file before him, pointing at it shakily. "It's all in there."

He looked at her before opening the file. "Your recommendation?"

"Yes sir." She nodded, convinced. "They are barbaric and have no waste management plan."

Chief gasped. "That can't be possible. They slaughter more than a hundred cows every week."

"Every day, sir. They slaughter an average of forty to fifty cows, and who knows how many pigs and goats. They serve four local government areas and part of others in the neighbourhood, but they virtually rinse their waste down a drain."

"What?" Chief almost came out of his seat. "Impossible."

"A place as big as that and the department does not have any records on them. Urban development does not, neither does the navy. I called our approved agencies and companies. None. No one does any business with them."

"My goodness." Chief looked strung up. "Do you know what you're saying?"

"They are so far from civilisation everyone virtually has left them to their own."

"No, I don't think so. I think we just believe they should know what to do and to do the right thing after we sent out the communiqué." Chief opened the file. "I was worried the management of the abattoir would not understand it but going from the way the man sounded on the phone, he seems knowledgeable. The poor old bastard must think he is very smart."

Christine almost said he wasn't old at all but swallowed her comment.

"So get the raid team together. We should visit them tomorrow morning," Chief said.

She stood, satisfied. "Yes sir."

"I'll look through your file and if I have any further comments, I'll let you know. Otherwise, go ahead," Chief said.

"Yes sir."

"Thank you."

CHAPTER FOUR

O DE ABATTOIR WOKE UP at 4a.m. The butchers collected and sharpened their knives and the masters allotted slabs. Butchers had permanent locations except where there was a vacancy or extra hands would be needed. Most of the time, everyone remained on their slabs.

Chico did a walk round before the butchers gathered. He'd do a head count of the cattle to be slaughtered every morning at three. After getting their allocated spaces, the butchers indulged in a ritual of drinking so early in the morning. Some eat a light meal but most just shack up with alcohol in preparation for the day's work.

Chico had insisted they had their bath before climbing the slabs, so they troop to the public bathrooms on the ranch and clean up. The slaughter boys walked the cows out to the slabs, and the butchers filed out at almost six o'clock. Within minutes, blood began to flow.

It wasn't a typical day at the abattoir. At about quarter after five o'clock, shortly after the butchers got finished with filing their knives, two army trucks drove into the premises, seizing the activities and ordering the butchers out.

The leader of the band was a stoic looking soldier, with a huge build. He couldn't have any senior rank in the army, but he took his job seriously. Ode Abattoir was on a large expanse of land, but the soldiers had full control within minutes. Especially since no one showed any signs of resistance.

Chico had just finished dressing up and came out to the slaughter yard to see what the fuss was all about. The day had only just started. He stared at the soldiers for only a second before he knew who to walk up to. The soldier was half a head taller than Chico and much heavier.

"Good morning, officer. My name is Chico Ode. How may I be of help?" Chico said assimilating the attitude of his confused butchers and masters, the stern soldiers surrounding them, the trucks, the weapons—

"We are shutting down the abattoir by order from the ministry of environment task force," the soldier said stiffly.

It had never happened before in all his years of butchering. Chico looked into the man's eyes as he spoke. "Do you have an explanation for it?" he said, just as stiff and unfriendly.

"Go to the ministry of environment. Task force unit. They would give you your explanation. My job is to close this place down." He turned away rudely and shouted at the men. "Man the exits till I give you further orders." The men responded with a loud 'yessir' and went into position.

The 'nameless' soldier marched back to the first truck and got in, speaking to a couple of the soldiers as he went. Chico stood looking at them, a mixture of emotions running through him. He couldn't even understand where this was coming from.

Bala walked quietly up to him accompanied by other masters. "Oga, what is the meaning of this?"

Ejiro, another master shrugged. "It has never happened before in my life. What is this?"

"Let us call DPO Ojo. He would deal with all this at once," Okey, another master said and made to move.

"No." Chico stopped him. "This is not police matter. I'll go and see them at the ministry. Calm the men down. Tell them to go home to their families. They should not make any trouble with the soldiers. The slaughter boys and stable men should be given supplies for the cows. Do we have any special orders today?" He knew the answer to that, anyway. He had all the orders for a month in his head.

"Chief Aliyu's father's burial is this weekend. We should deliver five cows—slaughter and deliver," Bala said.

"Call them. We would slaughter in their compound or anywhere they want. If they don't have a venue, call the barracks at Oke-ido. Ask them to let a slab to us. Take care of the other orders and the regulars. If you have any questions or challenges, call me," he said.

"What about the other slabs at the piggery and goat farm? And the—" Ejiro started to ask.

"We have been shut down. I declare holiday for Ode Abattoir," Chico announced, raising his voice.

The men laughed. They thought that was funny, but Chico found nothing amusing. The town would practically shut down. Meat would not be in the market today. Few sellers would travel the several miles to Oke-ido to buy and return to sell at ridiculously high prices. There was nothing funny about Ode having a holiday, even for one day. Chico had never had a holiday, never seen an abattoir closed, and not one like Ode which served several local governments because they were the biggest and the cheapest. People travelled a hundred miles at times to Ode.

Okey looked worried. "The customers?"

"The task force, I'm sure would send them back," Chico said.

He had talked too much already. He left the murmuring and grumbling behind and walked back into his office to prepare for whatever this was.

Bala was chewing on kola and spitting it as he spoke. "Go organise your men. You heard Chico say there is holiday," he said.

The men continued to cluster, and murmur. Chico was the most upright businessman they had ever known what could he have done to incur such wrath?

"Ejiro, you'll handle the order for Chief Aliyu," Bala said.

The men were used to taking orders, even from colleagues. Chico had drilled that into them. Ejiro nodded, glad to have something to do after all. He moved away and gathered his men together to address them about the situation. Okey frowned in the direction of Chico's office.

"Don't bother. He would take care of himself," Bala said and looked at the uniformed men already making themselves at home on borrowed land. This didn't look good at all. "I wonder what he has gotten himself into," he murmured.

"I'll find out," Okey said and walked toward the closed doors of Chico's office.

"You'll have yourself to blame," Bala called after him.

"Talk to my men," Okey called back and jogged past the clean and dry slabs to the office.

Chico saw him approach. Strategically located, he could see everything happening in the slaughter area. He wasn't surprised Okey had come to him. The young ruddy man had benefited from his generosity.

Okey had come to the abattoir, a homeless orphan. Initially scavenging and hiding, he had been scared of being thrown out. He didn't know his whereabouts at the abattoir, and this made him conspicuous. He had been about eighteen years then. Five years later, at the same abattoir, living a 'decent' life, married with a child and grown to be a master under Chico's tutelage, he never voiced it, but his gratitude felt thick enough to cut.

He knocked and waited to be summoned in. Chico struggled. At this moment, he was gathering his documents and his thoughts. He didn't want any intrusion. He continued picking at the files he had brought out from his lockers, ignoring the young man staring at him from the other side. He didn't want to send him away. But at the same time, the men would need some coordination, and Okey was reliable. Yet, he may need a quiet assurance.

In many ways, he and Okey had a lot in common. Out of all his masters, Okey was one of the few quiet, careful ones on and off duty. The others drank and womanised. Not Okey. The young girl he married was one of the butchers' daughters, who had lived and grown up on the ranch. She was a pretty girl who satisfied her husband in every way. Chico had no reason to distrust this master.

He pulled the door open and allowed Okey in.

"Thank you, Chico," Okey said softly. He didn't ask any questions but stood still till Chico spoke.

"I have a feeling it has to do with the ownership of this place. I'm putting the papers together," Chico said.

Okey stared uncertain, his hands hung loosely beside him. "I'll go with you to the task force unit."

Chico shook his head. "It won't be necessary."

"Two are better than one."

"I forgot to talk about the hotels—"

Chico felt strange. He never forgot anything, and the look of pity he saw on Okey's face made him scared. What was he afraid of? For a moment he needed to gather his thoughts. This couldn't be happening—But the strong leader came back almost as soon. "You handle that," he ordered.

"Bala is dividing the masters to tasks. He's taking Aliyu's orders. May I ask him to handle it too?" He added softly, "So I can go with you."

There was a long pause as leader tried to intimidate his protégé with his glare.

"Ask him to do that then," he said and continued to separate files. He was going to get to the bottom of this embarrassment, he thought warily.

Okey moved to the now-dispersing group and gave Bala the instructions.

Chico was ready to leave minutes after Okey returned.

"It's just after six, Chico," Okey said incredulously. "The office won't be open now."

Chico walked to his door as though he'd heard nothing. He looked around and stepped out. Okey followed him. Chico locked the door behind him and climbed into his pickup truck parked at the back of the office away from sight of the slabs. Okey jumped in beside him.

While Okey was away, Chico had tucked in his rain boots under his brown chinos trousers and rolled down his white shirt sleeves. His man still looked unkempt and ready for the slabs but Chico did not complain. That was the kind of person Okey was. He knew the younger man was self-conscious about his appearance, but it didn't matter one bit.

They noticed the military task force were sending some of the customers back at the entrance and they drove past. Chico knew the ministry of environment premises well, but he had never entered the building. He found a good place in the lot, far from where he assumed the regular workers would park and parked his truck. The black, two-cabin Toyota truck was an old model but well-kept and it served his master's purpose.

The two men sat in the truck both entertaining their private thoughts. Okey glanced at Chico several times and opened his mouth as though to make conversation but changed his mind and shut it.

Chico's silence sometimes spoke louder that wailing. As much as most of the abattoir crowd admired him, everyone wondered at his lifestyle. He didn't have a family, save his grandfather who lived like a hermit up on the ranch hill in a shack. The old man had no one either except his silent grandson who ran one of the largest abattoirs in the state, as though it was a small stall.

Chico commandeered hundreds of able-bodied, skilled-butcher, family men as though he ran a kindergarten. Once when Okey accompanied him to see the old man, it had been a very strange experience. Chico had sat mute for over four hours with the man. Neither spoke a word till

Chico stood up and left. Okey had never volunteered to follow him for visits up the hill after that, much to Chico's amusement.

The offices of the ministry began to open after about two hours of silence in Chico's truck. Chico got out without any announcement and Okey followed. The receptionist directed them to the task force offices where they were asked to wait till the man handling the closure arrived.

Chico had not expected to see the officer who came to the abattoir for the operation in the morning, but then he did not expect to see the pot-bellied civilian who came in at about eleven o'clock. Composed, he entered the secretary's office and endured another hour's wait.

"Oga is going on break." The secretary looked up from her work, "but he would see you now briefly," she said.

"Thank you," Chico said and followed the lady's direction to the boss' office.

The office was furnished with a large finely-finished wooden table, a swivel chair that occupied all of the fat man in it and two visitor's seats. Chico and Okey took the seats without invitation. A ceiling fan circulated air from a creaking room unit air-conditioner. One dusty bookshelf with old books sat against the wall beside the room unit.

"Ode, Ode," the man said with a voice that usually surprised its listeners. For such a heavy-set man, the voice was too feminine. He shook his head and wagged his finger at the abattoir owner. "Why do you do this to yourself? I have been receiving calls all day from angry meat sellers."

"I don't even know what I've done."

"You have done terribly. Your offences are so many I don't know how to start with you."

"Does it have to do with taxes?" Chico said.

"Taxes?" The fat man laughed, bobbing his stomach. "If you had come with a cow from your abattoir, maybe we could limit it to taxes," he said.

"I have all the documents for my taxes here." Chico put the files with him on the table. He had wondered why ministry of environment would be interested in his tax records. The fat man looked at him incredulously before his expression became stern.

"You'd rather think of getting a lawyer because your abattoir is going to be closed down for a long long while. Let me see the tax receipts," he said.

Chico handed two files over to him and he inspected them.

"I must confess you're good with your documents—"

Chico and Okey waited as the man perused five files holding all sorts of documents.

"Well, you need a lot of explaining to do." He pushed the files back to Chico.

"I'm ready to do so."

"It won't be here or now. I have a meeting right now—"

"I can wait."

"I have other things to do." He looked at Chico and scowled. "Come back day after tomorrow."

"The ranch was shut down, sir. I would think it's better we sort this out today, if you don't mind." Chico held his anger in tight rein.

"Please excuse me now," the man snapped.

Chico stood grasping his files. "Have a good day, sir," he croaked.

Okey followed him, almost running after his long angry strides. "He wants a bribe," he said as soon as they got into the truck. "He wants you to give him something. I don't even think we have done anything wrong!"

Chico swerved the truck back on the road and rode out of the state complex under the speed limit, his focus doggedly on the road.

"I hate all these state officials. Corruption is their middle name," Okey said after a silence stretched between them.

"That's why I left the other man I was working with. He was a civil servant. One big man in Governor's office at the security post. Every day, they just bring all sorts of envelope for the man. You see all kinds of yams and bush meat and gifts, cloths—" Okey paused and looked at Chico, who concentrated on the road. "I was washing his clothes for him then. You'll see money in the pockets of his shirts and trousers. Thousands." Okey kept quiet for a beat. "He wasn't even a senior staff in the security department but they're always sharing things." He shrugged. "I'm sure people like that don't even touch their salaries." He sighed. "Now this one is asking for a cow."

Chico swerved into his parking lot and stepped out. Okey followed him into his office.

"Keep the doors open," he muttered as Okey closed it. "I'll be around if you or anyone need me."

"Yes, sir," Okey said quietly and left him.

CHAPTER FIVE

O
DE ABATTOIR SOON DISCOVERED they were facing a standoff. Nothing was slaughtered for a week. Chico made arrangements with the slaughters in Oke-ido and Idi-iroko, neighbouring communities with much smaller abattoirs, to remove the older cows due to be slaughtered. The masters agitated about the deadlock. They lost money with each passing day, and though Chico proceeded to feed all of them and their families on the ranch, they felt the pinch. No one understood the issues.

There was talk about the ownership tussle at the abattoir, which was unfounded and then other matters hung on Chico's lack of cooperation with authorities which was just as vague as everything else. Chico showed up at the task Force office each given day and time only to either be referred to another office or rescheduled.

As he stood listless in the corridors of the ministry of environment, the second week of the shutdown, waiting for yet another officer to clear his abattoir from the defrauder list, a familiar face approached, carrying a folder and a handbag. She passed, stopped and turned to face him.

"Well, who's here?" she said cheerfully. "What are you doing around here?"

He sized her up before responding. She was dressed in a baby blue shirt and black skirt suit with high heeled formal shoes. She looked like one of the officers in the ministry.

"I happen to be waiting for someone in waste disposal unit. The director, I guess," Chico said, as though speaking to an inquisitive child.

"Hmm, really," Christine said. "Well, have a nice day." She shrugged and started to walk away.

He leaned against the wall. "What are you doing around here?" His mocking tone as well as his question must have halted her.

She swung round her eyes fixed in him. "I'm seeing some of the officers concerning my research—project," she stuttered.

She had the strangest look, drawing his attention to her eyes. "Oh, really."

"Have a good day," she said and walked off.

"The abattoir was shut down," he called to her. "Almost two weeks ago, now."

She stopped short and turned again, her face drained of life. "Why?"

Her genuine look moved him. No business premise was allowed to be closed for more than forty-eight hours without criminal indictment. Even then, the business would be reopened while the arrests were being made.

He shrugged. "Search me."

"Is this why you want to see the director now?"

"Yes."

She frowned. "Strange. You don't know why you were shut down?"

He shrugged, a bland shift of his shoulder blades that could only be described as a shrug for lack of any other word to use. "No, I don't. I have been given every reason you can imagine."

She glared at him. "Maybe it has to do with the man you—killed the other day."

He chuckled. "He didn't die. I slapped him and he fainted. You can come and see him today if you want."

"A grown man like that faint because of a slap?"

He licked his lips and allowed himself the luxury of staring at her, and not just her face. She was delightful to watch. Her feminine features popped. He assumed she was a young woman who knew her physical strengths and capitalized on them. Her clothes fit, whether casual as he'd seen her previously of formal like now, and her make-up and jewellery complimented her size and colouring.

"Maybe he hadn't eaten," she said. "What was his offence?"

He paused before answering her. "He was caught stealing. I don't tolerate that."

"Wow. Well." She checked her watch. "I really must go. I'm sorry your abattoir was closed down."

He shrugged.

"Bye," she said and made it away this time.

He stared hard at her retreating figure till she turned the corner of the long corridor and disappeared.

⫸⫷

Christine hurried to her office. She had wondered why he would be waiting to see her director, but to learn he'd been shut down for so long? Since turning him over to the task force, she'd finished her report and started working on other projects. She had essentially closed his chapter. She had wished she could witness the horror on his face when he discovered who she was, but unfortunately, she hadn't had the pleasure.

Christine did not breathe until she was in her office and then she became restless. Many questions ran through her mind all at once. Why had she continued the lie? If he'd known she was indeed a staff of the department, what difference would it make? He couldn't do anything about it. So why had she not been truthful. And what was it about the continued closure of his business? Especially if he didn't know the reason? Was this some foul play or what?

She dropped her folder and bag and headed out of the office only to stop short. She didn't want to see him again. And he would be waiting for her director. She marched back to her seat and picked her LAN line. Maybe she should do some investigation of her own. She called the task force office.

Mr. Agoro had taken over the management of the task force office from its inception two years earlier. Everyone witnessed his show of relief and promotion from redundancy in the ministry of defence. Agoro had thought he would be retrenched but when the task force units were opened in some of the ministries, many from the ministry of defence staff applied and got transferred. Agoro got environment.

Ministry of Environment had been considered 'all work and no play' by those who had no ambition. But Agoro was good at making the best out of every situation, and his potbelly expanded. He delighted in defrauders. His joy was full when offenders were caught but for the wrong reasons.

Christine got a response after the call had almost ringed out.

"Hello, Agoro on the line, how may I help you?"

"Hello Mr. Agoro, Christine Bello from research," she said.

"Hello, Ms. Bello. Longest time. We only see your files," he said with his high-pitched treble.

She smiled. "It's not my fault. Work. Just work all the time." She hated his voice.

"I should come to your office some time and share in the work with you," he said and laughed.

"Hmm, you want me to lose the job then."

"No o. It's just so I can also enjoy what you research people have been enjoying."

His gurgling was disgusting. Christine closed her eyes for a moment for control. She changed the subject. She wasn't about to get carried away with listless talk. Besides, she was very busy and had other things to do.

The earlier she cleared the abattoir thing the better for her. At least that was her genuine feeling.

"Sir, I wanted to find out what the update is on Ode Abattoir. You know, since I sent over the files, I haven't been in on the case."

He gasped. "Ode Abattoir?"

Christine tapped her finger on her table. "Did your men carry out the closure?"

"Oh, of course. Yes, we did. But that was about a week or more ago, it's a closed case. I thought you had another location—"

"No. I was just checking in on the abattoir." Christine paused. The man was lying. She had to break him somehow. "I got a call from the abattoir they had a cow for all of us here—"

Agoro laughed. "So that stubborn man breaks."

Christine moaned. "But when I sent my driver to collect, it was shut down."

"What? I thought your guys have given the—huh. Wait, a minute, let me call—"

"What could have caused such a delay in reopening them? I'm going to take this up with the director-general because it is so unfair." Christine found her voice shaking and realised she wasn't acting any more.

"The DG? Would that be necessary? Let me call the people at—"

"Why did it take so long? To think our cow would just be lost like."

"Impossible. Don't worry. I'm sure the man just realised he has to play ball. He'll keep it till we open them. He may even add one more." Agoro chuckled. "About time too."

"Please make sure they are opened."

"Once they are cleared, why not?"

Christine sighed. "Let me know. Thanks a lot, Mr. Agoro. I'm counting on you, please. I promised Tolani I would give her my share of the cow toward her daughter's birthday."

She was beginning to have a head ache. She hung up without giving him a chance to respond.

If Agoro was not holding it as he insinuated, who was and why? He had seemed genuinely concerned the place was still shut down though he'd also implicated himself about Chico's 'stubbornness.' She was glad Chico did not give any bribe but could it be the reason to shut him down for so long? If Agoro was not in control, then who was and why would they not tell Chico his waste management plan was below standard.

It was a simple procedure. He would be shut down for forty-eight hours maximum, by which time the urban development people would come in and take charge. It would cost Chico a lot of money and a huge fine but he'd have his business back. Christine had never followed up on other projects before and had a funny feeling on her inside. Could it be the procedure was not as simple?

She stood again to see her director and then remembered the butcher could still be there. Impatient, she went back to her seat. She forgot about the job on her desk, the review of a company profile for waste management in the local market which needed a follow up on but now it had to wait.

She picked her phone and dialled Ayo Lawrence's number.

"Hello," a woman answered.

"Hello," Christine said. "Please can I speak with Lt. Cdr. Ayo Lawrence?"

"Who's this please?"

"My name is Christine Bello from Ministry of Environment."

"He's on leave. How may I help you?"

"Huh, I guess I'll call his mobile," Christine said. She could deal with the official aspect with this woman any way—No, she wanted to talk to Ayo—Lol.

"Okay then. Have a good day."

Christine dialled the mobile. He picked after the second ring.

"Hello, Ms. Bello. Waoh, it's good to hear from you again."

"Yes Lt—"

"I thought I told you Ayo is good enough for me," he chided.

"You said off duty—"

"I'm on leave and this is a private call I believe?"

"Alright, you win. Ayo it is then." She smiled, he chuckled. "So, I was calling to find out about the waste management of Ode Abattoir we talked about. You said there are no records of their using the navy?"

"Huh? I thought this was a social call. I'm on leave, lady."

"I know—I called your office." She paused for one full second. "I wanted to talk to you."

"Oh then. I'll answer your questions." He laughed. "About the abattoir, none. I re-checked."

"Really?"

"Is there a problem?"

"Yeah. The abattoir was closed but the owner is crying foul. He said he doesn't know what he's done wrong."

"Really?"

"Yeah. He's confident he hasn't offended."

"Maybe he used other means he can defend but I am so sure it's not us. We have no records on him."

"Alright then. Thanks again."

"I was thinking—" he said. "If you and I can see, maybe later? This evening?"

"Huh, this evening?"

"Yeah, if you're not too tired after work, I could pick you up and we can go for a drink or something." He tried to sound casual. He failed.

"Why not? I'm free this evening," she said.

She wasn't a child who needed excessive nudging. She wasn't in a relationship with anyone, and she would welcome this one. He was good-looking and polite. It was a good starting point.

"That's really great. Thanks," he said. Christine smiled and gave him her house address. "I'll pick you up at seven."

"Seven is fine," she said.

He thanked her again and hung up. Christine smiled at the phone before thoughts of the abattoir came rushing back, stifling her momentary joy.

She made several calls to the urban development officers and waste management contractors and came up empty. This was worse than she expected. And the Ode man still did not know his offence?

Fishy. Very smelly.

CHAPTER SIX

S AFFRON BELLO HASSAN'S RESEMBLANCE with her sister couldn't be missed, though she was a fairer than Christine. She looked as though she just came out from soaking in the pool, when she opened the door to Ayo Lawrence. Her light skin bordered on pale, almost whitish. She wore a flowing white silk boubou that fitted her so well she could have been straight out of a digital photo book. She smiled at the handsome suitor standing on the doorstep, dressed in tight jeans and a white shirt, tucked in. The outfit completed with brown leather belt and moccasins.

Saffron drawled. "Hello?"

"Hi. I'm Ayo Lawrence. I'd like to see Christine," he said.

"Really, hmm." Saffron looked him up and down. She remained in front of the door, blocking his advance. "Are you a new friend?"

He chuckled. "Well, yeah. You can say that." He seemed to analyse who she was. She was too young to be Christine's mother maybe an aunt with a young face. Family, definitely. A younger sister who had the gall?

"Wow, my sister has stepped up. You're not her spec," she said. "Have you met Janella?" He arched an eyebrow. "Sorry, I'm Saffron." She stuck out her slender, well-manicured hand to him.

"Saffron." He grabbed the hand and nodded. "Nice meeting you."

Saffron's features were soft, almost homely but her make-up was sharp, and spoke more of her character. The dark colours made her look like a gothic queen of some sort, though they were not loud. She wasn't as pretty as Christine, but there was a likeness between the two that made Ayo believe Christine had a family of beautiful people.

"Please come in. I'll get Christine for you." She stepped back and closed the door after him. "Feel at home," she called over her shoulder.

The room was plush and spoke of affluence. Ayo took a single leather sofa and sank into it with a sigh.

⟫⟫ ⟪⟪

Saffron walked into Christine's room without knocking. She glared as though she'd seen a dreadful thing, her lower lip slacked, and she shook her head.

"What?"

Saffron shrugged. "Nothing." She gave Christine a once-over. "Your new bobo is here," she said.

"Really. Right on time," Christine giggled. She dabbed herself with a touch of designer perfume and took one more look in the mirror.

"And I think your dress is awful."

"Thank you."

Saffron perched on Christine's big bed and snickered. "He's not your type."

"What do you mean?" Christine searched for her purse on the bed. Saffron picked it like it was a piece of dirt and handed it over. "Thanks." Christine breathed.

"He's tall, dark, handsome, decent—"

"He's a naval officer," Christine added proudly.

"My point exactly. Even the rowdy type doesn't stay, how much more this clean one. Has he met Janella?" Saffron slurred, crossing her legs daintily.

"No," Christine snapped. "And I take exception to your—your analysing my relationship."

"It doesn't matter what you take exception to. Don't waste his time." She strolled to the door. "You won't have sex with him anyway—so what would a virile man like that be doing with you?" She opened the door and turned to look, her eyes cold. "Poor poor Christine. Don't worry, you'll come around sometime." She stepped out and slammed the door.

Christine stared after her, aghast. "Well, thank you for wishing me luck." She took a few calming breaths, looked in the mirror again and stepped out.

Ayo stood to his feet when she walked in. He looked at her with admiration and whistled. "Wow, you look so nice."

Christine wore a soft knee-length floral gown which clung playfully. "Thanks," she said. "You look very nice too."

She knew he had been striking in his uniform at the office but there was an edge to his looks tonight as though he inspired the blue-jean design. Models should be envious of his physique.

He flashed even, white teeth. "Well, thank you."

An awkward moment later, he ushered her to his black Honda Accord parked in the driveway. He opened the door for her, both unaware of Saffron's disdainful gaze from her first-floor room.

"Your house is beautiful," he commented and manoeuvred into the light evening traffic. "You must really love nature and you have the land for it."

"Yes. My parents have this Victorian mentality, so everything is properly done. Our house even has a name, you know," she said.

"Is that so?"

"Yeah. The Rose Manor."

"Hmm? Who named it?"

"Well, as the history goes, my great grandmother loved roses and had only roses in the garden when the house was built so there goes the name."

"What an interesting story. I didn't know families like this still exist. The house must be very old."

"Over a hundred years," she said unable to hide the pride from her voice.

"Wow. It looks like it was built a few years ago."

"My father is a maintenance freak. We overhaul every two years."

"He must be a very proud man to own a Victorian mansion, and here in Ode town!"

"He was. He really was." She chuckled. "He died three years ago, and it was on his breath—the very last."

"I'm sorry about the loss."

She shrugged. "Hmm."

There was no love lost between her and her father. She never even missed him. But she couldn't tell this man she was on a first date with.

They drove into the premises of The Roaster, a high brow restaurant renowned for their ribs. Christine had been there several times before and it held some memories for her, some good, some painful.

Ever since her affair with her last beau, Jon, ended, she had not been at the restaurant. But she had moved on from the terrible experience and was ready to enjoy the night with Ayo. The Roaster's chicken apart from the ribs, was the best in every state they were franchised in.

Ayo got out of the car and like a perfect gentleman, helped her out. The chef welcomed them himself, making sure they were comfortable and exciting them about the chef's special roast ribs. A waiter came over to take orders and Ayo opted for the chef's special while Christine stuck to her chicken. They chatted about their jobs. Christine was excited to learn about his work. He had never been in combat before, he was an administrator.

"But it's just because this is peace-time. May we not see a war."

"Amen," she said.

"Contrary to how the world seems to project war, it is nothing to want to experience. Mere boundary conflicts are distressing enough."

"I can only imagine." She shook her head. "War for some is a lot of money."

"Of course—Some make policies to breed war. Horrible."

"Why did you join the navy?"

"I had always wanted to be involved in security, protection for my country and all that. But why navy in particular?" He chuckled. "It's funny really."

"Tell me about it."

"The uniform. So neat and nice. White is my favourite colour," he said and they both laughed.

"Who could have imagined."

"But I stick to my patriotic reasons in public," he said.

She realized she enjoyed his company a lot. They were both relaxed like old friends.

"I like the navy uniform as well. In fact, I toyed with the idea of entering the military, the navy precisely." She giggled. Her father had kicked the thought out of her like a demon.

He corked his neck. "So, why didn't you?"

"I was too short, I guess. Or I thought so."

"You are short." It was the way he said it and they laughed.

The night wore on and when they'd both had their second round of drinks Ayo suggested he took her home. The ride was short and tense with emotion.

When they arrived, Ayo escorted her to the front door.

"Are you sure you don't want to come in for a few minutes before you go?" Christine said, self-conscious.

Ayo shook his head. He stood so close she could barely breathe. When leaned into her and bent to capture her lips, she turned away and chuckled.

"I'm sorry," she mumbled.

If she so much as tilted her head a small fraction, she would kiss him, so she kept her head bent.

"What's wrong? It's just a kiss," he said into her neatly wrapped hair.

"I'm really sorry, I'm just not—" She looked for words.

He tilted his head so he could see her face.

"Your lips are so pretty, so inviting," he said, and tilted her chin up, as though to re-examine what he already knew.

She stepped back to put more space between them. "Thanks. I don't feel we should be so fast."

"Why? I like you a lot and I believe this is the beginning of something that would last," he argued.

"I believe so too—I want to see you again, but my faith does not —" she stammered knowing where she had faltered. Her faith hadn't come in at all when she'd accepted the date.

"I am a believer, Christine, and I would never compromise my faith," he said, looking at her in disbelief. "Kissing you tonight is way off any kind of compromise."

She noticed he moved a little again, creating some space. She took it as a bad sign. She saw it coming, he was going to say goodbye—forever.

He heaved a heavy sigh. "Are you free tomorrow?" It was a Saturday.

"Yes," she nodded and smiled at him as a form of encouragement.

He smiled back. "Ode Boat Club premieres tomorrow and the Navy is escorting them on the first cruise. I want you to come with me."

"Wow, really. I would love to." Short of jumping on him, she clapped. "Really Ayo, I don't mean to hurt you about the kiss or anything—"

"Sshh. Look beautiful tomorrow," he said. "I'll pick you up at noon. There'll be a cocktail party and then the cruise, and then a dinner party."

"It's the whole day?" She dared not complain. She was glad.

He laughed. "It is, dear. And I'm looking forward to every minute of it. With you."

"Anything you'll like me to wear?"

"Party formal."

"Okay. Thanks for this evening. I really enjoyed myself."

"Me too. Till tomorrow dear."

"Thanks. Goodnight."

He blew her a kiss and she smiled again self-consciously. She stood at the doorstep and watched him leave before opening the front door. She had expected it would be open because she was still out. What she hadn't expected was Saffron sitting in the parlour, sipping chapman, fully dressed.

"Waiting up for you," her sister said before she could mutter a greeting.

"Really? How kind." She headed for her room.

Saffron glared at her. "How rude of you, Christine. Not even a greeting or some chitchat of how the evening went?"

Christine stopped and turned to look at Saffron. "I wasn't expecting to see you or anyone this evening. Besides, I am tired and would like to retire."

"He left disappointed. I saw it in the way his shoulder sagged as he walked back to his car," Saffron stated calmly.

"You always were good with analysing situations so, I guess you're right."

"He's not seeing you again, I presume?"

"Think what you like, Saffron." Christine sighed. "I'm going to bed. Good night." She turned back and started walking away.

"Why would you not oblige a kiss? One kiss on the first night is too hard for you? What is wrong with you?"

Christine stopped and turned. "Are you alright? What's your business?"

"It's every bit my business what happens to you." Saffron screamed, jabbing the air between them with her finger. "I accommodate you. I own you. Your father made you my responsibility in his will."

"You are crazy." Christine half-ran out of the room and slammed the door after she got to the safe confines of her room. She heard Saffron's laughter follow her all the way up the stairs. She almost hated her sister sometimes.

CHAPTER SEVEN

CHICO STRODE THROUGH THE thick brush, parting them as he did whenever he made this trip. His maternal grandfather lived like a hermit, but he was the most precious possession Chico had. He had been instrumental to the young man's progress from the day he received breath, many times physically fighting for the boy's rights. Especially with his father.

Oloye, as he was fondly called by everyone because he had been a chief in his village community had retreated into the bush after news of his daughter's death got to him. Over a decade, he had lived on bush rats and wild fruits and vegetables. No one had ever been able to convince him to come down from the hilly path. Chico visited him often. They rarely talked anyway, but it was the young man's ritual. And the few times Oloye spoke, it catapulted Chico to another level. The old man was full of wisdom.

Though Chico had visited him every day since the abattoir was shut down, they had not spoken a word to each other but the mere serenity in the presence of his grandfather helped him to think and to plan. While he was mostly alone in his office, the mere sight of the abattoir left him with physical pain. He had lost so much money he couldn't even begin to think about it. Almost all the butchers had left to find work on other abattoirs. The doctors stopped coming after all the animals were sold or transferred. Cattle owners moved their cattle elsewhere. To many, the death of the thriving Ode Abattoir was here.

The soldiers sent to guard the place were angry and restless and the women living on the ranch no longer felt safe. The masters couldn't just leave like that but were already making deals at other abattoirs and complaining about the cost of doing business outside. Chico had stubbornly remained true to his land. Several calls had come for him to lease a temporary property in other local government areas, but he'd refused them all. Not because he could do without the gains. He was just too proud for his own good.

The self-made wooden hut and thatch roof looked newly changed. The entrance was narrow enough for only one person to pass through, the wooden flap made from crooked tree branches half-open as Chico had always found it to be. The room could only just accommodate three people even with no furniture. Small grass weeds grew by the side and Chico pulled at them once he sat on the ground and his eyes became accustomed to the dark room. He found Oloye on the floor in his usual corner.

"You'll die of hunger," Oloye said.

He chuckled. "I won't move up here with you if that's where you're going. How did you know?"

"I stole into the abattoir at night and saw the soldiers," Oloye said.

"They must have thought you were a mad man."

"They were scared to death," Oloye laughed, something he'd done less than once a year in over a decade.

"You're lucky they didn't shoot at you," Chico reprimanded. He couldn't think of this man ever dying. He had no one else in the world.

"Has government seized your land?"

"No. Never," Chico said viciously.

"You'll die first. You'll die anyway—of hunger."

"I have more money than you can imagine. I can't die of hunger."

"It's almost a month now."

"You don't know that," he said. The old man snickered. "I know one of my boys came here. You don't need to fool me about entering the abattoir. You haven't left this hill since you came up." Chico yawned.

"They want me to beg you to do whatever you can—"

"Beg, Oloye," Chico snapped, and stood to half his height, which was all the head space available.

The old man went still, and Chico walked out to take fresh air. Oloye never begged anyone for anything. It was part of the demon that had plagued him all his life. It was also part of the legacy he'd left for his only grandson.

When Chico returned into the hermit's hole, it was just as still and stifling as he'd left it. Oloye sat quietly, staring into space.

"I won't give bribe. If this is the end of my famous Ode Abattoir, so be it. I was accused of not meeting up with environmental standards and that is a big lie. All my documents are complete. So if Bala and the rest want out, you, Oloye, tell them to get out," Chico said.

"You. Get out," Oloye said softly.

The remaining three hours was spent in total silence by the two men.

Ever since he had been told ho-ha that he had violated environmental standards, and given the penalty, Chico had stopped going to the Ministry of Environment. At first, he'd tried to reason with different officers, but none had been ready to bulge on his behalf. If his documents were complete, then why did the monitoring organizations have no record? All along he had been paying to the urban development office, and the ministry of environment and the navy and he had all his receipts complete. This alone had informed part of the frustration he'd expelled on his grandfather. The wise old man understood his plight. And knew exactly how to handle him. His soft rebuke had calmed him and put him where he belonged. But Chico was a fighter, and a stickler for integrity. He was going to bulldoze through if he had a say.

He didn't have a say in the type of visitor he got though when he climbed down from the presence of his family member, feeling refreshed despite the confrontation. Christine, the student was waiting for him with a soldier at his office. The soldier had advised her to wait because the man slept in his office. It was already after working hours and dusk was fast approaching.

Christine dismissed the soldier politely as Chico got closer and the officer left them alone. Chico opened his office without a word and ushered her in by a mere sweep of his hand.

"Good evening to you too," she said.

"I thought I greeted you—" he said and continued as she started to protest. "With a nod?"

"I didn't see the nod," she said.

He ushered her to the same seat she'd used the first time she entered his office and watched him casually stride to the sink and washed his hands.

"How may I help you this time?" He turned and dried his hands on a towel hanging off the wall. She stared at him for a moment and he stared right back.

"Sorry. You wash your hands all the time I find it interesting," she said.

"Ladies like you would stare at my hands in disgust if I don't wash," he snapped, then added softly, "Now what brings you here? My drains are dry."

Christine shrank back at his unkindness. "I came to inform you," she sat up straight, poised to face him. "I have made some terrible and disturbing discoveries about your abattoir."

He turned to face her. "On what authority should I assume your information is based?" He walked to his work desk and leaned against the edge, his arms loosely folded across his chest.

"I am a research student, remember?"

"I am not in the mood for words."

"Okay, so you are not happy at all and I understand why. But your own men have been messing you around and this kind of stealing, I'm afraid, you may kill someone this time," she said.

Her excitement was glaring though he noticed she tried to maintain a stoic front. Her fingers twined and untwined, causing him to notice how slim and dainty and pale, and utterly attractive they were. He told himself she was a mere child. More than a decade younger than he was, he assumed.

He muttered, "Too young."

"What?"

He shook his head and waved her on. "Continue."

"I was worried for you, so I did some snooping around." She stole a glance at his bland face. "My boyfriend works in the navy, and he was very helpful."

His rigid jaw twitched.

"Now I know why you're still shut down—besides the fact that there are a lot of corrupt officers in the—"

"Get to your point," he bit out.

She sighed. "Someone has been eating your money and providing fake receipts. All those receipts in your file are fake. And this is so huge, heads may roll. They are not going to open your abattoir in a very long while if you don't bribe or get the police involved." She shrugged. "You're between the devil and the deep blue sea." She stood and headed for the door.

"And where do you think you're going?" He surged forward as though to follow but he did not.

"You're not in the mood for words. Bye."

"Wait. I want to know more."

"Well, I can't be here to help, and you'll snap at me and glare at me," she said, and he looked away.

He softened, just a little. "Look, it's not been easy. I want to hear what you have."

She went back to the seat. "I discovered there has been no record at all of any transactions from your office and that is so strange. Three different organisations are indicted. My friend in the navy said—"

"Is he a friend or a boyfriend?" he interjected.

"It doesn't matter—"

"It does."

She rolled her eyes. "Okay, my boyfriend. Well, his office has no records, but you claim you've been paying so I snooped and found out there is someone in the navy who provides the paper work. And it's the same for the other two, environment and urban development."

"I don't get it."

"Who goes to pay for the taxes and the services?"

"Bala."

"He's a big thief. He hasn't been doing the right thing. You need to get him to confess."

Perhaps she expected a reaction. He didn't move from where he stood. "Bala has been in this place since I was a child. My father and his father worked together. He has never cheated me," he said.

"Then you need to find out if he's been sending someone who's been cheating," she said. "As for my side, the officers stink. I have found the man behind it."

"Your side?"

"My—the ministry," she faltered. "Someone in the accounts has been issuing receipts that are not duplicated. It's really ugly."

"Are you a working student?"

"No."

He arched an eyebrow. Her lips trembled for a moment and he thought she had something more to say.

"You saw me there the other day gathering materials for my project. That's my second home, so I know all of them," she said.

"Okay." He nodded and chewed on that piece of information. "So."

"I have enough evidence implicating three officers. If the director sees this, they are out of work," Christine continued. "They have been practicing corruption so blatantly, it's appalling, and people just fall into their hands."

"Is the fat one in the task force office one of them?"

"He is the ringleader." Christine laughed. "His name is Agoro."

"You should be a detective," he mumbled.

Her eyes twinkled. "I am," she said. "Some people are just talented."

He enjoyed seeing her so relaxed and chatty.

She sighed heavily. "What I think is you should confront your men first, let's see who's the leak here and then you can work it from here."

"I'm curious," he said. "How did you see my receipts?"

She faltered again and shifted in her seat. "I stole them from the director's office," she burst out. She waited. He just stared blankly. "I was worried for you. And I got to return them back before it was discovered missing." She opened her folder and brought out a bundle of sheets stapled together. "I needed to show them to my frie—boyfriend so he could see them too. So, I photocopied them." She put them on the table.

He didn't touch the heavy stack. He didn't spare a glance. "You went to a lot of trouble."

"I hate cheating," she said. "My friend said the receipts were not from the navy. They are fake. They have the logo and everything on the real receipts, but they were not." She flipped through and brought out the ones affected. "See here and here." She pointed on one specimen. He remained where he was, looking at her instead of what she was trying to show him. "Are not the same way. Subtle difference, but it's there. I saw the real one."

"Okay. Thanks for all the trouble," he said.

"It was no trouble. I'm glad I followed my instinct." She sighed. "Truth is, I couldn't sit back and watch such oppression going on in—I couldn't let it go."

"I'll do what I can."

"You need to. Corrupt people must be brought to book. I want to know what you plan to do."

She looked at him. He stared back, mute. When he refused to talk for several moments she sat back and started to strategize for him. When she paused for breath, he nodded toward the door.

"I need to do some thinking alone. Please go."

"I should go? That is so rude of you." She stood and packed all the documents she brought. "Not a thank you?"

"Thank you."

"Shove it."

※

Bala was already approaching Chico's office before Christine left the slab area. He had commanded the master to report at once. At the time he began to head the abattoir, Bala had been a near-do-good who could not be trusted with even a kilo of meat. He had picked him, brushed him up and established him as one of the masters. The man had been ever grateful and faithful.

The land mass of the ranch was so massive many of the masters had built their personal homes there. Bala had a simple ranch-style three-bedroom house where he lived with two wives and seven children. Right on the outskirt of the abattoir was a government school which most of the children on the ranch attended. When the going was good, the ranch was a small city close-knit community of peace and progress.

Chico remained at the exact spot Christine had left him when he summoned Bala on the phone to report in his office. As the older man walked in, he began to tremble at the look on his boss's face.

"Just tell me who your allies in all those agencies are," he said.

Bala looked back as though there was another person in the room. There was a long pause.

"I don't understand, Chico."

"Bala. Bala. Don't make me ask you again. The navy, the urban development, the environment ministry. Talk, and your time starts now," Chico said softly.

CHAPTER EIGHT

CHRISTINE STOMPED OUT OF the office after her tart statement.

The abattoir was deserted. It broke her heart to see it so. She tried not to blame herself. She had done her job. But corruption in the system had made Ode Abattoir a victim and she was determined to root it out. It wasn't any easier defending the brute Chico. And the seductive way he constantly stared at her made things worse.

She had thought she was mistaken the first time he ogled her, pausing at suggestive parts of her body, but the glare stayed with intermittent scowls. As Christine walked to the exit of the abattoir, she was sure she had mistaken a lot of things. She may be confused by his angry tone, and lustful gaze, but was determined to set the ball rolling to clean the corrupt practices in her office. He didn't deserve to suffer for that.

Then she remembered Tolani had asked her to make enquiries about meat for her daughter's party. Christine hissed a hundred times before she got back to Chico's office. If she didn't do this for her friend, she would feel bad. She had been the one who whet Tolani's appetite for Ode Abattoir's meat and now she had set herself up unknowingly. She could tell her friend to walk into the market anyway, but she decided to do the right thing and swallow her pride.

Sure she would be making plans with Chico about the thugs in both their work systems, she had thought seeking assistance on where to get good and cheap meat would be part of after-plans chit-chatting. Now she wished she'd just told Tolani to forget about it, and buy from the market, which was where they'd both bought their meat in time past when they had only heard about the tales from the abattoir.

The ten-minute walk back from the entrance helped to take some weight off her. There wasn't anything more he could do to offend her, anyway.

Bala sat on the floor weeping like a child when Christine knocked and entered. She was embarrassed by the scene. Chico sat behind his desk his hands dangling between long legs stretched out, his head hung low.

When she opened the door, he looked at her with bloodshot eyes. What had happened within the ten minutes since she left him? Bala looked at her as well, and for a moment, she thought somebody may have died. He must have come in as she left because his garment was soaked with tears and sweat.

"I'm sorry I interrupted you," she said softly. Both men continued to stare at her. "I can wait outside for a few minutes." Without waiting for their replies, she stepped out.

She was outside forever. When her legs could not carry her again, she knocked once more, and this time waited for someone to answer. No one did. She opened the door. Both men were still in the same position.

"Mr. Bala, please can we talk for a moment?" She asked when neither said a word, again.

"Go back to your family!" Chico growled and Bala flew to his feet.

Christine stepped out of the way, afraid he would stomp her in his flight. Chico got to his feet in one swift fluid movement and faced her. "Did you forget something?"

She swallowed hard. "What did you do to him?"

"I asked him why he betrayed my trust."

"Just that?" She blinked, and she curled her lip in disgust. "You are so intimidating, and you think you can bully—"

"Listen to me I have come a long way. All my life, I have fought for something. I have survived on my own. You have no right to judge me, or snob me. Now pick whatever you forgot and get out." He spoke in the same tone he had used for Bala.

Christine's mouth dropped open. She forgot she was supposed to be a timid student seeking help. She saw herself as the senior research officer being stood up by a defiant subordinate.

"How dare you speak to me like that?" she said, her voice rising. "Do you think I am insensitive to you or the surroundings you are in? Do you even know me, and you'll talk to me like that? Excuse me, don't ever, ever in your life ask me to get out. Who do you think you are?" she snapped. Her body began to vibrate, her breathing quickened.

As she spoke, Chico resumed his sitting position, making sure his gaze on her did not falter. His eyes softened but he didn't say a word. She took a deep breath, and found she wanted to cry. She hated to lose her temper, but Chico had just driven her so far.

She gulped in air. "My friend wants to buy meat in some quantity and thought you could suggest where to get it since the abattoir is closed." She pressed her lips together. "I know there are other smaller abattoirs in town and of course there's the market—"

He narrowed his eyes. "Your boyfriend?"

"No. My friend—female friend." Colleague, she almost added. "She has a five-year old daughter and wants to throw a party for her." For the umpteenth time, she questioned her continued deceit. She ought to tell him she wasn't a research student—

"What quantity?"

"I don't know." She shook her head. "She just felt I should seek your advice on an alternative."

"When's the party?"

His questions irritated her, but she was past debate. "Next week or oh this coming Saturday."

He pushed a notepad to her with a pen. "Write her name, number and address. I'll contact her."

"Thank you," she said, eager to leave. She supplied the information and kept the pad and pen on the desk.

He took a quick look at what she'd written and nodded.

"Thanks. Bye."

She felt she should apologise but refrained. He should apologise. He didn't reply her greeting and that was just fine. Her legs couldn't carry her fast enough away from him. She had always prided herself for being able to control her emotions and felt sorry for losing it with, especially a total stranger like him.

All the way back home, she reflected on what had happened. She had been wise enough to drive her car down since commercial vehicles would be scarce. Days when the abattoir was open were different. Everywhere was busy till night-time. Not now.

Why was she so bent on remaining in the lie? She had never been an adventurous person, despite the nature of her job which she was good at. Normally she would not be on a project longer than was necessary as this case had now turned out to be. It made her reflect on Chico. He couldn't be more than thirty-five years old, and yet she'd seen him "slap" a man to "death" and reduce a family man to tears without any emotion.

His bloodshot eyes had been the only sign of stress. What kind of man would own Ode abattoir? He struck her as cold-blooded, indifferent, rude and mean. And ironically, she couldn't imagine any other type of person in charge of so many men with violent tendencies.

No matter how one tried to view it, butchers were violent – butchers, animal murderers, murderers. She shuddered at the realisation. These were men who took life daily. It would not be far-fetched to assume they had little value for it. It would not be unbelievable to assume Chico also behaved like the animals he butchered.

These were Christine's disturbed thoughts when she got home.

Ayo's car was parked on the front drive. She hadn't been expecting him. She parked her car in her lot and ran into the house. Her relationship with Ayo had skyrocketed in the past two weeks and though he had not proposed, he had mentioned twice he was ready to settle down with her. It was just a matter of time before he popped the question.

Through the kitchen door of her beautiful triplex home, Christine entered the guest parlour. No one was there. She walked into the living area, hoping to find someone to ask and found Ayo with a glass of wine, looking through an album.

"Sweetie," Christine called and walked over to him, giving him a side hug. "I'm so sorry. I went to the abattoir to see—"

Janella, her immediate-younger sister walked into the living area wearing a gorgeous black dress. She was the beauty of the family. Her oblong face glowed despite the light make up on her beautiful eyes and full lips, high cheekbones. The small black dress stopped just before her knees exposing fair-skinned long, straight and dainty legs and feet clad in high heels. She packed her hair away from her face, and the long, curly tresses rested in the middle of her back. Janella was a perfection of beauty.

Ayo stood to receive her to Christine's dismay. "Jan, hi."

Her sister nodded in her direction, her eyes sparkling with excitement.

Ayo walked to her side and looked at Christine, an apologetic tilt to his lip. "I came to pick Janella for an outing. I thought she'd have told you."

Christine frowned, confused. "She's my sister, Ayo. Where are you taking my sister?"

Janella sighed. "Chris. What can I say? Ayo and I met yesterday and he—" she giggled. "He just wants this one date to satisfy his whim," she said with a slight shrug. "He said he'd never dated a beauty queen before."

Ayo's deep voice was low, and grave. "It's not quite as simple as Janella is making it. I came a bit earlier today, hoping I'd meet you at home, and explain myself to you—"

"You know what, Chris I'll excuse you guys for a few minutes. Ayo, I'll wait out by your car, if you're ready, we leave," Janella said and walked regally out of the room.

"Christine."

"No, really. If you want my sister, you can have her, but you can't have two of us at the same time," Christine said, struggling hard not to cry.

"How can I ever say this without being cruel? You are a wonderful and beautiful lady and I have a lot of respect for you—"

"I don't want you to patronise me, Ayo," Christine said with the last shred of composure. If she had to say anything more, she would lose control.

"I'm not patronising you. God sees my heart, Christine, please. Let me explain this to you. Please."

She folded her arms and leaned back on her heels, holding her eyelashes back so she wouldn't blink. Then cry.

"It doesn't look nice but the first time I saw your sister, I felt something different. I would be unfair to continue to deceive you into thinking we could be together, really. Please understand how I feel. I know it is painful and I wish things would be different—" He sighed and rubbed his eyes.

Christine adopted Chico's style and remained mute. Ayo stared at her for a moment and shook his head. "I don't imagine you'll understand so fast. I wish you the best, Christine and I pray you meet someone who really deserves you, 'cos I don't." When she didn't say a word, he gave a small bow and left her alone.

She rocked back and forth on her heels and hugged her arms around her waist. Tears clung to her eyelids, refusing to fall. She hated herself for it but walked to the large window facing the front of the house. Ayo walked tall and brisk—away.

He closed in on Janella and gave her a peck on her cheek, before opening the door for her. They drove away.

CHAPTER NINE

CHRISTINE SHUT DOWN ON her emotions and walked through the house to her first-floor rooms. The house had been designed in an all-encompassing manner. There were four apartments on the two upper floors and the general rooms on the ground floor, where there was the guest parlour, a massive family room, kitchen, dining room, a guest room and guest bathroom.

When Paul Bello's ancestors built the house, it had had just two floors and designed to accommodate the large family. Paul had desired to keep the legacy and massive renovations and reconstructions had been done so each child could still settle in the mansion even after marriage. The three sisters occupied the middle floor apartments while Paul and Wendy Bello used the last floor with Pebble.

The apartments replicated the basic contemporary three-bedroom flat so a family could still occupy it. Though the apartments had their kitchens, food was centrally prepared since none of the girls had large families. The only married one was Saffron and she joined the family at mealtimes with her husband, Hassan.

Christine had long since been independent of the communal lifestyle of her family. She opened her refrigerator and brought out a chilled bottle of water. She wouldn't dare try to hold down anything otherwise. All she wanted to do now was just fold herself in a ball and cry till she couldn't anymore, and it was what she did. She removed all her clothes and wore a thin nightgown and turning the air conditioning to the coolest, cuddled up under her blanket and wept. She didn't want to think of her reason why, she had more than enough reasons. Chico and Ayo made her cry.

She cried so hard, she lost her breath, her nose blocked, and her attack came upon her. She groped in the dark, struggled to breathe, and sought her bedside drawer for her inhaler. The first three puffs left her weak and hiccupping. She knew the cold air was not good for her, but she just wanted to be sick or to die. Why was her life so tough?

She must have slept off from fatigue before the attack came back again. She felt so cold. Her heart was constricted. It was a bad sign. She groped for her inhaler again, but the puffs did not relieve her, soughing aloud, her eyes bulging, she searched for the air conditioner's remote control. When she saw it, her eyes were watering, her nose blocked, and her chest tight. She managed to switch off the coolant, and move to her small parlour, gripping the inhaler and dragging the blanket along. It was warmer there. She took another three puffs and suppressed the longing to cry. She felt like dying.

Saffron found her cuddled on the rugged floor of her parlour. As a sick child, she had been taught to leave her doors unlocked in case she was in danger. Her sister sat on the couch close to where she cuddled and peered at the bundle in the blanket. Christine stirred and sluggishly sat up. She had no idea what time it was, but Saffron was fully dressed. Though her sister was always like this as though going for an important event. Clad in a flowing sari with gold jewellery and accessories, her face made up, with hair wrapped on top of her head, it could be any time of the day or night with Saffron.

"Hmm," Christine groaned from the aftermath of her dreadful night. She had no pains anymore but felt weak. "What time is it?" she slurred.

"It's close to midnight," Saffron said. "Janella just came in with clouds in her brains." She chuckled. "I thought I'd let you know."

"Really?" Christine mumbled.

"Look, I know it hurts but that's just the best thing for you. Janella is more suited," Saffron said. "And she was just full of the guy. She couldn't stop talking about him. And guess what, I watched them kiss!" she exclaimed. "Goodness Christine, the guy didn't want to leave her. They didn't want to leave each other."

"Hmm?" Saffron wanted to kill her, she was sure. How did Chico keep mute when being provoked? She wished she could do it too. "She's my sister, Saffron. And he was my date," she said, her voice thick with emotion.

"And they are better suited than you and him. And it's better for you they met now than later when you might have been more deeply committed. Don't you see the reason?" She shook Christine. "It's for your own good."

"I love him," Christine whispered. "How would I be able to see them together?"

"You're tough. You got over Jon and you would get over this one. I told Janella this would happen when they met, and it did. I don't know how you could have thought you could keep such a—man. Such an exotic man." Saffron giggled. "You should have seen his face yesterday when they met."

Christine gasped. "They met here?"

"Yes. I told him I wanted him to meet someone. I got his number from your phone," she said.

Christine could scream but instead reached for her inhaler sure her attack was close. "You arranged for them to meet? Here?" Could she overdose on the inhaler—she'd never thought of it.

"For your own good," Saffron whispered in her face before she stood.

Christine sobbed. "Why? Why Saffron?"

"Because I knew they would hit it off. Because I knew he would end up breaking your heart anyway." She walked to the door and stopped when she reached it. But she didn't turn. "Take care of yourself, Sis. Your spec would come one day."

"You set my man up with my sister—"

"Who I know has better taste in men than you do. Besides, Jon called me," Saffron mumbled.

Christine sat up. "Jon called?"

"Yes," Saffron said, and turned to face her. "Why else would I really want to go ahead and set up Janella with Ayo? Jon wanted me to talk you into coming back—even though it's not a good idea what with what happened and all."

Christine held her head. She had a headache. "Please go away, Saffron." She burst into tears and covered her head with her hands.

"When you're like this, you don't listen." Saffron shrugged and slammed the door behind her.

Christine jumped at the sound. She walked to her dining area and poured some ordinary water into a glass, with which she took three tabs of paracetamol. It always helped her to sleep. She regulated her air conditioning and with an inner strength she'd always depended on, turned down her bed. Jon was gone and Ayo was gone. And this, she had to live with. Saffron had come to gloat—she wasn't crying anymore when she drifted off to sleep again.

Despite Chico's bad attitude the day before, Christine went ahead and reported her findings to her director.

"If the Permanent Secretary or the Commissioner sees this, those men are gone, do you know that? Mr. Agoro is due for his full benefits next year," the director said.

"I know, sir," Christine said. "And I really appreciate your sensitivity but look at what this man has done all these years. He's gotten more than his share of the full benefits. I looked at his activities and this year alone, he's made millions off extortion."

"I know. I can't even believe this has gone on this long without anyone detecting it. I'm amazed," the director said, looking through the pages of confessions, bank transactions and blatant evidence of blackmail and coercion from Mr. Agoro's office. The man had fed fat.

"What hurts me the most is many of my cases got to this man's desk and he just cheated those men off their money. I should have known. My instincts should have told me," she said.

"Ms. Bello, I hope you are not taking this personally," he said.

"No, sir. You know I am a very objective person. Look at the abattoir's case. Everyone is affected. The place is so relevant to this town, the local government chairman even talked about it. Because the place has been shut down for so long, people are suffering," Christine said.

"The price of meat doubled but that's only because the owner of the abattoir refused to move, do the right—"

"He was shut down, sir. What did you expect him to do? He may have thought all this would blow over in a couple of days. And Mr. Agoro here insists on sitting on the place till the man pays about five hundred thousand naira." She sighed. "What is his offence, anyway?" She knew but did her director know?

"He wasn't paying his taxes. He had no environmental standards body inspecting him, he was not doing the right thing."

"And we have evidence this is not true. Someone in his workforce was ripping him off."

"And it is no concern of ours. He still needs to pay for his offence. What I don't agree to is the bribe Agoro is demanding but the man has to pay."

"He should be reopened, sir." Christine sighed. "At least to maintain the integrity of our office. He should be reopened, and then we can serve him a letter stating what he must pay and when. Follow the proper procedure at least, sir."

The man sighed. "I'll talk to Agoro."

"Yes, sir." Christine swallowed. "I have the final report on the Papeeng Oil Mill. I'll bring it to your table first thing tomorrow morning."

"Okay. There's an oil spill on the river. I want you to join the team to inspect it later in the day."

"Yes, sir." She stood and started for the door.

"Ms. Bello," the director called, halting her. "We have good intentions. We just must not let them seem as though they are not."

"Yes, sir." Christine nodded and left the office.

She didn't agree with him. Having good intentions and executing them was the only way to "not let them seem as though they are not." The only reason Chico is shut down till now is because he refused to give a bribe, she thought. The Ode Abattoir had been on the news for weeks and to think the fault came back to her office was quite appalling. This was the same kind of bureaucracy she blamed the backwardness of her country on.

She rummaged through her directory and found the commissioner's numbers. She called the secretary. Within minutes, she got an appointment with the man. Though her director was a man of integrity and would not be a part of what Mr. Agoro did, he was also not assertive enough for her. His position was not a political one, yet he needed to please the politicians, and Christine found this depressing especially because it often interfered with due process. But she wasn't going to wait for anyone on this. She started this and owed it to all of Ode and anyone who patronized the abattoir to follow through.

The Commissioner of Environment was a man who saw his job as a calling. He had been a hardcore grassroots politician, serving at the council before climbing through the party ranks to get the appointment but it was well-served. During his campaigns and tenures, he had always sung the song of protecting the environment though he was a graduate of philosophy. As a ward councillor, he had introduced regular sweeping of the streets and washing of the gutters. He introduced penalty for roadside litter and executed it. Christine was confident the last thing he wanted was controversy amongst his ranks.

Another fantastic aspect of the commissioner was his easy accessibility. Several times he could be caught strolling down the corridors, peeping through offices and generally making himself visible. Despite his good attributes, rogues like Agoro still thrived in his ministry and they needed to be sifted out.

Christine had to travel a hundred kilometres to the state capital to meet him for her afternoon appointment but when she walked out of the commissioner's office, she was beaming.

CHAPTER TEN

CHRISTINE HAD TAKEN TWO days' sick leave because of her turbulent night the evening Ayo broke up their relationship. But on her first day back at work, everything was rolling again into action. She saw her director, finished up her outstanding reports on her current projects, saw the commissioner, escorted DPR officers to inspect oil spills, and returned to late lunch with the inspection team. She was on her feet arranging her desk ready to close from work when Tolani trudged into her office.

"Christine my dearest," she cooed. "What can I ever do without you? You don't cease to amaze me, girl. What did you do all that for?"

Christine looked up at her friend with a smile. "Do all what?"

Tolani had always been a dramatic person and never ceased to make theatre. She lunged at her neck and squeezed. "You are a blessing to my life."

"What did I do?" Christine pushed back. "I don't understand."

"Oh, you this girl. Stop the pretence. I know it's a really big do, but you like to make light of everything—"

Christine frowned. "I didn't do anything. What are you talking about?"

Tolani leaned back. "You didn't do anything?"

Christine shook her head "No. I can't think of anything."

She moved pending files into its tray. Whatever Tolani was up to, she didn't have the time for it. She had a programme to attend in church.

"I got a call on Tuesday from Ode abattoir—the man said you gave him my number and he would get back to me today on the meat," Tolani said. "I totally forgot to tell you about the call."

"Oh. Yeah. I should have told you I gave him your number so is that the reason you want to break my neck?" Christine laughed. She knew Tolani could be so overwhelming.

"Dara called from the house. There was a delivery of two laps, hunchback, tongue, tail and four legs." Tolani screamed. "I still can't believe it!"

"Wow. That's almost a whole cow." Christine gasped. "But is that not too much meat for one party?"

"Exactly what I said. I wasn't going to pay for two laps and Dara said they were huge. I was already rebuking her and demanding to speak to the delivery man when she told me I didn't need to pay. She said the order had been paid for." Tolani shrieked. "Christine. That meat would not be less than fifty grand if I want to go by Dara's description."

"Paid for?" Christine lowered herself into her seat. "Is your sister joking?" Why would Chico give Tolani free meat?

"That's what Dara said the man told her," Tolani said, her excitement drastically reduced. "Or maybe the guy was mistaken," she said and chewed on the insides of her cheek. "God knows it's better I get home and if I need to return—"

"Do you still have the number for the man who called on Tuesday?" Christine interrupted.

"Yeah. I saved it." Tolani opened her handset and scrolled through. "I should call him?"

"Yes. Just acknowledge the receipt of the meat and ask him for your charge, I guess," Christine said. "If we need to return some, we'd better know now."

"Okay." Tolani placed the call and then put her phone on speaker so they could both hear. The receiver picked up after the third ring.

"Hello, my name is Tolani, Ms. Christine's friend. You called me on Tuesday about the order for meat."

"Yes. Good day, Madam," the voice said. Christine's heart pounded. She tried to focus on the voice. It didn't sound like Chico. "Have you got your meat?"

"Yes, it's the reason why I'm calling. Please how much is it? The meat is too much oh," Tolani said.

"It was paid for by the person who placed the order," the man said.

"Who placed the order?"

"I don't know, Madam. We were given your name, number and address and told what to deliver."

"Really?" Tolani gazed at Christine who shook her head, just as confused.

Christine cut in. "Do you work in Ode Abattoir?"

"No, Madam."

Christine scratched her neck. "Do you have any number we can call in Ode because we placed the order in Ode, and we don't know who has paid for it."

"I have a number you can call in Ode, Madam. I'll text it to you," the man said.

"Thank you so much," Tolani said.

After hanging up, she shook her head. "Strange, isn't it?"

"You know what, let's go to your house, I want to see the meat—" Christine jumped to her feet and carried her bag. "Are you ready to leave?"

Tolani headed for the door. "Yeah. I'll just pick my things in my office."

"I'll meet you at the house," Christine said.

She was wary. Why would Chico order for the meat and pay? Especially after the way they parted. It had seemed like nothing would bring them together again. When she'd sought his advice, she'd expected him to give it, not ask for Tolani's contacts.

Christine got to Tolani's place before her. Her sister, Dara welcomed her at the door.

"Aunty, hello." Dara let Christine into the house. Tolani's daughter, Toke ran to Christine and jumped on her.

"Dara hi. Wow Toke, you're such a big girl now, can I carry you." She lifted her and faked fatigue before putting her down. "Dara, where's the meat?" Christine asked as they heard Tolani's car in the driveway.

"In the kitchen. Let me welcome Aunty Tolani," she said and excused herself.

Christine walked into the kitchen and greeted the young lady helping in the house. The meat had been separated in large bowls and placed on the kitchen floor. Two of the bowls had water in them signifying the washing process. The special parts were also placed in bowls. There were four bowls with meat and four others with the specials.

"Wow. Wooow." Tolani screamed when she entered her kitchen. Christine had been too shocked to talk. "Huh, you have cut all the meat? How were you able to do that so fast?"

"The butchers cut them up for us before they left. They said they were asked to," Dara said.

Christine looked at Tolani. "Did you get the number?"

"A text came in while I was driving," she said and brought out her phone from her bag. The text was from the meat-man, as she had saved the number. Tolani dialled. It rang for several seconds before it was picked up.

"Hello?" a voice answered. Christine signalled for her to speak and Tolani nodded.

"Hello. Please, meat was delivered to my house today and I want to know who I'll pay to," Christine said.

"The meat was paid for," the voice said.

"By who? I am grateful for this, but I want to know who paid, or is it supposed to be anonymous?"

"I really don't know. I was asked to order the meat—"

"Who can know then? Who asked you to order the meat?"

There was a long pause and Christine thought the person on the other side had hung up. "Hello. Hello?"

"Yes, may I help you?" another voice came on. Chico's. She knew it and had to hold her tongue not to acknowledge him.

"My name is Christine Bello, and I helped a friend make enquiries about buying meat at the abattoir, and some meat was delivered to her house today, paid for. We are just curious as to who would have done such a thing. The meat is so much and would be expensive and we want to know who to appreciate." She was rambling, she knew.

"I paid for the meat, Christine," he said it so low Tolani frowned and mouthed, "what?"

Christine was overwhelmed. She meant to ask, "who are you?" but found it so ridiculous because she couldn't even find her voice. Somehow, the conversation felt so private. She wanted to take the phone off the speaker mode but knew it would be rude and unfair to Tolani.

"That is so generous of you. Thank you very much," she said. Tolani mouthed again, "who?" and Christine made a "hold on" sign to her. "My friend wants to say thank you too."

"It's not necessary," he said but Christine beckoned on Tolani.

"Hello sir. I am so so grateful. The meat is so much we can't finish it," Tolani gushed. "Thank you so much, sir."

"My pleasure, Madam."

"We would love to have you at the party, too. I want to meet you, sir," Tolani said. Christine's mouth dropped open and she shook her head.

"Okay," he said in a low voice.

"Okay, sir. The party starts at about two o'clock. Please bring your kids along. We have more than enough meat to feed everybody," Tolani added jokingly. There was silence at the other end.

Christine took the handset from her friend and removed it from speaker. She didn't care what Tolani felt. Why invite someone she knew nothing about?

"Hello."

"I don't have kids."

"It's Christine."

"I know your voice."

She was mute for a second. "Thanks for the meat again."

"Don't mention it again."

"Bye then," she said.

He hung up without a reply.

Tolani frowned. "Who was that?"

Christine wanted to retort she should have asked before inviting him, but instead said, "The owner of the abattoir."

"Wow. He must be very generous," she said. "This meat is too much for us alone."

"Maybe you'll add meat to the party pack," Christine joked. She checked her watch, and it was time for her meeting already. Tolani laughed but Christine was preoccupied. "I have to go to church."

Both ladies walked out to Christine's car.

"I won't be in the office tomorrow," Tolani said.

"Okay. I'll come early on Saturday," Christine said.

"Come and sleep tomorrow night?"

Christine shrugged. "Okay, no problem."

The ladies parted, Tolani elated, Christine distant.

Through service, she couldn't concentrate. Why would Chico be so generous to Tolani, someone he probably had never met before? Her emotions were still raw. Since the beginning of the week, after the bitter betrayal from her sisters and Ayo, she had kept to herself, avoiding the others in the house.

Her mother, who scarcely participated in the activities in the home because of her own anxieties, had asked her only once why she wasn't eating with everyone else and her simple explanation of not having appetite had satisfied the isolated widow.

She hated the way she felt about Chico and his attitude – the way he looked at her, talked to her, and now his actions. She hated her feelings towards him as well. If this person was different and the circumstances different, she might have assumed he was flirting. The man maybe had never flirted in his life. She should be irritated and upset with him instead she was just muddled. She wanted to call him and ask questions—but she knew it would be wrong or come out wrong. She just had to wait and pretend she didn't notice anything unusual.

Tolani was not at work the following day as she said but she called. Chico had sent two young men to assist with preparations for the party.

"Extremely generous of him. The boys work like horses."

"You're sure they are not horses?" Christine joked. "I'll come to your house from the office."

"That would be great."

Tolani paused. "Hmm, is there something more to this? Is he trying to give a bribe?"

"He's your guest tomorrow. Ask him."

"I look forward to his answer."

"Not me. I'm going to focus all my energy on enjoying the day."

She knew she would have fun, and Chico's presence hopefully would not spoil it. She had avoided her sisters on purpose since her personal tragedy because she didn't have enough courage to face them yet. Through the day, she kept to herself occupying her time with work. With

Tolani, she had an ally, and she could relax and even confide in her but whatever she had to say would have to come after the party.

Sunday evening was most likely the best time. She packed for the weekend and told only her mother she would be away. As usual, Wendy Bello gave her a hug and told her to enjoy her weekend.

And she planned to. Everything that had happened to her over the week would be consumed by the peace and joy of the weekend.

CHAPTER ELEVEN

T HE BOYS WORKED LIKE horses put the description on point.
When Christine arrived, they were frying meat. They had gone
to the market earlier and fried the stew. When they'd arrived, they had
told Tolani they were cooks and if she needed the service, they would be
obliged. Of course, Tolani had already paid for cooks to come so she only
asked them to hang around, but by the time the day's job was done, the
boys were the only ones working. Even Dara was idle.

Christine checked into the guest room and after a shower, changed
into work clothes. She joined Dara and Tolani at the shed outside where
the ladies chatted idly while the two boys tidied up.

Christine pulled a low stool close to the others. "What happened to
your cooks?"

"They left. I don't need them. When I tasted the meat these boys
seasoned, I told myself I would not need those ladies. Dara, bring meat
for Christine to taste," she said. Dara stood and entered the house. "The
man must really want to impress you," Tolani added.

Christine exclaimed. "Huh?"

"Did you buy sweets for his kids?"

She couldn't answer. He's trying to make up for upsetting me, she
thought, and wondered why. Dara came in with a plate full of meat and
Christine inhaled.

"We would finish the meat before the party."

"I counted about five hundred big pieces from the two laps—I'm expecting fifty children and max another fifty adults. Double that if I am a celebrity—if it is meat, I have more than enough. I'm adding meat to the party pack like you suggested, Christine," Tolani said and they all laughed.

"When you said the meat was much, I thought you were joking," Christine said.

"No jokes o, my sister." Tolani picked a piece. The three ladies ate. Christine hummed in delight. Dara and her sister laughed.

"Aunty, I have eaten so much, my teeth ache," Dara said.

"Dara, bring chin-chin for Christine." Tolani laughed. Dara stood. "In fact, bring everything those boys have been doing since morning."

Christine arched her eyebrows. "I take this to be dinner?"

Dara took a while and showed up with a variety of cookies and local snacks, gurudi (coconut snack), kokoro (corn snack) and a couple Christine didn't know.

"The boys are good." Tolani sighed. "I've been trying to guess their ages."

Christine shrugged. She didn't feel like discussing the boys—it made her want to discuss the person who sent them. "I'll think they should be early twenties?"

"I don't know. I'm a poor judge of human age and character," Christine said.

And how oh so right she was. She never imagined Ayo would ever disgrace her the way he did. She thought he was a naval officer, a perfect gentleman—she made herself change the subject of her thoughts.

"When is Toke's daddy coming back?"

"He's been back since yesterday. He went to see some friends," Tolani said.

The two ladies chatted idly about everything, from Toke's father's job as a structural engineer to the girl's school, and then back and forth from the birthday party. Later when Tolani's husband returned home, they had a light meal for dinner. Christine declined because she had stuffed herself with too much junk to permit any more food.

She had already turned in when Tolani knocked on the door and came in.

"The boys insisted on going but I forced them to stay. Please can you share the room with Toke and Dara, so they can use here?"

"Definitely." Christine stood and picked her things.

"I just felt it was better. It's late already and they want to start cooking by five in the morning. I'm sorry," she said.

Christine laughed. "Of course not."

Toke's room had two beds. Dara slept in one and Toke the other. When they entered, Toke and Dara were cuddled on Toke's bed. The other was neatly made.

Christine assessed the set up. "This is nice. Thanks." She chuckled. "It's good, I won't be lonely in the night."

Tolani teased. "You've been lonely in the night for too long. You should get married this year."

Christine didn't expect the comment. Tolani never teased about marriage. She felt sore and tired.

"If I see husband, won't I marry?" She meant it as a safe comment, but it came out hard and snappy and Tolani visibly recoiled.

"I'm sorry to tease you," Tolani said and turned to leave.

Christine felt bad and rushed after her. "I'm sorry for snapping at you, Tolani. It's not as if it's your fault, is it?" She wanted to giggle, but a sob escaped.

Tolani pulled her into her arms. "Ha, Christine, is something the matter?"

Before she could say more, Christine was in tears. Tolani exclaimed and closed the door, glancing at Dara and Toke. She knew Dara was still awake though the latter's eyes were closed. But Christine, oblivious to her environment rather was consumed by her grief.

"What happened to you? Tell me," Tolani urged. "Is it Ayo?"

Christine had excitedly told her about her new date, and she had even noticed the glitter about her colleague. Christine was too overwhelmed to speak and only nodded.

Tolani took her to the empty bed and sat with her. "What happened? What did he do to you?"

Christine sniffed for a while, hiccupped and swallowed in a bid to coordinate herself. Tolani let her. When she was sure she could talk she looked at her friend.

"I'm so sorry. I feel embarrassed."

"It's okay," Tolani said. "Tell me what happened."

Christine proceeded to tell her friend everything from the way she met Ayo, to how they felt so good together, and then what happened the evening she came back to find him waiting to take Janella out.

Tolani gasped. "That is so callous of him."

Christine sniffed. "I love him, Tolani. I wanted it to work."

"He doesn't deserve you, Christine—"

"That's just what he said." Christine cried. "As though I am some foolish child who needs a kind of—"

"You don't deserve him. I'm sorry to say but not sorry, Janella does," Tolani interrupted Christine's self-pity. Her words were weighty, and Christine's mouth drooped. "I mean no offence to you, Christine, but that's the truth. I think it's high time your sisters got what they deserved, and if stealing your man, that kind of man, is what they want, they deserve it," Tolani said with conviction. "Look, Christine, you are a good person, and God will give you a good man, okay? Ayo does not deserve to be mourned, honestly," Tolani said, patting Christine on the back.

"I never knew this could happen with him. He was just a very responsible, respectful—"

"Forget him. If he was responsible or respectful, he would not do what he did," Tolani cried. "You are too kind. You should be raining curses on him—and your sisters," Tolani said passionately.

Christine sighed. "Oh Tolani. I just feel very sad."

"Please. I know it would be hard, but you should snap out of the sadness. Focus on people who appreciate you—like me. Like this abattoir owner spoiling us left, right, and centre."

"Oh Tolani. That's ridiculous." Christine snickered. "I'm sorry I lost my composure. I am just overwhelmed by their betrayal."

"Be overwhelmed by joy and peace, especially that you are moving forward. Do you know he would have still left you? If not now, later? Men like him are better done away with. I don't know how he got into a reputable organization like the military. Mtschew!"

Christine hugged her friend. "Thanks a lot, Tolani. I really feel better now. I do."

Tolani stood. "We both need to check in. Make sure you sleep well. Tomorrow is a long day."

"Yeah. Thanks a lot."

The following morning, the boys were up and about by the time Christine dragged her feet off the bed and prepared for the day. The night had seemed too short and she didn't feel rested. Tolani joined them to give instructions and Dara got ready as well.

"A lady has come to join the boys. It seems our new friend has his own crew," Tolani said to Christine. "When are you telling me to what we owe this extreme kindness?"

"I think we will have to ask him if he comes as I am oh so curious myself. When I met him, he wasn't even in a good mood, and the abattoir is still closed," Christine said.

"The lady said it was reopened yesterday—"

"Halleluyah!"

"Her name is Lucy. She has to go back to her shop at the abattoir. She's only here to start off the cooking," Tolani said. "I think she sells meat there as well?"

"Yeah. I bought liver from her once," Christine recognized her. "Ah. This is good news. They'll be busy today, catching up."

Tolani frowned. "You think it was possible for the abattoir to be shut down completely?"

Christine shrugged. "As far as I know—though of course, I think they collaborated with other abattoirs."

Again, she was surprised by Chico's concern. Could he be trying to appreciate her for her role in the reopening? This took the appreciation too far.

There wasn't much to do while the cooking was on so Tolani and Christine assisted with other preparations. One of Tolani's friends had volunteered to decorate the canopies and the house, and the ladies chatted while they worked.

By two o'clock, all the cooking and preparations were done, and the guests began to arrive. Toke wore a lovely pink Cinderella dress with a tiara and looked like a princess. Dara, a great lover of children, coordinated the party. There was plenty of food and drink and music and soon, the party was in full swing. The butcher boys had been joined by another two to help with serving the food. Tolani was elated by all the excitement, and perfection of the party. She kept saying Toke had never had a birthday party before and this was just such a befitting compensation.

Most parents dropped off their kids and came back toward the evening period, but even the ones who stayed back enjoyed themselves with the music, the kids' games and the excessive food and drink. The men sat together with Abbey, Toke's father while Tolani shuttled between co-ordinating, supervising and sitting with the women, chatting. Christine was too busy to sit with guests. Many of them were from the office and

Tolani's church and were known to Christine but she opted to stay off the stage and make sure all went well with service.

Chico walked into the party during a children's dance competition. It was quite interesting, and even the adults got involved. He found a vacant seat under the canopy and sat. One of the boys walked to him and greeted. They spoke for a moment and the boy returned with a bottle of water, and a plate of vegetable salad. He ate and watched the children dance.

There was a deadlock between the last two contestants. The boy and girl were just too good to pick a winner. Dara told the DJ to stop the music and asked both kids to bring their mums to dance with them, and the mother who danced best would get the prize. The DJ started the music and both women dug into it, while their kids encouraged them. At the end, the boy's mother won the prize and the girl burst into tears, forcing Dara to find a gift for her as well.

Gradually, parents started to leave with their children. Christine remained mostly in the kitchen, supervising the boys with clearing up when not peeping to watch the party.

"I hope all the guests have eaten?" she asked one of the boys, who responded positively and added that they had someone stationed outside to ensure people coming newly would eat.

"No abattoir owner. Our new friend ended up not coming." Tolani walked into the kitchen, tired.

"Oh, poor you," Christine said lightly. "Don't worry, I'm sure he knows we're very grateful."

"Wow, what a day?" Tolani slumped onto the kitchen stool and yawned. "I don't know what I'll give these boys o."

"They've started clearing up. I think we'll just ask how much their charge is and then beat it if it is outrageous," Christine suggested. "Where's Dara?" she said. "I want to start putting the plates away so this place can be cleared up."

"Some kids are still outside, so she's keeping them company. Wow. I don't know what I would have done without her." Tolani sighed. "Why don't you just come out and sit with the rest of the guests. Everyone we both know has asked after you." Tolani jumped to her feet.

"I'd better be here to make sure these boys do the right thing," Christine said.

Tolani laughed and dragged Christine. "At this stage, they can't be wrong."

"At least let me come along with a plate of food. I haven't eaten anything yet," Christine said, and her friend screamed, making her laugh.

She didn't have much of an appetite. She was always like this when she helped out at a party. She got herself a wrap of moi moi, a small serving of rice with fried meat and salad and followed Tolani to the front of the house where the party was winding down.

A couple of men sat with their wives and Abbey. Toke, now wearing a pretty, floral ruffle dress, with her friends, probably the children of the couples, played a game amidst a clutter of scattered chairs. Four women sat chatting idly while their children climbed on them and did hide and seek.

Chico sat alone, sipping from his bottle of water. He wore a crisp white shirt, brown corduroy jeans and leather boots and a real cowboy felt hat. Christine saw him at once and her heart thudded. She wasn't expecting he would be there at all. She whispered into Tolani's ears, who couldn't hide her startled expression even though Chico stared at them, and both walked towards him. He stood.

"My oh my. Permit me to say I now know why you've been sooo kind." Tolani cupped her hands around her cheeks. "Christine, I didn't know he was a bloke," she added, embarrassing Christine beyond reason. Oblivious of how tense her friend was, she held out her hand and beamed. Chico took the hand. "I am Tolani Okueko, mother of the celebrant. Thank you so much for all the meat and those boys of yours are made in heaven. Wow. They can cook." Tolani held on to his hand.

"My husband wants to meet you. Let me just get him for you right now." Tolani made to leave his hand but then held on. "I'm sorry I didn't notice when you came in. Really, when I saw you sitting, I thought you were probably a friend of one of our friends, or a brother or guest of one of our friends. I would have come to welcome you, I cross my heart. Let me get my husband," she said in one breath. Still, she didn't leave his hand. "Have you eaten, drank anything? You know there's still plenty of food, snacks—everything. Your boys are wonderful, and that lady too—are they all caterers? See I'm so excited, let me just get my husband." She giggled and let go of his hand.

Chico did a small bow and Tolani rushed off. "Thanks, Madam."

"I'm sorry for her outburst. She's not normally like that," Christine said. He nodded. "Thanks a lot. You didn't need to go through all the expense and the boys? Really."

"I told you not to thank me again," he mumbled. "I want us to talk before I leave," he added, looking at her—or rather, her mouth.

"About what?" Christine asked and he arched his eyebrow at her as Tolani came with Abbey.

Abbey was polite and appreciative. Like one would, meeting a new friend, he chatted briefly with Chico, and then excused them. As though sure his wife would be a nuisance, he called her along to see some friends off.

"Please forgive my husband," Tolani said in a whisper. "I'll be back in a jiffy."

When she was out of eardrops, Chico murmured, "I'll be going." and Christine chuckled.

She placed her food on his table before they walked out of the compound and towards a pick-up truck, parked by the roadside. It wasn't old, and rickety like most butchers she knew had but it definitely had seen better days.

"You said you wanted to talk," Christine said.

"Yeah. The slaughter was opened yesterday. We had a full day. All the butchers are back. I wanted to thank you," he said.

Christine shrugged. "I don't think I did anything about it—really."

"Really?"

"Well, I snooped around, and reported Agoro. I guess is all. But I'm so glad you're open now. Your man, Mr. Bala, how's he?" she asked. He shrugged. There was an awkward silence between them before Christine sighed.

"Your food is getting cold," he said.

"Yeah, I almost forgot about it," she said. "Bye." She turned and walked away.

She felt rather than saw him drive slowly past. She wanted to stop and wave but decided against it. It closed the chapter of Ode Abattoir for her and this made her very sad.

CHAPTER TWELVE

CHICO DID NOT BOTHER to change up when he got back to the abattoir. The pick-up was parked in front of his office before he took the bush path to see Oloye. It was already getting dark, but he knew the trail like the back of his hand. He didn't know why he was sprinting, but he got to his grandfather's hole in record time. He wasn't panting when he stooped to enter. He was fit and used to controlling his breath. As usual, the tiny space was dark. Chico tripped over something and almost fell, letting out a low groan in disgust.

"You only keep your bowl in the centre when you've pilfered my fish," Chico said.

He picked up the substance that made him trip, confirmed it was indeed a bowl and smelt the smoked fish in it, and laughed. "You can never change."

Oloye made no sound. Since taking up residence as a hermit, he had survived on wild fruits, bush rats, meat and sometimes snakes. He would make his fire and eat his food like a stone-ager. The hillside was virgin and fruitful, and Oloye lived healthily. There was a spring from the rock where he took water from but once in a while, he had a craving for other things he couldn't find in his immediate wild, and then he would wander into Chico's lands and take whatever he wanted.

He was good at catching fish from his grandson's man-made pond with his bare hand, and sometimes, a chicken would happen along and meet with unavoidable howbeit, untimely death. Much of this amused Chico who had taken up a wide range of animal farming just for the fun of it. It pleased him though that his only living relative lived "well."

He sat on the same spot where he had removed the fishbowl, and took off his cowboy hat, placing it on legs he had folded in his customary yoga-style. He wanted to talk today despite his grandfather's usual silence. It hadn't bothered him before and he really couldn't care less now though he wished the old man would comment.

"Did my fish sting you? I can feel you sulking," Chico said.

Mute.

"You believe you have found all sorts of herbs for your wounds, but I'll still send up some disinfectants for you."

Mute.

"I know you won't use it anyway. But I'll still send some up. I may even bring it myself and spend the night with you.

"I know that would make you very glad though you'll never admit it." He chuckled. "Funny how you have turned me into a weirdo like you. I'm being talked to and I just stare like a moron." He sighed. "Time spent with you is too much, now I realise that."

Mute.

"I can't believe I now behave so much like you and it makes me comprehend, you really are not normal anymore, Oloye. I wonder what she thinks of me staring when I should be talking or responding in some way but I'm there thinking it's perfectly normal to be talked to and not respond. Huh." He scratched his scalp, a smile lingered on his lips. "It's perfectly normal with you because your quiet is rowdier than ten of my butchers talking at once." He thought that was funny, but he only shook his head in the dark, as his eyes became acclimatized.

"But I find comfort in it, only that I wish you'll talk tonight. You see." He sighed. He had never had to organise his thoughts before Oloye in the past but now he felt a need to do so—so the old man would not misinterpret his actions.

"The lady who helped to reopen the slaughter has a friend whose child had a party today. That's where I went—remarkable lady." He paused. "Was it proper to have sent meat for the party?" He half-expected his grandfather to surprise him and respond. He had no such luck. The old man was as voiceless as the sepulchre. "They just carried on and on about the gesture. I hope I don't have them imagining things about what I did—I mean.

He moaned. "What do I care anyway? I won't be seeing either one again." He shrugged. "But it bothers me that my actions could have been misread."

Though looking critically, he did think he had overacted. He couldn't even use the reopening as a reason. The moment she mentioned the meat, he decided to supply it. He'd only taken the details of the friend's address, so he'd know where to deliver.

The reopening, in as much as he was glad about it, had just been used as a reason and anyone who cared to think about dates would know it had absolutely nothing to do with it. He was a man of few words, and deep thoughts and it bothered him how he may have been misunderstood. It was just a spontaneous decision—and that was not him either. Being impulsive died a long time ago with his emotions. He was stone cold where others had a heart. He did nothing spur-of-the-moment. If actions had to be taken, no matter how unexpected it was, he took his own decision—one he remained responsible to, one he could account for. Impetuosity was not one of his traits.

Chico sat quietly in front of his grandfather as darkness from within and without closed in on them. He may have been there for another hour, pondering on her and how he had acted since she walked into his space with her notepad. Christine.

He stood when he thought he should and as he reached the door, Oloye said in a low growl, "Marry her."

If he didn't know better, he would have spun around and demanded an explanation.

He paused for a breath, muttered, "You're crazy," and left.

CHAPTER THIRTEEN

T HE PILE IN FRONT of Christine reduced enough for her conscience to free her for the day. She had been working overtime for a week. With the oil spill becoming an international concern, her director had more meetings and field trips, and she was left to do much of what was meant for both of them. In addition, a new project to expand the waste disposal centre within the state just commenced, located between Ode and Gureje, another commercial hub about 80 kilometres away. The project was being monitored by Christine's unit.

She had had to drive to that new site every day before facing the workday. She felt weary and used up and was contemplating a few days away, though her job had helped to distract her from the emotional trauma of the previous week and her own personal tumultuous feelings and thoughts.

For her it looked like it would be a long weekend since her office did not open on weekends but with the site on the outskirts of Gureje, she had little choice. To exonerate herself on Sunday, she would have to stay all day Saturday on site, so she could attend all three services after which she was sure she would be so tired, she'd not be able to do any other thing but sleep till Monday morning.

Like the coward they called her, she had painstakingly avoided her sisters though Saffron made her understand she was just giving her space to lick her wounded pride in private, and she was so preoccupied with the sizzling romance between Ayo and Janella she didn't have time for her. All well and good. The love birds had been in and out of the house almost every day. It was so bad her senses were almost attuned to the sounds around the two. She heard Janella's stilted heels on the marbled corridor as she came in and went out, and was almost sure she heard Ayo every single night, kissing her sister—

The thoughts were too provoking.

She stood and stretched. "Time to leave."

She hadn't had much time with her friend since the birthday, even though Tolani had spread the news of how Christine's friends took care of all the meat, and the catering, almost causing a serious upset for her. Well, her job had taken her out of play at work, as well.

For a moment, she toyed with the idea of spending another weekend with Tolani but kicked against it. She didn't want to start being a liability especially since she knew Tolani would never complain.

She packed some of the books she needed to read on water treatment with her bag and walked wearily to her car. She didn't want to join the family at table and decided to stop by her favourite cafeteria, Mama's Soup, to buy food. She had done that the whole week and knew she would soon be fed up with take-outs. The car park was near-deserted, and dusk had approached when Christine drove out of her office premises.

Mama's Soup bustled with customers, and Christine had to park her car along the road. It took another several couple of listless waiting before she was served. She carried the takeaway pack back to her car to find a young man standing by it.

"Excuse me?"

"Brother said you should give me the keys that I should bring you home," the young man said.

Christine frowned. She'd never seen him before. She shook her head. "Pardon?"

He couldn't be more than eighteen years old. He was thin and gangly. His face had a boyish handsomeness to it. She didn't meet many people, but she prided herself of being good with faces even years after.

She batted her eyelids. "Do I know you?"

"Brother said I should bring you home." He snapped and snatched the car key from her hand.

Christine gasped. "What is the meaning of this? I don't know—"

The boy was swift. He opened the back door and pushed her inside. People were all around, but none seemed to notice them. Fear gripped Christine. Was this a carjacking? Then where would they take her to? She opened her mouth to scream but not a single sound came out. The boy was talking to someone outside. She scooted to the door and opened it.

"My brother's girlfriend is always taking the car—" he was saying. The boy slammed the door back almost hitting her leg. "She's always putting me in trouble. Brother left the car key with me and she just sneaked out with the car—" he continued talking to a man.

Christine tried to open the door again, but he stood against it, blocking her. She kicked at the door and screamed, "I don't know him before, please."

Seeing this may not work, she scurried to the other side and tried to open the door, but it had the child-lock firmly in place. She shrieked and squeezed in between the front seats. If only she could get out of the passenger's side in time.

Another man came out of a car across the road, walked up to the boy and slapped him hard. "Give me my key." He growled.

The boy burst into tears and gave him the key. A few of the customers started gathering. The boy started stammering the explanation to the small crowd. The man who'd taken the key got behind the steering. The boy quickly got in the back with Christine as the other man drove off at a neck-breaking speed.

The impact threw Christine back into the seat and she wept like a child. What was she going to do? She had to pull herself together. She was too scared to jump out of the car while it was moving, if she got to open the door. What could she do?

The car slowed and she sat up as they approached an intersection. Maybe she could poke her fingers in the boy's eyes to distract him and find a way to jump out but not with the car moving. The driver slowed down, and she lunged forward to try out her plan, but the boy's hand came up and cleaned her face with a handkerchief. She slumped.

Christine knew she wasn't asleep or unconscious. She wasn't herself either. The substance rubbed on her face stung and made her eyes watery but otherwise, she seemed alright, but stupefied. She couldn't speak or see clearly, and her mind was in a maze. She struggled within herself to focus on her situation, where they were going—the driver had slowed to within the speed limit. Christine noticed the landscaping changed. It seemed as though they were leaving town. She tried to sit up but was too weak to do it so she remained slouched, stretching as much as she could, hoping to see something, remember something.

The car slowed to a stop and the driver took in another passenger beside him. They chatted until their voices soon began to drone in her mind. She thought she was beginning to doze but wasn't sure. The voices seemed to stray to a distance and soon, she lost consciousness.

When she came to, she was alone in pitch-blackness, and had a splitting headache. She couldn't see anything and had to use her hands to feel around her. The floor was cold, so she stood. With baby steps, she moved around. Her enclosed space was small just enough space for not more than two people. The wall felt like rough stone and she couldn't decide if it was cement or mud. The door however was wooden. She turned the handle several times and wanted to scream in frustration, but the mere effort drained her of strength.

She held her pounding head and sobbed. Oh dear God, help me. Help me. Where am I, why have I been kidnapped? What do they want from me? The questions ran through her mind. She searched round the room for her handbag. It was hoping for too much. She was isolated. She threw all her anger and frustration into the wind and banged the wooden door, screaming till her voice ceased of its own volition, and she slumped on to the ground, weak and weary. She would probably die here. She thought of all the crime stories she'd heard about, and how abducted people died of mind confusion and hunger. Or asthma.

A favourite Psalms came to her mind, and she recited herself to sleep.

The Lord is my shepherd I shall not want. He makes me to lie down in green pastures: he leads me beside the still waters. He restores my soul: he leads me in the paths of righteousness for his name's sake. Though I walk through the valley of the shadow of death, I fear no evil: for you are with me your rod and staff they comfort me—

Christine woke up in the dark room and sat with her back against the cool, uneven wall. She had no idea how long she'd slept or had been missing. Who would notice her absence? Her mother would, and her sisters too. But would they care to look for her? She took stock of her relationships. It hadn't amounted to much. Her sisters were selfish and hateful, and her mother was self-consumed and insensitive to others.

She burst into tears. Tolani would miss her but her colleague would not notice and raise any alarm till Monday afternoon. She may be dead by then. What would she do? Her pastor would notice she wasn't in church on Sunday—that gave her some hope. He would call her and when she didn't pick up, he'd check on her—more hope, but that wasn't until another two days, by which she may be...gone.

She wasn't sure what day or time it was, but she needed to help herself. All her life, the people closest to her, her family, had treated her as someone weak and cowardly. She needed to disprove this now if for no other reason than for her rescue. She culled on her inner strength and went for the door. She banged on it with all her might. Then raised her voice and called out for help. But she soon got tired. Her throat felt parched and sore and she slid back to the floor, too weak to even think.

The door opened inward, and she remained mute behind it, afraid of the unknown, coiled up in cold fear. Light from a lit room trickled in and Christine saw the silhouette of a man walk in and look round. It gave Christine the impression she was locked up in a storeroom of some sort. The light outlined the man, but it didn't illuminate his face. He must be tall and hunky because he filled most of the doorway, unlike the two who abducted her.

"She's not here," he called out.

"Check behind the door, idiot," a voice called back, and he turned to peep.

Christine was so scared she couldn't breathe.

"Oh." The hunk laughed at his own stupidity. "She's here," he said over his shoulder.

Christine heard the second man walk in with a strong searchlight which he pointed on her face, causing her to squint and prevent her from staring at them. She bent her head between her knees and folded her arms over her head. They stood over her for several seconds without saying anything.

"You are going to stay here without making any noise again, or else I will flog you," one of the men said.

Like a stubborn child being reprimanded, she remained in her posture. Right now, she was helpless, terrified they could kill her if they wanted. She just prayed they would not cause her bodily harm.

"If you want anything, you can knock and ask and someone will give you but if you shout and bang the door again, you will die here of hunger and thirst. If you want to use the toilet, then you knock and say what you want quietly. Do you understand me?"

She remained frozen. His booted foot pushed at her and she screamed.

"Shut up," he snapped. "Now look at me." He raised his voice. "Look at me."

With the flashlight still on her face, she lifted her head and blinked.

"I don't know you and I don't care who you are or how much they want on your head but if you make noise, I'll kill you and there's nothing anyone can do to me."

He lowered the light to an angle which enabled Christine to see a stocky, average-height man, and another huge one. She couldn't see either face of both men.

The shorter man, the one with the light growled. "Do you understand?"

She nodded, trembling. "Water. Please I want water," she whimpered.

She had a lot of questions, but she needed to get in their good books first. If they were just hired to abduct her then she had a long way to go and needed to have as many friends as possible. She still fought with the fear, anger and frustration of her situation.

The two men left, slamming the door shut. The hunk came a few minutes later with a bucket of water. He placed it in the centre of the room and left the door half-open. Christine wanted to tell him she meant drinking water, but he had turned away, guarding the door.

She crawled to the water and dipped her face in it. It was clean, cool and refreshing. A low rumbling sound from the man laughing at her made her look up. She took some of the water in her hand and rinsed her face and mouth out on to the floor. To hell with modesty.

"You're using drinking water to wash," he bellowed and laughed.

"Don't talk with her!" the other man called out with an angry voice. Christine turned back to the water and sipped. "Take the water from her. It's taking too long."

She sneak-peeked the other room. It was bare. Even the other man was on his feet. The room looked like a reception but that was only a feeling she had because she just saw a shadow of a floor too bare to tell since it was poorly lit.

The bucket of water was removed in a flash and the door slammed shut.

Now what? She wanted to use the toilet but couldn't bring herself to knock for that. A thought occurred to her maybe they would take her out and she could find a way to run. If the hunk came again, she could sweet-talk him. He seemed like a moron. The body of an elephant with the brain of a mosquito. The thought made her almost smile. It turned out as a sigh. She took in several deep breathes and knelt down to say a word of prayer. Then she moved to the door on legs she was glad still worked and knocked.

"Please I want to use the toilet," she said. She waited a second and the door opened wide. She leaped back like a lion retreating before an attack.

"Where is she running to?" Hunk laughed. "Follow me," he said.

It was broad daylight. And they were in the middle of a thick forest. No wonder she wasn't bound. There was no where she could run to. The other man was nowhere in sight. What she had thought was the reception area was just a paved frontage which was at the mouth of the forest. The bush was so thick they had to push branches aside to walk. This must have been an abandoned building project. It amazed her it was a red mud hut with thatched roof.

But who'd think of building such a—thing so close to the jungle?

"Move forward and do whatever you want ahead," Hunk said and lit a cigarette. "If I was you, I'll go all the way because tomorrow may never come." He laughed.

Thoughts about making him a friend vanished. She only wanted to run. She walked forward a little and looked back. He smoked and kept his eyes on her. There was no path and he seemed so sure she had nowhere to go, still his gaze disturbed her.

Christine moaned at how her simple Friday sky-blue and grey asymmetrical Ankara dress had blotches of dark brown. She didn't think the stains would ever go away, and she mourned her beautiful outfit. She walked forward a bit and pulled tall shrubs from her way so she could squat. She didn't feel pressed any more. She looked back at him again and he sneered.

"Please can you turn away so—"

He shouted. "You're joking. Do what you want to do and let us go now."

Self-conscious, she squatted with her back to him and peed. Never had anyone made her feel so violated. When she stood, she was still turned away from him. She contemplated running forward though she didn't know how fast she could go in this nasty forest. She thought she saw a deer dart across the forest and screamed. Hunk jumped over in two huge leaps and gripped her with tremendous strength.

"I saw an animal," she shrieked. "I saw a big animal. Where is this? Where did you bring me?" She struggled.

Hunk dealt her a dirty slap on the side of her head. She blanked out.

CHAPTER FOURTEEN

Chico hit on the centre of the bone, splitting the meat at its most vulnerable joint. The cut was a clean one. A huge drop of sweat landed on his nose and he used his sleeve to wipe it off before it got to the meat.

He dismantled the lap and pushed the large chunks to Ladi, the new boy working with him. "Do you want pieces, madam?"

"Oga Chico, is that not asking for too much?" A middle-aged lady said with a wink.

Chico smiled. She had been his customer for ten years. Somehow, he always couldn't allow anyone else to sell to her. "Ladi will cut it for you."

She sulked. "Hmm—will he know what I like?"

He pulled the chunks and stripped them with an accuracy only he could achieve. He was a stickler for detail and excellence. The volume of meat was much but Chico tackled it and left the packaging to Ladi.

Within minutes, he was done with the meat. Though he didn't like to interfere with retail in the abattoir, he still worked in the shops every once in a while. And some customers were just too precious to pass up. When the lady left, he gazed out of the shop and sighed. He had joined the butchers today and slaughtered a cow along with them, and then proceeded to hawk and find buyers. He did this often to keep in touch with what went on firsthand. The lap had been the last to go and he'd purposely kept it for the woman.

It was another uneventful Saturday. Fifty cows had gone to market and not come back.

"Ladi, clean up," he said and left the shop.

Most of the meat was now on retail trays. Chico walked to the offal shop and inspected as the trading and haggling went on. Lucy sat preoccupied with counting her money. Chico leaned over, and she looked up at him, a fond smile playing about her lips.

"You killed today," she said, still counting but now giving him her attention.

"I like to keep that skill in view," he said. "How was market?"

She shrugged. "I bought from Ejiro today. Stiff but not bad."

He laughed. "Ejiro has no sentiments," he said. "Business is business for him."

She batted her eyelids. "He learned from a master of the trade." He arched his eyebrow and she nodded. "Yes, he did." Her money complete, she tucked it into her apron purse. "It looks like there were not enough cows to kill. Seems meat was scarce today?"

"We had a little shortage. The trailers came in late last night," he explained. "The vets couldn't finish with their check-ups." He straightened as though visibly trying to straighten something. Though the trailers did come in, he would never sell meat he wasn't sure of.

"You've not allowed me to come," she mumbled, lowering her lashes alluringly.

"Lucy."

"I know. I know everything you have said—"

"Not here. Not now. Come to the house at the end of the day," he said.

"I have some offal left." Her eyes brightened. "I'll make pepper soup for you. Just the way you like it."

He smiled back at her and nodded. "Thank you."

He walked out of there, with mixed feelings. His relationship with her had always been one-sided and as tough as he was, he hadn't been able to tell her the truth. He didn't want anything more than a simple friendship with her. She was an attractive woman, and like him had grown up in the abattoir.

For him, it was her greatest disadvantage. Most of them ended up either living at the abattoir or leaving. Those who left hardly ever came back. And those who continued to live hardly left. If Chico didn't own the land and the business, he probably would have left and gone to find something else to do with his life.

Another major minus for Lucy was her lack of education. At Chico's insistence, she had reluctantly attended evening classes and when the exams came, failed all the subjects, and pleaded with Chico to let her just sit in her shop and sell.

Lucy's mother, who had a thriving business selling pepper in the main market, met her father who sold retail meat, and fell in love. When she got married, she got a stand in the abattoir and continued to sell pepper. Later, her husband convinced her to go into the offal business and it worked for her.

Lucy was born the first child of eight children and naturally took to her mother's business. As a young adult, even when Chico was just an ordinary butcher, she had been attracted to him, and the feeling was mutual. They both had never been able to deny the attraction and soon everyone called them together. Then came the huge split in his family and he left.

When he arrived Ode Abattoir, then jointly owned by several masters, he was determined to do better for himself. He started taking his education serious. Shortly before he took over the ownership of the abattoir, Lucy moved from the smaller abattoir run in the military barracks, where they had all been to Ode to be with him, and the relationship blossomed.

He liked her. He would have loved to be with her. She was hardworking, respectful, and beautiful. But she represented the lifestyle he detested. She represented the life he wanted to rise above. He had tried to let her understand his dreams, his aspirations. He wanted to revolutionize his profession. He wanted to be respectable. She couldn't give him that, ever. They were just not in the same world anymore, and he couldn't see them being there. If only she could understand.

Chico pushed thoughts of Lucy aside. The time had come for him to let her know he didn't want her any longer. He knew one or two of the masters who were crazy about her. She had a huge advantage over other women around. She was young, beautiful and enterprising. Once she took her mind off him, he was sure she would see someone else. He hoped she would not take it too hard.

Over the years, he had tried to make Lucy feel special while also trying to make her understand he would not be good to her if they ever ended up together. That had been so hard to comprehend, even for him. How did you tell someone you love them, but you didn't want them?

He knew on several occasions, he had sent mixed messages to her. Now he had to set it straight—and he refused to acknowledge it could be the presence of another woman making him assert his decision. There was no other woman in his life.

It was going to be a big evening in his life. Though he had offered her accommodation on the abattoir, Lucy had declined for reasons best known to her. She lived in the middle of town with her younger sister who now followed up with their mother's pepper business. Their parents still worked in the smaller abattoir.

When Lucy arrived, he wanted to be prepared for her. Since she was bringing the pepper soup for him, he was sure she would go home first, and this gave him time to get ready. He had a long bath and wore clean clothes. He didn't want to dress down or too well, either would send messages he didn't want. He wanted her to be relaxed and he hoped to be too.

For months, he had done his best to avoid her. He had stalled from paying much attention to her. Then Christine had talked about her friend's daughter's birthday party, and something had gotten into his head and he'd asked Lucy to help out. Of course, she had been only too willing.

He sighed heavily. He hated what he had to say, how to say it. He decided to see Oloye for a couple of hours. The old man's presence had a calming effect on him. When he returned, he was sure Lucy would be waiting. He wished he knew what she would do when he cut all ties with her. The great Chico was so jittery by the time he opened the door to leave, he jumped back at the sight in front of him. If he was a woman, he would have screamed.

Oloye stood by his doorpost, looking at the fish farm just across the fruit orchard, which sprawled over a large expanse of land beyond the lawn.

"Holy Moses."

"Move back into your house. I've been watching you since. What are you doing in this place? Are you not supposed to come and see me?" Oloye spoke rapidly.

Chico stood back and stared as the old man walked into his house. "Am I dreaming?"

"Listen carefully. I was checking on my traps today, and I saw something strange. I don't know what is happening but there are strangers on your land," Oloye said. He never wasted words.

Chico frowned. "Strangers?"

"Shut up and listen. They have a woman with them. I saw two men and a woman," Oloye said.

Chico took a deep, calming breathe. "Come and take me there." He stepped out.

Oloye remained in the house. "Don't be silly. I said there are two giants and a woman. She would be sent to seduce you most likely."

Chico scowled. "Take me there."

"Get people to help you."

"No." Chico walked back in and looked darkly at his grandfather. "Show me the place."

"We would go together then," Oloye said.

"No. You know I will never allow you to face such danger."

"I followed them, and they didn't see me, or maybe the woman did later because she screamed. Anyway, you know I am very careful, and I am smarter than you."

"Smarter, not stronger."

"I won't let you go alone," Oloye said stubbornly.

"You won't?" Chico gasped. "Watch me go then. I know all the places you set your traps anyway," he snapped.

He marched into his bedroom and changed his white shirt and grey trousers to black khakis and cowboy boots. He brought out a wrap of sharpened knives, tucking them into different angles in his belt as he walked out. He had ten knives by the time he was done. He stopped by his kitchen and picked two small knives he tucked into his boots. He strolled resolutely out of the house but stopped short halfway down the road.

Angry at his grandfather for remaining on the same spot, he walked back and snapped. "You lead the way."

"I need some knives too," Oloye said, and Chico glowered. "I'm better than you with the knife."

"Maybe. But you're old. Better but not faster."

He stood his ground. "Eighty plus not dead."

"There are more knives in the kitchen." Chico folded his arms across his chest. "Help yourself."

The old man sighed in relief and after picking two good knives, led the way out.

Chico's house was on the plateau of the closest of the hills facing the abattoir. It enabled him to see much of the plain and business areas of the ranch. Oloye's hole was up the big hill at the edge of the untamed forest.

"You remember that mud hut you started building for me in the middle of the jungle? Before we saw the huge snake in it one day and you chickened out?" Oloye said.

"I can't forget it," Chico said, as they made the uphill walk. Oloye could argue all day and night he "chickened" out so he'd decided to accept it, and now wasn't the time or the occasion for useless bartering. The truth in fact was that Oloye swore he would never live in a house even up in the jungle, and Chico angrily stopped the project.

"That's the place. The woman was screaming she'd seen a wild animal and fainted. The man carried her away. I think she saw me."

Chico said nothing. He wanted to joke Oloye was a wild animal, but his mind was too occupied on important matters. There had been threats of thievery before, but they had never hidden in the jungle. This looked like an organised set-up and he was ready to scatter it before it blew open.

When Chico and Oloye got up the hill, there was murder in Chico's mind. He loved his land, and he would die, or kill for it. They walked stealthily. Chico had to give it to his grandfather—fifteen years of solitary living had not reduced the man's ability to hunt. He was like a champ culled back from retirement. You could feel the excitement oozing from his every pore. They sneaked close to the hut and when it was in sight Oloye stopped and turned to Chico.

"I am sure they went inside," Oloye said.

"The place looks dark and deserted," Chico said.

"Maybe they've left—"

Chico lifted his hand to indicate they wait. "Stay here. I'll look round."

"When last did you set traps? You stay here, I'll look round, and boy, if any of my traps catch you, don't scream."

"I'll wait for you," Chico mumbled and felt rather than saw Oloye's smile.

Again, no need to tussle. He had to give it, the old was fit and strong. He didn't even pant when they reached the top of his hill, and as he stole away, he made no sound.

Chico kept his eyes fixed on the hut, watching for any strange movement. Oloye was back at his side within a few minutes.

"I heard two distinct male voices in the dark. One is about to leave."

Chico knit his brows. "What did he say?"

Oloye mimicked. "Stay here and be smart, idiot. And stay awake."

"It doesn't mean he's leaving."

"He is."

Chico let him have it. "The woman?"

"No idea. She didn't say a word. She might have left."

Chico stared ahead. "We'll wait and see if the other man leaves. I don't want them to see us coming. Most important, I want to know what they're up to. I think we should take a captive."

"I think so too. The idiot seems like a good candidate," Oloye said.

"Or the woman."

"If she's still—" Oloye paused at a slight rumbling sound. "Get up on this tree. You'll see the place better."

Chico could not believe the speed Oloye used to go up. He was slower. But he got up. The tree swayed slightly but the branches balanced as they saw a small flashlight. Wow, thief needs a torch, Chico thought.

The man walked as stealthily as he could, passing right under their tree. Chico estimated it couldn't be more than four o'clock, but the clouds were thick, the jungle was dense, he didn't see the face of the man, but the silhouette was impressionable. The man was short and heavily built. He looked like God had too much to pack in the body and too little space. His biceps were almost bursting the seams. Oloye and Chico watched him leave and stayed for another hour or so. Both were trained in the fine art of waiting.

"My leg is becoming stiff," Oloye mumbled.

"I'll go and bring one of them," Chico said.

"Wait. Don't mind me. We wait till it is dark," Oloye said.

Chico could feel excitement vibrating off every pore of the old man's being. When last was there some fun in his lonesome existence?

"It is dark," Chico said emphatically. "I can't see if it gets darker."

Oloye chuckled. "Then I'll go."

Chico snickered. "Are you eighty or what?"

"You know arithmetic, don't you?"

A sulky silence ensued. An hour couldn't have passed.

"I was thinking—" Oloye said. "We can go together. We need to know if there are other people. I would distract anyone awake—"

"How?" Chico whispered.

"I can make monkey noise. There are a lot of monkeys in the night."

"It's not yet night. And I haven't heard a single one—"

Oloye's voice hardened. "Wait till I make the sound then you'll hear them. Go down. This is my show."

"I should have sent you off this land long ago," Chico murmured.

Oloye couldn't come down from the tree if he didn't get down first unless he jumped, and his old man may think this was a "show" but he'd break his aged bones if he tried to jump. Again, Chico let him lead the way, and followed just as quietly.

Avoiding the open frontage, they circled the back of the hut with its overgrown shrub and waited for what seemed like eternity and then Oloye screeched. The sound agitated the quiet of the evening. There was a long silence and then he made another sound as though calling out to some animal. Soon, there was a distance response, and two closer ones.

A man swore aloud, cursing the sounds. A woman moaned so low they almost didn't pick it. There was no room for words. Chico knew the option he would choose of the man and the woman. Oloye nodded sharply, hoping his action would translate his message and scrambled off, ruffling the dry leaves in the night. His rough movement sounded like a trumpet blowing. The man moved forward, unaware of the bait.

Oloye made one sound like a baby crying. There was a response from different angles of the night. He moved toward a ninety-degree angle of the frontage and gave a loud cry. From the back, Chico heard the woman knock on a door and whisper, "water." He wasn't sure anyone else would have heard it. It came out so low. Was the woman sick? Even better. He moved closer to the front and heard the man walking to the edge of the thick brush.

"How does one chase these evil spirits away? I won't spend another night here."

Oloye must have seen Chico approach. He squelched again, drawing other night animals out. Then he scrambled fast in the man's direction. The man walked back to the front of the hut and picked a stick and his torch. Chico heard a lot of scrambling and then a huge thud and a loud curse. He moved like lightening to the door, unhooked the bolt and entered the dark room.

The woman scrambled and he grabbed her by her hair. It wasn't his intention, but he couldn't see her and that was what his hand touched first. The hair was bound in a bun that seemed to have started scattering. She screamed and he covered her mouth with his hand. It didn't take him more than a moment to subdue her. She was small. He clamped one hand round her small waist and the other kept her mouth sealed off. He moved out of the room with his back and with his shoe kicked the door shut, making sure he made as little noise as possible. He didn't have time. He took the back with the small woman and scuttled to the tree they had climbed earlier. Oloye was there.

"Let's go," he snapped and both men launched into the night.

Chico flung the woman over his shoulder like a sack. Whoever she was, he planned to use her to draw out the criminals on his land. All manner of night animals howled and squeaked. Chico had a feeling Oloye had roused the night life early. Only God knew what he had raised and for a moment, Chico pitied the "idiot" who would spend the night with them.

They got to the edge of the forest where Oloye lived in record time. Chico noticed through the run, the woman had remained calm, almost consenting. Oloye turned to him and signalled for him to continue.

"Lucy would be in my house," he muttered. "I don't want her to be part of any of this." He breathed hard. Oloye glared at him and shook his head. "Bring some light out here." Chico said. "Do you have a rope? I would tie her to your door—" The woman lurched with such strength, he staggered but held her tighter. "Stay put," he snapped.

Oloye raised an eyebrow. "Are you marrying Lucy?"

"Get the rope for me."

Oloye trudged to his shack muttering incoherently.

"Chico," she whimpered at first, unsure. Chico stiffened. His grip on her waist tightened. "Chico, it's Christine," she said weakly and burst into tears.

He lowered her to the ground, mortified. As soon as she was on the ground, she covered her face and sobbed harder. Chico bent over her and removed her hands from her face.

"Christine?" he roared. "My God. What on earth are you doing here?"

Oloye walked out of the shanty with a short rope and a lantern that merely illuminated the square foot they stood on. "This is all I can find. My past hostages have never been bigger than a short, wild—" Oloye stopped short when he saw Chico leaning over the hostage, soothing her hair away from her face. "Well well. Who's the captive now?" he mocked.

"She's somebody I know," Chico snapped, walking past Oloye into the shack. He looked for water in the clay pot and brought it out to her.

"Drink some water, Christine, and rest. I have a guest in my house I don't want involved in this, so I'll go and send her away and come back for you," he said.

"No, please. Don't leave me here," she screamed, her eyes bulging at Oloye.

Chico couldn't help but laugh. "He's harmless. Though he doesn't look it."

Oloye looked far from harmless. He hadn't shaved or cut his hair in fifteen years. He looked like a lunatic.

Christine knelt and grabbed Chico's leg. "I won't stay here, please. Please."

Oloye laughed. "Let her go with you."

"Okay, I guess I'll need to have an explanation for Lucy," Chico muttered. "But first, I want to know how you got here."

Christine's eyes widened. "I don't know where I am. How did you get here? What—?" She covered her mouth with one hand as though she had a new discerning of her plight. She lowered her voice, but it still shuddered. "You're not—"

"Don't get any ideas. I'm just as confused as to why you're here. This is part of the abattoir. I am on my land." Chico rubbed the back of his neck. "Now, how did you get here?"

Christine gasped. "What day of the week is it?"

"Saturday evening. Should be about—" He checked his watch. "It's about eight o'clock. I can't see well."

"Oh my goodness." Christine began to sob again. The men allowed her time to calm down and then got the story from her.

"I was going to tell you I'll camp over there for a few days till we get the full story," Oloye said.

Chico looked at his grandpa with gratitude. "Thank you."

"He must have been the one I saw today." Christine's gaze remained averted from the old man's.

"Are you strong enough to try and act normal?" Chico heaved. She nodded. "Oloye, I'll check back later." He turned to his grandfather. "Thank you for today."

The old man nodded. "I guess I get to keep your knives then?" It wasn't really a question.

Christine was shocked when Chico picked her up in his arms. She was weak and tired and welcomed it but feeling ashamed, she protested. "I can walk, really," she said softly.

"You'll walk when we get close to my home," he mumbled.

Oloye looked after them as they left and muttered to the dark night. "Marry."

Chico heard it as though it was in his ear.

CHAPTER FIFTEEN

CHRISTINE HUGGED HIS NECK, pressing herself close. She talked throughout, vain ramblings. She looked weak and tired, dirty and hysterical. Chico allowed her to talk, crooning his sympathy every once in a while. His heart was heavy. Who could do this? He feared a huge conspiracy against him but why would anyone kidnap Christine to get his attention? Oloye would find them first. Then he would know what to do. This didn't seem like a plot to destroy him, and he had a strange feeling he knew the culprits. And if he was right, then the war would be bloody.

He descended the mound just behind his house and changed his mind about hiding Christine. He would get into the house through the back door. Lucy would most likely be in his room, just to assert herself. It didn't bother him. He would still end whatever he had started with her today.

The house was all lit, which was against his principle. Though there were curtains, he preferred to have little or no lights around the house. Over the years, his eyes had grown accustomed to dimness and he liked it that way.

He lowered Christine and found the backdoor key where he usually kept it. She held on to his sleeves, and trembling, observed her surroundings.

"You're safe here." He stared at her. "You're shivering, are you cold?"

"No. I'm fine." She dropped her trembling fingers from his sleeves and hugged her waist.

"Come," he said, and led the way through the kitchen into the main house.

There was a sweet aroma of scent leaf and fresh fish and her stomach growled.

"I have an extra room. You can have a bath, and rest."

Lucy came out of his bedroom, as he'd predicted and leaned against the doorpost. She looked drowsy as though she'd been sleeping.

"Welcome dear," she mumbled. "I thought there was an emergency." She kept her gaze on him, as though Christine was part of the wall.

"There is an emergency," he said stiffly. He turned to Christine. "Come with me."

He led her to a clean room though not prepared for a visitor, and opened the windows to allow a full rush of cool night air come in.

"I'll bring things for you to use and something to change into," he said.

She stood rigidly in the middle of the room while he checked the bathroom to be sure all was alright.

"I want to go home," she said hoarsely.

He came back to face her. Her lips quaked and her eyes watered.

He shrugged. "You can still have a bath. You won't want to be seen like this." He stared her down. What was the matter with her? Well, she had been abducted, he chided himself.

"I don't care. I want to leave," she retorted.

"Give me a few minutes then." He sighed. "I'll take you home." He marched out.

She wanted to ask him where he hid her car but knew she would cry trying. She dropped on to the unmade mattress as soon as he left and burst into tears. She felt dirty, violated, cold and insecure. Why would she be abducted and brought to his territory. Was he in the know? Had something in the plan gone wrong and the reason why he had come for her? She shivered. Why was there no one in sight when he got into the room and how had he gotten in without help? Of course, except for the mad man who he seemed so comfortable with.

His tone had annoyed her, but she only cooperated with him, so he'd let her go. She could never feel safe until she was back in her own house. She recognised the Lucy as the lady who came to help with the cooking. Okay, so she's the lady of Chico's manor. What did it matter to her? He could be married to one of the cows he slaughtered for all she cared. That she was thinking about this made her even more irritated.

Would he let her go? She had cramps in her stomach, and knew she was going to be sick anyway. What next now? She couldn't go home like this as he had pointed out, but she feared for her life. With her car missing, she would need to get into action, report to the police, find the car.

She struggled to her feet and walked into the bathroom. When she opened the tap and warm water came out, she was too tempted to resist. There was a bar of soap in a dish. It was used but she didn't care. She took it and stood under the shower, with her clothes on and began to rub herself, crying—wailing.

She didn't know how long she was in the shower but when she came out, dripping all over the tiled floor, drenched from her hair to her shoes, shivering from the cold air and her fears, she found a clean shirt and jeans on the bed, no doubt Chico's, a towel, and toiletries. The new soap and sponge, and toothpaste with toothbrush were too tempting. She let out a soft gasp and took them right back into the bathroom. At first, like she had lost her mind, she rubbed the soap on her clothing on her body and then she pulled them off and soaked in the warm water, relishing every single feel.

⟫⟫ ⟪⟪

Chico's mood went from bad to horrible and though he hated being mean to Lucy, he couldn't hide the fact her being around was a bad idea. The dark clouds shadowing his face spoke louder than words as he came back from taking the other lady to the guest room and walked with jerky steps to his room without saying a word to her.

He stayed for long moments, rummaging through his wardrobe, looking for what could be acceptable for her to wear, and getting himself more upset by the moment. Lucy, who followed him into the room, sat on the bed she must have earlier made and followed him with her eyes as he moved around frenetically. He threw toiletries on the bed and when everything he needed was complete, stomped out of the room with them. He was back within seconds.

"How's she?" Lucy asked softly. She knew how to just calm him down. Her words softened him.

"I don't know." He didn't want to talk about Christine. "She should be fine, I guess."

"Do you need any help?"

"Help. No."

She took his hand and drew him to her side on the bed.

She cooed. "Come and undress. Let me rub you down, then you can eat and rest."

"No, Lucy. Thanks for the meal but I think I should take you home now," he said as kindly as he could muster.

"I want to stay with you this night."

She entwined their fingers, her eyes huge and childlike. It was one of her most endearing features and she knew the power they held. But he couldn't afford to be moved by those eyes tonight. He had a crime to investigate, intruders on his property.

"Come on." He pulled her up from the bed. She purposely fell and clung to him. "Lucy, no. We can't. I can't."

She groaned. "Is she staying the night?"

"I'll take you home." He withdrew from her and walked out to his truck, forgetting totally to tell Christine he was leaving.

Lucy grudgingly followed him out. She got into the truck and they drove away into the night.

"I paused on my way out, and put my ears to the door in front of the room—"

He gritted his teeth. "And?"

"She was in the shower, humming. For it to sound so soft, the lady must be humming above the shower—she's spending the night with you, right?" Chico did not reply. "You know me, Chico, I'll fight her—I'll fight anyone for you."

"I'll tell you about that lady someday, Lucy, I know what's eating you," Chico said when he stopped in front of her house. He had headache from too much talking since seeing Oloye at his doorstep. "But I found her on my grounds and that is why she must stay with me till I know what she wants there, okay?"

She held his gaze for a long moment. She was the first to blink, and nod. She drew him into a hug and kissed his cheek. He sped off before her door closed.

Chico hated what was happening to him as he rushed back to the ranch. He wasn't erratic and couldn't be easily fazed but he had a strange feeling within him. The deadliest wars were between brothers and he had an awkward feeling he was about to face a comrade in the war ahead. He knew for sure Christine would be scared to death, being all alone again.

Even if she was part of a conspiracy against him, she would be scared being in his presence. He just wanted this night to end. And that meant more than darkness turning to day.

He drove into the ranch and decided to go round the ranch just out of a hunch. Several times he was tempted to go up the hill but that could disrupt what Oloye was doing and greatly irritate the old man.

When he got back into his house, all was quiet. Panic gripped him and he thought Christine was not in but when he knocked lightly and opened her door, she was sprawled across the bed, wearing his oversized clothing, sound asleep. Her hair which he'd only seen tied in a ball was spread out on the pillow in long, tangled tresses, as though she spread the wet curls to dry out. He never knew they were so long.

He smiled involuntarily and his first thought was leave her alone, but he wanted to talk and know if she was alright, so he nudged her and after several trials, she came to, and sluggishly sat up. His outfit was ridiculously big on her, but she had folded the sleeves and trousers to make it wearable.

"Sorry I left. I had to drop Lucy off," he said, arms akimbo. "Did you eat?"

"No."

Her hair dropped down to the middle of her back and she subconsciously brought it forward and twist in a bid to dry it. The motion distracted him. He walked to the window and parted the curtain. For a moment he gazed at black nothing and then he turned back to her, ignoring the motions with her hair.

"Lucy brought pepper soup," he said. "I don't stay here much so I don't have food in the house. But I can check out what she left."

She closed her eyes and rested her back against the headboard. "I'll live."

He didn't have spare bed sheets, unfortunately. He wanted to apologise for that but shook his head and went back into the kitchen to see what Lucy had brought. It was pepper soup, just the way he liked it with a variety of seafood, and yam chunks. It wasn't as hot as the name implied because he couldn't handle too much pepper in his system. It was perfect for someone who hadn't eaten for a while. He had means of warming it but didn't. He didn't think she could handle anything scorching and she was too weak for his liking.

When he got back into the room, she was dozing off again.

He nudged her. "Sit up and take some."

"No." She shook her head. Just as she said it, her stomach growled in protest.

"Come on, sit up," he said. "It's quite tasty."

She dragged herself up, took a sip and groaned in appreciation but dropped the spoon. He took it from the bowl, and fed her, one sip after the other, one yam lump and then another. When the plate was empty, she asked for more. He quietly went back into the kitchen and filled up the plate. She cleaned it and then sighed contentedly, after washing it down with cold water.

"Excuse me." He left with the empty plate, leaving the water with her. He returned shortly and leaned against the wall.

"I have to go home." She yawned and slid back into her reclining position.

"It's too late. Besides, I don't think you'll be safe at home."

"I think I'm closer to my captivity here than at home."

"When does your school resume?"

Her eyes widened in lack of comprehension and he took it for her trauma.

"You're a student, remember?"

"I'm in session. I just came home to do my research." She placed her palm on her forehead and closed her eyes.

"I didn't know your hair was so long," he mumbled before he could stop himself. "Is it natural?"

Her eyes popped open and she chuckled. "Yes, it's my hair." Then, "Do you have a comb?" She looked at his head and noticed he had some coming on, not long enough for a comb though.

He shook his head and smiled. "Unfortunately."

They both kept quiet for a while.

His mind wandered to the genesis of a war in which he was ready to fight to the death. It wasn't the first time his life was on the line for the ranch. He had worked himself to a point of death several times to make sure the abattoir survived and endured unbearable stress to make sure his right was not taken from him. He knew anytime he needed to fight, he would.

"I have to be in church tomorrow," she said.

Just as he said, "Who would be looking for you now? Do you have family here?"

"My family is here," she said. "They may not miss me, though." She sucked in her breath. "But my pastor will expect me in church tomorrow."

He tilted his head to the side. A young lady whose family would not miss her caught his attention. He wanted to know more about her.

"Are you a pastor or what?"

"No, nothing of the sort. I'm just—" She paused for a minute. "I'm a committed member. Pastor knows me very well," she stammered.

"Hmm," he murmured. "So, if you must be in church, what do you wear?"

"I have to go home."

He shrugged. "I can do that for you in the morning, anyway."

"Do what?"

"Get your clothes—"

"Of course not."

He shrugged. He would not argue. "How old are you?"

"A lady doesn't disclose her age." She pushed herself up and sat with her back straight.

"Tell me."

"No."

"You can't be more than twenty-two." He angled his head and studied her. She began to comb her hand through her hair. "I'm probably right," he said. Or wrong, he thought. Why would he care? Her reason for being in his house now was more important. He wished he knew her age though. She looked so young, yet an edge around her eyes and her mouth depicted maturity, knowledge. Age.

"I have to find the car," she mumbled. "And who wants me and for what."

He continued to study her. "What car?"

She jolted as though in realisation. "The one they brought—My car. My father gave me—" she stammered and then closed her eyes again and took a deep breath.

"I guess whoever wants you, wants to harm me too. Or why would you be brought to my land," he said.

"You may be right." She nodded. "I wonder why anyone would want to try to hurt you by hurting me."

"That's the puzzle I'm going to solve," he said with a softness underlain with cold steel.

She flexed her fingers, a sort of reflex action that distracted Chico. "The old man?"

"Is my grandfather."

"Is—does he—why—"

"He's a recluse." He enjoyed her confusion but wouldn't offer any more explanation. "He won't sleep till he knows what the puzzle is though."

"I see." She sighed. She was tired and scared still and it showed in the way she shuddered. He had the premonition to leave her but not till he knew more. As it was, he knew nothing about her except the fact that she was a very committed member in her church.

"What do you do as a member to make the pastor notice you? Especially as a student that you are?" If she didn't like direct questions, like what her age was, then he would unveil her anyway he could. He would make her babble about herself.

She shrugged twice and stared at him, and then shook her head. "Nothing in particular. Just being available I guess," she said.

"Running errands," he muttered. What errands would a young beautiful lady run for the pastor? He thought carnally. "And when you leave for school?"

She shrugged. "You speak exceptionally well for a butcher," she said. "What's your qualification?"

He folded his arms across his chest and crossed his legs. "I schooled myself," he said. "So, I wouldn't know if I taught myself to a doctorate level, but I can read and write my name."

"How old are you?" she asked probably expecting a sure retaliation.

He glared at her. "I'll soon be thirty-three. In a few weeks." He looked his age, though his achievements ranked him much older.

She nodded. "You are a success story," she said.

He wasn't moved by her flattery. He had to know more about her. All his life, he had excelled in dismantling resolve. Hard cracked men yielded under his gaze, and he couldn't even get this small girl to answer one question to his satisfaction. Instead, he was talking about himself. She would soon be asking about what profit he made at the abattoir and he would be babbling.

"You should rest." He lifted himself off the wall. He was a man who knew when to retreat in battle to fight another day. At the door, he turned and looked at her. "What time is church?"

"I should get home to change before seven," she said. "So Saffron and the rest won't be awake when I get in, and see me in your clothes—"

He arched an eyebrow. "I'll be your driver till this puzzle is solved."

She shrugged. "Okay."

He thought her reply was arrogant. Small pretty girl was sharper than he'd ever envisaged. "Do you need to be woken up?" he asked, as she closed her eyes again. She nodded, not opening them. He thought she was really beautiful at that very moment, and it disturbed him. He was too old for little children like this.

He had said too much already, and he hated the way he was beginning to feel, thinking she was pretty and all. He opened the door and exited quietly. He doubted if he would sleep much. He wanted to go back to see Oloye but thought against it. He could disturb the bight and that would drive the old man into frenzy. He walked to the kitchen and ate the remaining meal. Lucy was a perfect cook.

Then he went back to his room and lay on the bed, doubtful of his ability to sleep.

CHAPTER SIXTEEN

CHICO DIDN'T DREAM OR snore or have sleeping dramas, so he surely knew he wasn't confused someone was in his room. He remembered he wasn't in the house alone as soon as he became conscious and wondered what Christine wanted here. He remained still as his mind followed her movement around the room. Of course, he had reason to suspect her. She had been removed from his forest and though she had a kidnap story to tell, anyone could say anything. Unless she wasn't the one opening his wardrobe right there.

It was a woman anyway because the footsteps were not silent but soft. She walked into his bathroom and he opened his eyes. He had a knife in his hand when she came out. She stifled a scream when he revealed himself to her from where he had hidden beside his wardrobe. As soon as he saw her walk out of his bathroom, barefooted and carrying a bottle of water, he showed just a side of himself, with the knife in his hand.

"Do you sneak around strangers' houses in the middle of the night?" She stood rooted to the spot, shaking. "I could have killed you," he spat, putting the knife away.

She gasped. "For what?"

"Don't you understand?" He glared at her. "You're not here by invitation."

"Thank you. And I'll be out of your house before you know it." She headed for the door. He shot forward to block her and towered over her in a sinister way.

"What if it was an intruder—or your captor who had come back? I could have thrown the knife if I had just a few extra seconds without seeing you," he snapped. "And I never miss."

He held her gaze, and she licked her lips but didn't look away.

"Why are you in my room?" he asked even though she had the bottle of water in her hand.

"I wanted to take some tea." She lowered her eyes. "I was looking for a flask with hot water. I saw only this bottle of water in the kitchen."

"I don't have tea or coffee—" He sighed and rubbed his head. He must have slept for only a few minutes before she came though he was a light sleeper. "Go back to your room and sleep." He stepped out of her way.

"I'm afraid," she gasped. "I can't sleep—alone."

"Stay here, then." He walked to his wardrobe and brought out a thick blanket which he threw on the floor. "Take the bed."

"Thank you," she sniffed. She kept the water bottle on the floor and climbed on to the bed. She was fast asleep before he'd settled in on the blanket.

Chico had only a couple of hours to sleep before he got up in the morning to follow his routine. He had woken up an hour earlier so he could be thorough. This time more than ever, he had reason to look round the abattoir.

Usually, the slaughter was closed on Sundays, but the masters were permitted to go out and work or make sales of live animals, and the doctors came in to do routine, extensive check-up for the animals. There was no killing on Sunday. After the two-hour routine walk which he judiciously did, he went up to see the recluse. The old man's snoring was heard a mile down the path and Chico smiled fondly. It only meant the man had kept watch through the night.

"Oloye," he called from the middle of the hut. Oloye groaned a response. "What did you find?"

"Go back in the evening. The idiot ran in from the bush and jammed himself into the room. Nothing else," he moaned. Chico burst into laughter. Oloye must have been disgusted having to stay and see nothing.

"But you should be there—what if something happens?"

"Get out boy," Oloye growled. "I want to sleep."

Chico decided if he went to the forest, he could see something but then he would be back late. Christine would be awake and worried. And then he may not see anything and that would infuriate him. He decided to leave it to the old man.

⟫⟫ ⟪⟪

Christine was up and dressed in her own dress when he arrived. She stood listlessly in the sitting room when he breezed in and rushed to his room. Within five minutes he was out, shaved, bathed and clothed. It was six thirty.

"Good morning," he said. "Let's go." He headed for the door.

She felt self-conscious. Her tangled hair had been tamed to the back and braided somehow into one neat lump. Her dress, though rumpled and damp, was wearable. He took just a quick glance but kept his comment to himself, and rightly so. After all, she was going home to change.

In the truck, he made it clear he intended to stay with her in the church and bring her right back to the abattoir.

"That's not possible," she retorted.

Her nerves were raw though she had slept well. When she woke up and didn't find him, she had panicked. The least she expected was he would explain his whereabouts when he returned. Instead, he shunned her. Well, he wasn't going to be giving orders. Besides, she just wanted to hand this mess over to the police. Once the police came in, he would have to back down. They would part ways, and hopefully, for good.

"I have two good reasons. One, you were on my property I won't let you go till I find out why. Two, you're not safe anywhere else," he said and manoeuvred the truck out of the familiar terrain.

She wanted to laugh at him, but realised he had a point. Two good points. You wouldn't catch a thief in your house and then just let him go without finding out more. "Your guest room mattress doesn't have sheets and I won't sleep in your bed again."

"I can get sheets for you. And you may not be able to sleep anywhere else anyway," he said softly.

She rolled her eyes. "Don't you go to church? Won't you be missed in your church?"

"Yes and no," he said simply.

Her mouth fell open. "You don't go to church?"

He sighed indulgently. "I go to church, but I don't run errands for my pastor. I won't be missed."

She took the slight in silence. She was proud of her work in her church and had no reason to defend herself to him.

"I advise you to pack your clothes when you get to your house. A day or two and I'm sure the riddle will be solved and you can go home," he said. They negotiated the junction to town. "Give me directions."

She mumbled them and they continued in silence. He found the house quite easily. It was located in the old high-brow area of the town. Christine showed him a strange angle and he parked the truck.

She let herself in through the back door. The housekeeper was already preparing for the day. In her family, everyone went to church. Janella followed whoever she was dating—she always had a date. Saffron attended the family church, with or without her husband. Wendy took Pebble with her to her church. The day her husband was buried was the last time she attended the family church. Christine had stopped attending any family church from the day she could find her way unaccompanied. It had been the beginning of conflicts between her and her father.

The house was as quiet as she had expected. On Sundays, people began to wake up from eight o'clock. She slid into her apartment and though she'd had a bath in Chico's house, she felt compelled to have her bath again. As she showered and washed her hair, the events of the past forty-eight hours overwhelmed her, and she cried softly. Exposed to such danger left her overawed.

Feeling clean, she removed a small duffel bag from her box room. Despite her difference on his logic, she found sense in it. She pulled two good dresses out of her wardrobe and stuffed into the bag with a formal jacket she could use to work. Reluctantly, she put in a t-shirt and a pair of jeans, hoping she wouldn't need the casuals. Then she searched for a suitable pyjama. Her undies were thrown in and some toiletries, a bed sheet and wrapper, and a pair of slippers, and snickers.

Her wardrobe was painfully limited, and she ended up wearing a simple hound's tooth dress with a black scarf, and a pair of shoes. She brushed her hair and bound it in a neat school-mistress bun. Every strand was tucked away. She was dressed for comfort even though the colours and the simple dress complimented her.

She had some cash in the house and she took it, just in case. Her office bag had gone with her car, and all her debit cards. She did need to report to the police, and the banks. She picked another office bag and carried it instead of the usual small clutch bag that would have complemented her church outfit. The housekeeper greeted her when she told her she was off. In her house, it was not anyone's business what you did with your time or schedules.

Chico had remained in the truck though he left the door open with one leg dangling outside. He came out when she approached and col-lected the bag from her, throwing it into the space between them in the single cabin truck. She noticed his alluring gaze though he didn't say a word. His eyes roamed her body with a flourish she detested herself for indulging. It was as though he dared her to pose for him.

"If you don't mind, I want to leave a note for Tolani," she said.

He nodded, then mumbled. "Let your hair down."

Her hair's wetness and oiling made it shine and look glossy and attractive. She pretended she didn't hear him. If he was going to be making personal comments, she'd have to pack her things right back. She wasn't ready to be stared down and told what to do with her appearances.

Tolani was not at home as Christine had expected and she dropped a note on her door jam, telling her she had to be away from work for a few days and she would explain later. She didn't want to give any details that might instigate Tolani.

They drove to her church and she asked Chico to blend with the church crowd. She was going to forget about everything except worship and she advised him to do the same. Chico found a seat in the back of the hall.

⤐ ⤏

Christine's church was one of the new era Pentecostal assemblies. They preached holiness to mean love and defined love in all the terms Chico had never imagined it could be seen. He had been invited to several such churches for weddings and baby dedications, and he was surprised Christine would find fellowship in such a place. She didn't strike him as so—gullible.

He believed in religion the old ways where men wore men's clothing and women wore women's clothing. With almost all the women with their heads uncovered, he prepared his mind to see things he didn't like about church.

Initially, his eyes followed Christine around as she greeted people. He got the impression she would really have been missed if she didn't come.

To his surprise, church wasn't as bad as he'd expected, though the females in men's clothing disturbed him. Many of the young ladies wore clothes with their cleavages exposed, tight clothes, even some of the ushers and choristers wore strapless dresses. Several times, he had to look away from this or that side to avoid distraction.

After service, Christine was nowhere to be found. He sat patiently, as the church emptied. The newcomers had been asked to stand up and be recognised during the service. Not him. He sat mute and afterward, as they were encouraged to come forward for a reception, he remained on his seat. He wouldn't be appreciated by them for any reason.

While waiting for Christine, it occurred to him she might have bolted but there was no reason for her to do this. She was safer with him than anywhere else. It was ludicrous. He didn't even know anything about her except she was from a rich family that didn't care about her. Thinking about where she lived had his head reeling. When he was much younger—

"My pastor wants to see you," she said.

He hadn't seen her coming. He arched one eyebrow but decided not to ask her what the meeting was about. Maybe it was the church or her stiff behaviour to him or just plain nerves. It didn't matter. Whatever the pastor wanted, he'd give and leave.

The previous night, he hadn't slept much, most of the time he sat up to just stare at her. Her hair flung all over his pillow gave him a strange feeling. She was too young, he'd told himself over and over again. He had never lived in his house with any one before, talk less a woman. An attractive woman. Now she'd be with him a couple of days and he had mixed feelings about it.

The pastor's office had blue and gold furnishing and leather seats. The air conditioning was cool but not excessive. At least, the thirty-some-thing-looking, trendy pastor was comfortable with it. During the sermon, Chico had gazed at him endlessly. His suit glistened like a movie star's, and his shoes were the colour of a supernova. He spoke with an accent Chico didn't think was natural. Everything about him just seemed too loud for a man God can speak to. All these new age pastors were just the same. Young, flashy, proud. How the illiterate souls would be won in this environment, Chico did not understand. If you don't have good clothes here, you don't fit.

The pastor sat behind a huge mahogany desk with flags from all over the world in a fancy flag-holder. A fat concordance was open in front of him, beside a laptop. A plasma TV hung on one part of the wall, with his pictures on the wall right above the seat, and another, picture. Chico deduced it must be of another pastor. Maybe the owner of the church.

They were ushered to soft leather seats opposite the pastor by a young pretty secretary, someone very much like Christine. A small conferencing facility occupied the other half of the office. This pastor sure has taste, Chico thought. His jean shirt and brown trousers with brown leather boots did not fit into a Sunday outing but he had worn it on purpose, surprised now Christine had not made a comment about it. In his own church, he blended with the crowd wearing native outfits. Not here, and he thanked God for his nonchalance, as if he'd known he would need it.

"Mr. Ode, you're welcome," the pastor said in his authoritarian preaching voice.

Chico noticed he wore a huge ring on his right fourth finger. Was he a bishop? There was no wedding band on the left. A woman he assumed was the wife had sat beside him through the service at their exalted royal seats on the altar. Surely, she couldn't be his mother?

"Christine told me the whole story," he said.

Chico nodded. So? Despite knowing the man was married, he didn't like him. He didn't like Christine running any errands for this pastor.

"Pastor thinks I should come and stay with him instead of with you," Christine said, her voice high-strung.

The statement rang loud bells in Chico's brain. Hell, no. He turned to Christine.

"He's sure it's safer for me—" she said, refusing to return his gaze.

Why would she not look at him? He flinched and could hit the desk or jerk her chin up. Instead, he glared at her.

"We have police officers in the church who would handle everything. I already spoke with the deputy commissioner and he is sending his boys down," Pastor said as though he was talking to Christine alone. She nodded eagerly.

"Thank you, sir." She glanced at Chico but when she saw his glare, looked away. "The deputy commissioner of police is our member here," she mumbled.

"He is a son to me," the pastor said proudly.

Chico's brain began to ring.

"I'm sure Mr. Ode would have his cooperation, Pastor," Christine said. "Chico?" Her high-pitched call willed him to say something.

He jumped to his feet. Shocking himself as much as the others. "I'm leaving," he muttered. He walked to the door as Christine scrambled to her feet. It was rude but he didn't care.

"Excuse me, Pastor. I'm sorry. I'll be right back, sir," Christine stammered and followed Chico out.

His strides were so long she had to run after him, and even then, he reached the truck before her. He was half inside when she got to his side and yanked his shoulder.

"Get in," he snapped. He leaned over and opened the door for her.

"I'm not going anywhere with you," she screamed. "Did you have to be so rude to my pastor?"

"Get in," he spat. He pushed her away, slammed his door, and switched on the ignition.

"I'm not coming with you. Just let me get my bag." She ran to the passenger's side and leaned into the truck to get her bag.

He gripped her hair and pulled her in, simultaneously stepping on the throttle. She fell across his chest and screamed. Her door slammed on impact, and he sped off.

CHAPTER SEVENTEEN

S HE YELLED. "Stop this car."

"I must be out of my mind," he said under his breath.

He drove crazily, almost hit a man crossing and then swerved and climbed the walkway. Luckily no one was on it. He swerved back, ran into the other lane and almost caused a chain accident, tyres screeched, and drivers marched on their brakes to avoid it. Christine screamed.

If Chico knew why he was so angry, he didn't know how to explain it. It seemed everything was getting at him. He had a horrible temper which over the years he'd taught himself to control. Whenever he was about to lose his temper, he reined it in but today was different. It hadn't been like this for him in a long while and he knew why. Chico Ode cared.

Christine began to wail as he negotiated the turn to the abattoir. It took a while before he realised, she was not only crying and screaming anymore, she was having an attack. She grappled for her rucksack and tried to open it. When she did, gasping, and gulping, she pumped the inhaler in her mouth and gave a shrill sound. That was when he noticed her inhaler was empty. She shook it several times, wheezing, her eyes bulging.

He leaned over her and opened the pocket of the truck. Under his breath he mumbled an appreciation to God. The previous day, when he went out to drop Lucy off, it had occurred to him to get an inhaler for her, but he'd forgotten it in the truck. The inhaler almost fell to the floor close to her feet, but he caught it, swerving fiercely to keep control of the truck.

"Use this," he snapped.

Her eyes were watery, her face sweaty and he'd never seen such heavy breathing in his life. He put the inhaler in her hand. He didn't know how it was used. She tried to break the seal, but her hands trembled so badly it dropped on the floor. Her eyes seemed to be popping and she kept trying to grab on to the air. He parked the truck by the roadside and came out to her side, with fast, jerky steps.

"Show me what to do." He picked the inhaler from where it fell. "How do I break this seal?"

Weakly, she pulled on the seal and he broke it and then placed her hand on his for guidance. She took three puffs and slumped back in instant relief.

Chico was mortified. What if that inhaler hadn't been there? It would have taken another fifteen minutes of crazy driving to get to town and then begin to search for which chemist was open on a Sunday. He heaved a heavy sigh and slumped against the chassis. When he looked at her, tears trickled down her face. He wondered why she was crying again. He knew he had behaved badly, and it made him feel guilty. He took out a handkerchief from his pocket and wiped the sweat and tears off her face.

"You'll be alright," he said softly.

She closed her eyes. She didn't want to be alright. Usually after an attack, she felt sad and teary but this much more because he was here. Because he had caused it. She was embarrassed and ashamed, and weak. Yet grateful. He'd had a new inhaler in his truck for her? That made her feel more ashamed about the way she regarded him.

She hiccupped. "I don't get so sick so often."

She had been grateful when pastor offered to keep her in his house, relieved even. But now she didn't want to be anywhere else except with this violent and callous stranger. She had never felt so safe and—loved, accepted. Her attacks had annoyed her father and agitated her mother. Her sisters were just embarrassed and irritated. Over the years, she had had to take care of herself. No one had ever thought ahead for her—taking initiative on her account.

Chico turned back to his side of the truck and got in. If she slept, that would be good. He had planned to do a little shopping for food at the Ode mall after church but then, his anger had made him forget all about it. There was nothing to eat in the house.

His driving was gentle and smooth as he finished the ascent into the abattoir. He parked the truck, carried her into the house and placed her on his bed. She was awake he knew, but her eyes were closed.

"I have to get to town," he said.

Her eyes flew open. "Don't leave me," she whimpered.

"You'll be alright," he said and placed the inhaler beside her pillow. "Do you need anything?"

She sobbed. "Don't leave me."

"I have to buy some food. There's nothing to eat in my house," he said. "What do you want to eat?"

She shook her head. He took a decision as she puffed her inhaler again. He would stay and hope she slept. He left the curtains covered and helped her out of her shoes.

"Try and sleep," he murmured.

She gripped his hand. "Don't leave me."

"I'm not going anywhere."

She dragged him to her. "Stay with me."

He eased her hand away and sat on the bed.

"Hold me." She tried to pull him into a hug.

He didn't feel uncomfortable. In fact, he wanted to hold her and rock her to sleep. He slid on his back beside her and held her in a close hug. Her body was cool and small, and she trembled making him feel a greater need to protect her. He pulled the ruffle holding her hair away and combed his hand through.

It took a moment before he realised her mouth was on his neck. She was caressing him with her lips, tracing the veins on his neck and his Adam's apple with it. He went still and tense, fighting for control. In order not to offend her he allowed her for a few torturous seconds before he gently placed his hand on the side of her head and eased her on to his chest. She went limp shortly after and he knew she had slept off. At the moment she trailed his neck with the caress, he was sure if he had been asthmatic, he would have had an attack.

He waited for several minutes to be sure she was asleep and then he stood, heart thudding, and left the house.

Ode town was in a lot of ways like a model town. Several years earlier when states were being created in the country, Ode had been lobbied to be the capital and true sons of the soil had gone all the way to advertise the town. Some had opened offices, erected buildings, set up their businesses—at last, Oshogbo got the capital but everyone, in the good spirit of Ode continued to portend they were as developed as the state capital.

Some of the Ode sons in diaspora came home to live and work and boost the town. It worked, Ode thrived.

As Chico drove straight to the Ode mall, a product of the development age, he pondered on Christine, and especially her boldness. Was it as a result of the attack? Why did he react so fiercely to the caress? He wasn't into women though in his life, and days of adventure, he had had a woman, maybe a couple of times. But he'd realised then women wanted more than sex more than he could give, commitment. And he thanked God he had not ever touched Lucy in that way.

Could it be his body longed so much for a woman's touch? He hadn't been close for at least the last five years or was it this particular woman? At least Lucy had pulled him into a hug just the previous day and tried to get close, he hadn't felt this strange longing.

By the time he got back to the house, his body was still tingling. He peeped through the door and saw she was still asleep.

"Very good," he muttered.

For a moment, he just stared at her. She was such a beautiful girl. She wasn't as tall as Lucy and was much fairer, facially prettier but less endowed bodily—

"What's my problem?" he said under his breath and firmly closed the door.

He had bought enough foodstuff and ingredients to last a few days. The only thing he never bought was meat or fish. He had more than enough for the town.

He strolled into his private yard, to his snail farm and harvested some. They were big and his snails were the best edible species. He then went to the fish farm and caught two big fish. If she wanted meat, she'd have to wait till the following day, he thought.

As a butcher and an animal farmer, he was a good cook, as well. He had taught himself to prepare what he reared. Just to impress Christine, he seasoned the fish and snails and barbecued it and then prepared a pepper sauce to take with rice. Food was ready in less than two hours and he dished it and carried to the room. He would wake her up if she was still asleep. He wanted her to eat before he went to see his grandfather.

She was up when he opened the door, looking sleepy though. She sat up and hugged the pillow to herself when he walked in with the tray. He noticed she avoided his gaze and placed the food tray beside the bed.

"Are you okay?"

"Yes. Thank you."

"I had to rush to town. I have anything you want now. There's tea and coffee," he said. "And I cooked rice."

She nodded and mumbled, "Thanks."

He made to leave. "If you need anything, let me know."

"I'm sorry," she spurted. He arched an eyebrow. "For the attack and and the way I was hysterical—" She lowered her voice. "And for—for kissing you."

He folded his arms across his chest and watched her, the tightness in his loins coming back with a vengeance. So she felt something, he thought.

"I'm not like that." She licked her lips. "I have never made moves on a man before."

"This man has no complaints," he murmured. "Only that you're too young for this."

Christine gasped, and not knowing what to do, threw the pillow she was hugging at him. He didn't dodge and it hit him square on the face. He laughed, and she joined in.

"Come on, let's eat," he said softly and took his seat beside her on the bed. He dished a portion of the food on the plate. "I don't eat much. I eat a lot of protein though."

"I don't eat much either, of anything."

"It shows," he mumbled and she smiled. He took the first spoon and she followed.

"Hmm. Very nice." She chewed on the rice and swallowed. "Who cooked?"

"Me. Try the snail," he said. "Many people don't know but the best way to cook snail is barbecue."

She daintily cut a piece. He watched her, enjoying her ladylike manners. He didn't have proper cutleries but she made do with the dessert spoon he provided.

"Hmm. Mmm," she moaned and he laughed.

"My thought exactly," he took a huge bite of another piece. "You can have as much as you want. I rear them. The fish too."

"Really? You know." She finished the snail and swallowed. "When you drove out this morning I was shocked at how big this place is. People just come here and see the slaughter area alone," she said. "What else do you rear here?"

"Everything I guess. I have poultry, piggery, and cattle."

"That's so impressive."

"I farm. The farm is huge too," he said proudly. "I'll show you round sometime."

She took some rice and went for another snail. "Wow. Well done."

"The fish is also very good," he said. "I picked them especially for you."

He had dressed and barbecued the fish whole just like they do in restaurants, serving it on a bed of fresh vegetables.

"Thanks. It looks tempting," she said.

"Try some." He cut out a generous portion off the tail with his hand and put on the plate. "My hands are clean," he mumbled.

"Obsessively so," she added and he smiled. He poured some water for her and she took a piece of the fish and ate. "This is really good. Who taught you to cook this well?"

He shrugged. "My nomadic lifestyle, I guess."

"I don't cook at all," she murmured. "My family always had a cook and my father simply forbade us entering the kitchen." She shook her head. "Unfortunately."

He thought that strange. "And when you left home to school?" He knew the answer anyway, even before she shrugged. "Of course," he said.

He hardly touched the rice. He went for the veggies and the snails and the fish, and ate a lot of them.

"I tried to learn but my mates would laugh so hard. They were not encouraging. And most of my friends are just like me so." She shrugged, feeling guilty.

"I should marry you then," he started and stopped. Why would he say such a thing? She was a child. A school girl.

She let out a nervous laugh that sent another message to him. Her laugh had a snobbish edge, and he felt a twinge of inferiority complex. He thought he'd dealt with this long ago.

In those days when he was young, he had gawked in awe when he had the rare privilege of seeing the kind of house she lived in. He had never imagined then he could have the opportunity to go into such compounds or even relate with anyone who did. He was just a poor butcher boy.

He jumped to his feet. "I have to go up the hill."

Her laughter was cut short and she straightened. "Don't leave me here," she pleaded.

"I have to. You're safe here. You could clear the dishes or you don't know how to do that too?" he muttered harshly. His statement offended her, he knew from the look on her face but none of the hurt showed in her pleading voice.

"I can do it when we come back," she said. "Please."

"I may be away for a while." He moved toward the door and she jumped off the bed.

"Then don't leave me here, please." She was close to tears again. She looked like a child, standing barefooted in front of him.

He gentled. "I may be in the bush for hours. You can't take the pressure."

He picked the tray and turned away from her, going into the kitchen. She followed him. He proceeded to tidy the kitchen, and put away the leftover. She made to assist but one wave of his hand put her off.

"I don't care. I'll die of fear if you leave me here," she said.

"Then sleep."

Within minutes, everything was sparkling. Then he washed and dried his hands.

"I can't sleep. Fear won't let me sleep."

He couldn't take her with him. She would be restless and end up being a distraction, and what if her abductors saw her and captured her again. That possibility was not applicable, he thought as soon as it crossed his mind, unless he was dead first.

"I would ask you to stay in the shack, but I wouldn't do that to you—" he said. "Wild animals stray to visit the old man," he added when she arched her eyebrow. And then she visibly blanched. She didn't say a word for a while.

"Do you really own this whole place?"

He ignored her question. "You can't wear a dress. Did you bring trousers?"

"Yes." She nodded and ran back into the room.

He followed her and she had to enter the bathroom with her bag to change. She wore her pair of jeans and snickers which made her look even smaller beside to him.

He changed into a figure-hugging T-shirt and jeans, rain boots, and was tucking knives into his belt when she walked back into the bedroom. She shrivelled at the sight of the knives.

"Now listen to me. You can't argue with my instructions," he said sternly. "And you can't play pranks with me. You don't want to know what I do with traitors either."

She nodded profusely. He said nothing more and led the way out of the house.

CHAPTER EIGHTEEN

S HE CHATTERED THROUGH THE short drive up the hill talking about how she loved the outdoors and thinking his life out at the ranch must be colourful and refreshing. Chico had nothing to say to her. Apart from the fact that he felt she was just talking to keep from thinking, he needed to think about the next few minutes or hours or days—Everything was just so unpredictable. He had faced uncertainty before on several occasions. But he'd always been alone, fending for himself. Whether he liked it or not, she was a total stranger. He wasn't even sure if he was being set up or not. But he was sure of something; he would never go down without a fight.

He parked the truck under a shrub a stone's throw from the shack. Oloye stood at his frontage, arms akimbo, ready to challenge whoever the intruder was.

"Why the truck?" he challenged and then Christine opened her door and got out as well. The old man looked at her, and then at him, and burst into laughter.

"She refused to stay," Chico mumbled angrily but the old man continued to laugh. Chico brushed past him and marched inside. "Well, come and tell me what went on while we were away," he barked.

The sun was up and high in the heat of the day. At this time of the day, the forest was asleep and Chico's voice echoed for miles away.

"You may wake all the snakes and lizards but I'll still say I least expected a mere child to conquer you," Oloye said elaborately.

"She's not a child. She's a university student," he snapped.

"Well, all the same. Your sacrifices paid off then," the old man chuckled.

Chico was so irritated with him he marched out of the hut again and stood facing both persons. "I want to know what you saw in that place," he demanded.

"Come with me," Oloye said.

⚜

Chico held her hand firmly and dragged her behind him as Oloye followed the path to the abandoned hut.

"Be quiet," he ordered, though no one said a word.

Christine thanked God for the snickers but still she stepped on the dry grass to minimise the sound coming from her. She could see the dark clouds of Chico's temper resurfacing and she didn't want to have the experience again.

"Can she climb?" Oloye asked as they reached the tree they had used the previous night.

"She will," Chico said.

He turned to her and commanded her to get up on the tree and keep her mouth shut. She had never climbed a tree in her life but she needed to prove being there was not a mistake. She hauled herself on a branch she felt was nearest and missed her step, almost splitting her thigh. Involuntarily, she let out a cry of pain. Chico grabbed her waist and Oloye muttered an expletive. To help her up, Chico had to climb at an awkward angle behind her and hold her waist. Tears sprang to her eyes.

"I'm sorry," she whispered.

His voice came in less than a whisper. "Shut up."

He balanced on the tree and lifted her up off the branch she'd fallen across from. Holding her waist tightly, he found a branch with his other hand and climbed with amazing strength. He found his balance and then went up again. Before she knew it, she was on a slab-like branch, firmly seated.

"Just look. Okay?" he murmured, and she nodded.

"Thank you," she whispered, swallowing her tears. Her left inner thigh hurt where she'd landed when she fell and she began to rub it gently.

"Don't rock the tree," he said between his teeth and effortlessly climbed down.

She nodded again, leaving the thigh alone and holding back tears with all her effort. Were they going to leave her on this tree? She was at least ten feet off the ground. She wished she had stayed back in his house and knew she would have been restless and miserable. But being on a tree—

⟫⟫⟫ ⟪⟪⟪

"I saw nothing," Oloye said as Chico jumped down soundlessly. "If your baby wasn't here, I'll swear on your mother's grave nothing happened here."

"She's not my baby," Chico snapped.

He squelched the urge to look up and see if she was okay. Oloye did it for him and smiled. "She's fine, staring down at you like her life depends on it."

"What do you mean you saw nothing?"

"No one is there. I even opened the door and looked in. No one," Oloye said.

"They must have come when you were sleeping," Chico scolded. He walked angrily toward the hut and the old man followed.

Oloye lowered his voice. "Did she turn you down?" The younger man swung round so swiftly he nearly knocked the older man down.

"Get this out of your mind, Oloye. Since I recognised that girl, you've been acting stupid. She is a little girl. I'm way too old for her, okay? Even if I like her, I won't make advances," he said.

Oloye shrugged. "Oh, so you like her. I knew it. The other day, you talked about her for an hour non-stop."

"Oloye!"

"Sshh," the old man said.

They both went still. He beckoned toward the back of the hut and they snuck there. They were silent for a long time before Chico heard anything. Someone was approaching. The approach was so noisy, Chico was sure the person could not be of interest—until he saw her.

"What on earth—" he began to curse but Oloye signalled for him to shut up.

Then he saw the huge man. He was trying to hide but the "idiot" was clumsy about it. Christine was limping badly. She walked to the hut and opened the door, and then she looked around, and stepped in, closing it behind her. The big man shot the bolt from behind and disappeared into the forest.

Nothing happened after that.

Oloye did not say anything. Neither did Chico. They both understood at once Christine was being used as bait for them to come out. Well, she would probably sleep there then.

"I can't take this anymore," Chico said.

The big man was no longer visible to them, and they had been lying low for probably three hours. No sound of Christine was heard. Oloye glared at Chico but it didn't work. It was getting dark and he wasn't ready to stick around all night.

"You'll blow everything up," the old man whispered harshly.

"I don't care," Chico spat. "I'm walking right up to that silly door and yanking it out." Chico straightened.

"You must be crazy, boy. Do you know how many of them are there?"

"I don't care." Chico pulled out a knife from his belt and shoved it right back. "If I never see you again, then, thanks and farewell." He looked at his grandfather and nodded bravely.

"I thought I was mad," the old man said and like a flash, leaped into the open as he spoke in a harsh whisper, "Cover me."

Before Chico could stop him. Oloye was out in the clear and walking to the door of the hut. Chico cursed so loud birds screamed in protest. But he had been posted without a chance to protest. He had to cover the old man's back. He moved closer but remained concealed. Oloye unlocked the door and opened it. Chico saw it but it was too late as someone from nowhere pushed Oloye into the room and jammed it. Within the second the person was out of sight. That was when Chico's blood began to pump. He needed to get out of here. How many people were involved and how was he going to find the root of this?

He remained mute and still till it was completely dark all around him. He couldn't leave both of them alone. Oloye, he was sure could defend himself but he would not be able to take Christine on. Christine, on the other hand, may have an attack or worse still, not be able to help herself or the old man. It was a miracle she hadn't had her attack when she was first abducted, going by the tale she told him. He needed to do something. He cursed himself for the umpteenth time for bringing her. They would have been back with the culprits tied together by now if he had not been foolish enough to let her come with him. He checked on the knives in his boots and stepped out. He was exposed. In the open. Nothing happened. Nothing moved. His instincts were as wild and as alert as that of a hunter in the jungle. He moved to the door and opened it.

And he let himself in.

The room was pitch black but something hit him hard on the face and he staggered heavily backward. He slumped against the closed door, conscious but pretending he was not. Had he missed something when he was outside? Had Christine and Oloye been removed without his knowledge? Impossible.

He felt his legs being moved. She couldn't move them fast enough for the old man and he moved over to assist her.

"Nice try," he mumbled and kicked into space. Both staggered back and almost fell, losing their grips to his trained movement. He bounced to his feet and flattened against the door.

"Chico." she whispered. "What are you doing?"

"Sshhh," he said. "Oloye, listen to me and don't do anything stupid again. You have to be sharp. Leave with her and get her to my house safely," he said in a rapid, harsh whisper. "Then go to your house and stay there."

Christine's voice trembled. "What about you?"

"He'll be fine. He's a jaguar," Oloye said.

⟫⟫ ⟪⟪

There was a hush as each geared for the next lap of danger. Chico opened the door and they slipped out. Oloye shot the bolt in place, and began to rattle like a snake, shocking Christine but she knew to keep quiet and close behind him. The environment was clear and Oloye led her quietly through the woods to his shack. The truck was parked same as where they'd left it.

"I can't leave him alone here. This is my entire fault," she sobbed as the old man began to lead her downhill.

"He'll be mad if I don't take you home."

It was the way he called it home. She grabbed his arm and pulled him to a stop.

"Please, sir. Let me stay with you. When all this is over, I swear, you'll never see me again but I can't just go and sleep. Please, sir."

He hesitated for several seconds. "Alright," he said and took her back to the hut. "He'll almost kill me but I will allow you to mesmerise me the way you do to him." He chuckled.

Chico would raise hell when he came back—For a moment, Christine feared he may not come back but killed that thought for the sake of her peace of mind.

"If the boy doesn't show up, I'll go," Oloye mumbled inaudibly. "I'll go mad, then I'll drop dead."

He led Christine into his dark hut, and found his small stool for her. When she tried to lower herself into it, she moaned in pain.

"Lie on the floor. It's clean," he urged and she did.

Her body ached all over. What had she gotten herself into and who wanted her head so badly. Why?

"I'll give you a balm to use when you get home—" There it was again. Home. "After you take your bath, ask Chico to rub you down," he continued.

What on earth does the old man think she was? Chico's wife? What were the men up to? Once again, her suspicions rose high. Was this all a set-up? Were they playing games with her or what? She was so confused, tears sprang to her eyes. Why? The question kept ringing in her head.

The floor was cool against her body and refreshing. She'd thought inside the hut would stink but to her pleasant surprise, it didn't. The old man didn't stink either.

She laid her head on the solid earth and began to doze. She heard the old man ask if she wanted to eat but she moaned a weak reply. He made her sit up and sip some warm herbal tea. It wasn't sweet but she felt an immediate calming she had thought would be impossible. He tried to put some food in her mouth but she couldn't chew. She didn't know what she said but he left her. All she knew was she just wanted to sleep forever.

She must have for a very long time because when she woke up, she was in Chico's bed.

CHAPTER NINETEEN

CHICO STAYED IN THE hut, drawing in every iota of strength. If he would leave here carried, he was ready. Nothing happened for long, and he closed his eyes, reserving his energy for the unknown. Then it came first as soft steps, as though someone was on a tip-toe. The bolt slid so slightly, obvious the person was being careful and stealthy. Chico became stone. Just as carefully, something small was used to wedge the door, so you could not know until you were at the door. He felt movement in the small space. Then the click of a belt. Was the man about to flog her? Them? They had put in the woman and the old man—Zip went down making so much noise the man cursed it.

"Old man. Get out and run now," he whispered. Nothing. "Leave now, or I'll kill you myself," he said. Nothing.

His flashlight came on just as Chico caught him between his legs. His scream was so loud, Chico had to clasp his hand over his mouth. He collected the flashlight from him and switched it off. He didn't know how many were outside so he had to contain this man. He took the belt just dropped on the floor by the side, and tied the bully's hands over his head, then pulled off his T-shirt and tore it into strips. The man was big but completely cooperative. Chico hooked the belt to the strip, dragged it down and tied them to his feet. It was a very painful connection and the man sobbed.

"Now I want to know who you are and what you are doing here," Chico rapped.

"They are coming. They are coming soon."

"Who are they?"

"I don't know, I swear. They just asked me to keep an eye on the girl."

Huh. And you wanted to sleep with her? Chico resisted the urge to punch his face.

"You would keep quiet till I tell you what to do. And I mean every word of that or you are a dead man." Chico switched on the light in front of his knife just so the big man would see it. A sob escaped his throat and he swallowed.

They continued to be quiet.

"This idiot has still not finished. Does he want to kill her?" a voice said into the stillness of the night.

"I wonder. The girl is so small, his weight alone can kill her," the second man laughed.

"We have to be fast and leave this place. Bala would go crazy if he knows we're still here," the first man said.

"We should not have come here in the first place. He told you the Chico is a mad man and can see everything at the same time."

"I want to meet the man."

"Chico? Mad man?"

Chuckle. "Yeah. I want to meet the mad man."

"Meet him now."

The bound man was flung at both men from inside the small room. They'd had their backs to the door. Chico's adrenaline was pumping litres per second. The two men staggered and fell. Chico hadn't been sure of their sizes but from the way they fell in the dark, it was obvious they were both smaller than the man bound. No one could see anything but Chico's ears were trained, and he had learnt early not to underestimate people.

One of the two men jumped to his feet and hit him on the shoulder. His strength was impressive but though slight in build, Chico was a fighter. And he fought more with his mind than with his body. He staggered back but was prepared for the next attack.

"Untie me."

"Untie him."

The men called on one another as Chico tackled the one. It was pitch-black and the fighters could locate themselves by breathing and movement. Chico had taken up more than three men who were stronger than him before, butchers who were bull-headed and believed might was right. It had been one of the tests of his leadership. His brutality had shocked the men to submission. One had lost his life. It had earned Chico physical respect and leadership. But he had taken on those men, in broad daylight, looking into their eyes. He had been able to predict their moves. Above all, he'd known how many they were.

As much as the darkness was to his advantage, it was a huge minus for his skills. He could not know if they had weapons or not. Or if they felt weak or were determined or distracted, discouraged—

His knee must have gone into the man's chin. There was a crunching sound and a groan then footsteps retreating at a run. But the battle was not over. The impact on the chin was almost as painful as that on the knee that hit it. Chico stifled a cry and staggered back. Thank God for the darkness there. He breathed in and found the man he was on, trying to loosen the bound man, obviously, the third man had gone to get help or simply absconded.

Punch and punch then some crunching and groaning sounds. Chico would have thrown the man against the wall to finish him off but the big man came on him with an elbow blow on the back of his neck. He fell on one knee feeling as though his shoulder blade had split. The big man really had the blows. Another quick one followed on the side of his head, making his nauseous. But he now knew where the man was coming from and the next blow hit air the man lost his balance.

Chico rolled away and held his breath. Big man lumbered around and tripped over Chico's foot. Chico kicked him in the same place he'd been hit in the small room. The man gave a pathetic shrill cry and fell face down. Chico stumbled to his feet and gripping his ribs, found his way out of the location. He couldn't walk upright. Surely, he had been damaged but what was on his mind was to get away as soon as he could.

He had a vigilante in the ranch. He would deploy them to the hillside. They would clear the place out within hours. Someone else would have done this first, but not him. He had to find out what his men would be facing for himself.

Dizzy and nauseous, he stumbled to Oloye's shack. "Water," he gasped and collapsed to his knees.

Oloye sat in front of the shack, wringing his hands. He leapt to his feet and brought a gourd with cool water. Chico took only a little and poured the rest on his head.

"Where are you hurt?" Oloye asked.

Chico fell on his back, breathing hard. "My ribs. He's broken my ribs." He coughed, his face twisted in pain.

"I can get something for the pain," Oloye scrambled back into the shack. He came out with a bitter potion which he poured down Chico's throat.

"That's awful," Chico spat on the ground but he knew Oloye's potions worked. He felt instant relief and drew himself up slowly. "There were three of them. One got away. Just be careful. I'm going to get the vigilante," Chico gasped.

"The woman is still here," Oloye said as Chico staggered to the truck. He stopped short and turned to the old man.

He breathed hard. "Why?"

"I gave her something to drink. She slept off."

"I told you to take her to my house. What did you give her? Marijuana?"

"I gave her tea," Oloye said and Chico sneered.

"You don't have tea. You have weed." Chico snapped. "She'll be out the whole day."

"She was limping badly. She couldn't walk and I couldn't carry her—" Chico stumbled back into the shack and picked Christine up. She was as heavy as stone. He staggered with her to the truck.

"When you get to your house, give her a rub down with this," Oloye said and gave him a balmy potion wrapped in dried leaves.

He took it impatiently and threw it in the bucket of the truck. With Oloye's help he got her in and drove off. With all the willpower in him, he took her in then went back to the ranch security post to alert the vigilante. The men knew the forest area. The land was vast and the brush thick but they had combed it before. At some point, a strong barbed-wire fence had been erected to keep the habitable area free of wild animals.

Chico returned to his house in the early hours of the morning. He was fagged out, hungry and feeling pain all over his body. It had been long since he did anything so energy-sapping. Though he was fit by virtue of his job and the way he did it, he hadn't been in combat since after he resumed control over the ranch.

It was the time when the butchers went on strike and he had stubbornly climbed the slabs and began to kill the cows. After the tenth cow he had collapsed, meat sellers had taken over and helped in shearing beef. Chico had refused to allow the men to come back to work. Those were the early days when ownership of the ranch was under contention. He had been stronger than a horse and been like a god compared to other masters. The weak had eventually given way to the strong. To him, Chico Ode.

He stumbled around his house to bath, eat, and use the balm Oloye had provided for Christine on his swollen ribs and chest and then he went to examine her. He was sure she had been given weed to drink. Oloye cultivated the plant and what else would he have given her to ensure she was knocked out. If he had given her food with vegetables, he could swear it was marijuana. The same with the "tea" he claimed. He was careful not to touch her unnecessarily. Her legs were okay but her inner thighs were sensitive. Angry red marks spread on both sides and was swollen a little. When he touched it gingerly, she moaned. He moaned.

Well, she'd have to take care of herself. He would never touch her so intimately again, he decided. He spread his blanket on the floor and slept within the minute.

CHAPTER TWENTY

THE ABATTOIR WAS IN an uproar the following morning. The two men caught in the hills were bound and paraded like criminals. The huge one had been beaten till one eye was shut and swollen. The smaller man still looked okay but subdued. Both maintained they had been hired by people they didn't know. Masters, butchers and customers alike poured sand at them at will.

Chico remained in his office, consulting with the leaders in the ranch. Ejiro, Bala and five others sat around and brainstormed on what to do with the prisoners. The vigilantes had kept a close watch on the mud hut in case any more people came by. None had.

As the men pondered the same questions on Chico's mind, he watched them, saying nothing except to provide needed information in clipped sentences. Yes, there was a woman. She's safe in hiding. There were three men, one got away— They were wearied of his anger and lack of enthusiasm. Some of them had seen him fight for his land, all knew how passionate he was about it. What they couldn't understand was his aloofness. He treated them with suspicion.

The heat in Chico's office reached a climax when Ejiro stood boldly in their midst and stretched.

"Looks like we're not going anywhere with this meeting," he said.

The others gasped at his effrontery. Chico ignored it and turned his attention to Asindu. Asindu was one of the newest masters but he had endeared himself to Chico by his hard work and business astuteness.

"You know who these people are, don't you, Asindu? You brought them into my land," Chico growled, startling everyone.

All eyes turned on Asindu who blanched. He wasn't a man who could articulate himself well and he didn't have formal education. In his mid-forties, he had weathered many storms in life, and had only recently settled with a third wife and eight children on the ranch. For several seconds, Chico glared at him as he fumbled in the respite.

"I would never do that," Asindu blubbered.

Chico. Wagged his finger. "You know me the least. You care the least about me. I know the least about you—"

"That is not true," Asindu said huskily. "I love this land and I would never bring evil men here."

"Asindu is not sharp enough to plot—" Ejiro teased. Chico turned to him with a steely gaze that hung him mid-sentence.

"This is a big joke, isn't it?" he said softly.

"Ejiro must be guilty of this crime," Bala said, pointing a crooked finger at the man.

Ejiro jumped on him violently. The men began to brawl while Chico glared them down. When it seemed they would not stop, he turned to Bala, and dragged him out of the mix.

"You go find the small coward who got away," he snapped.

His words stopped all of them. They separated and turned their gaze to Bala.

"How will I do that?" Bala gasped. Chico gave him a rare smile, and patted him on the back.

"I know you can." He looked at the distressed men and waved them off. "Go back to your businesses. Bala," he softened his voice. "Get to work. Find the man for me. Today," he said. "Or I'll hold you." His gaze locked with Bala's. They were hard, able to turn a man to an insecure twit. He did. Bala turned away from those penetrating and judgmental eyes and sought support from the rest of the masters.

"We would all look for the man together," he announced.

It sounded like counter-orders. A taboo in Ode Abattoir. The men went still, expecting, yet not expecting reactions from the boss. They got what they expected. He waived them away and continued to watch through the reflexive glass as staff and customer alike snubbed the prisoners.

As the day progressed, business wound down. Lucy walked into his office, looking worried. She was one who always wore her emotions on her sleeves, most unlike the man she loved.

"Market not good?" he asked softly. He was always concerned for her, always protective and gentle. His soft side always came to the fore with Lucy.

She shook her head and sat. "No."

It was getting to late afternoon. The sun had gone down and the abattoir was beginning to experience routine peace common for that time of the day. Most sellers were either moving to the evening market in town or going home after the day's job. Chico had stayed in his office throughout, observing from his vantage point. There was a lot on his mind and he knew he needed to be alone.

"Those men outside—are you going to leave them there?" she asked. "There is a lot of talk around. You are not safe," she said. "I'm worried for you."

He gazed at her then stood and circled round to stand behind her. She turned to look at him, her shoulders stiff. He didn't say a word, but watched her twist her fingers in her laps, her lips trembled ever so slightly and there was a thin film of sweat on her nose and forehead.

"I came to see you yesterday and waited for hours," she continued when he refused to say anything. "When you didn't come back, I went into the village—everything was alright till this morning."

He raised his chin at her, questioning her decision to sleep over. He knew she had many friends and colleagues on the ranch. Still. He didn't approve of her stay over.

"Continue."

"There was talk about terrorism. It was as though some soldiers had come to take over and you'd been taken away. I was so worried until I saw you this morning. What's going on, Chico?" she moaned. He stared her down.

"See, I know you don't like me poking but you may think I don't know anything but I know a lot. I could help you. A lot. And I have friends here and they are always talking. They know about these men more than you do," she spoke rapidly.

He folded his arms across his chest and leaned on his heel.

"Chico, I love you. And though you have your good reasons, we are meant for each other." She stood and leaned into him. "We are meant to be husband and wife, and I will do anything to make it happen."

She unwound his arms and pushed herself into it. He was taller than her but he found himself gauging her height with Christine's.

"I love you, Chico. I will do anything for you."

She rested her head on his chest. He smelt offal faintly, and flared his nostrils—On the contrary, Christine smelt of rose, and mint and exotic flowers.

"When the talk of the men came to me, I thought I'd die. The plot was such a grand one and they said you were missing," she said. "Do you know anything about those men outside?" She cupped his face. "What do you plan to do to them?" She tipped forward. "Do you want to leave them there? Chico? You can't be quiet this time. Those men are almost dying and they know nothing about what is going on, Chico. Chico?"

She rested her head on his chest. "I don't want you to be hurt. Tell me what you intend to do. I can sniff around and know what is going on. This is bigger than you, Chico. You can't bulldoze your way through this one, please my love." She began to sob. "Don't do any more harm to them. Let them go. They are innocent. Bala has assured he would find the culprits—If they die here, you'll be taken away by the police. You'll be charged with mur—"

Chico shifted her away and walked out to the open area where the two men had been tied to stakes as though facing an execution squad. It would be so easy to find both dead by morning and the police swamping the ranch. He passed by as though on inspection of the unwinding trading.

The big man's second eye was almost as swollen as the first one and he was slumped against his restraint. Chico had the strange feeling he was asleep. The shorter man, on the other hand, was alert. Both eyes were wide open and bright with observance. He had suffered a lot of bruises also but his body had borne it well. The ropes tying them both had eaten into their flesh and left visible marks.

Chico checked on the masters and butchers as he did at the end of the work day, and then he went back to his office where Lucy waited for him.

"Where did you go?" she asked him eagerly as he circled her and went back to sit behind his desk.

"To check on the day's business," he said absent-mindedly.

Since the beginning of his ownership of the abattoir, he had handled his accounts himself, even though Bala had still ripped him off with the environmental charges. On that account alone, he had lost half of what had been paid already. The authorities had insisted he would not get away with what they saw as his own negligence. They had only been merciful on him and asked him to pay half of what had been embezzled.

Daily, he reconciled what was spent on the stock, and received from sales. Daily he chewed over his books and made sure they balanced spending hours alone, doing what he had taught himself and adapted to suit his purpose. It was hours of careful analysis. There were several brands on the ranch and each had its own unsophisticated accounting system. Chico had carefully outlined each brand – the slaughter, the piggery, the goat-farm and the poultry. Then there were the other things like the fish pond and snail farm which had initially been started for personal use. And the farm. The farm had expanded beyond his imagination. Now he had suppliers coming in from the main town and environs seeking his fruits and vegetables and yams and cassava and—

Lucy gasped. "Did you not hear any of what I said about those men?"

"What men?" he looked at her blankly and pulled out a drawer containing files.

He had never believed in hiring accountants when he could sum his additions and remove his subtractions. He started with the slaughter. Fifty-eight cows sold. Sometimes more but consistently in the past year, never less than fifty. Except during the month the place was closed. Then he had sold as few as five a day, and only because they were on order.

Though he had a ranch and a herd of his own, much of the daily sales belonged to the masters and other colleagues and friends, and other ranch owners. Practically, he sold ten or less cows a day of his own gathering. But he accounted for all and then disbursed. He preferred it that way. Then he could be sure he hadn't been cheated in any way. The system suited the other owners, especially because he was honest and this took a chunky part of the accounting off their necks.

"Chico? They want you. They want your life." She screeched. "That's why they took that girl and brought her here. They want to kill her and dump her here so it will indict you but now you saved her, they will go on to another plan. Chico why are you being so difficult? What do you have in mind to do?"

"I'm tired, Lucy. It's been a long, hard day. I want to finish up here and go home to sleep," he said around a yawn.

Her anger rose like a demon. "Home? You now call your house a home? Just because of that lady?"

"Lucy. Please."

"Oh no, Chico." She rushed at him and tried to shake him out of his seat. "Chico? After all I've done for you. And all I've been to you—"

"It wasn't enough, Lucy. I want more," he snapped with such force she froze.

Tears coursed down her cheeks. Still, Chico held her gaze, tearing at his heart in the process but refusing to back down. It was time to let her go, he decided.

"Chico," she croaked.

"You can never give me what I want, Lucy. I'm afraid this is where we end," he said, his gaze unwavering, his tone just as cruel, and unfeeling.

She turned and sobbing aloud, stomped out of his office. He turned right back to his books, refusing to acknowledge the pain in his heart. It had to be over some time. Better now than later.

CHAPTER TWENTY-ONE

CHRISTINE ROLLED OVER AND sat. The sun was up and shinning bright. Though the curtains were still drawn, the warmth and light seeped in. She stood to her feet and stretched feeling the pains of the previous night. She must have torn a ligament or something when she slipped on the tree and when the huge man found her and dragged her down.

She limped to the bathroom to have a refreshing shower. Wow. That was so sweet a sleep, she thought. Only God knew what the old man had given her to make her sleep so soundly. She checked her watch and screamed. It was past noon. She peeped through the curtain hoping to make out her environment. She saw just a beautiful scenic view of a flower and fruit garden. The flowers flowed around the fruit trees on green manicured grass, the work of a perfectionist. She had almost expected to see the busy slaughter area and was pleasantly surprised.

Since she came to know Chico's house, she had had neither the chance nor the interest to look round. And though she felt a subtle pang of fear for the unknown, she was overwhelmed by her curiosity of her surroundings. She slipped on her shoes and limped round the house, ending in the kitchen.

The house was a three-bed four-bath bungalow. The master bedroom had a kitchenette, a walk-in wardrobe and balcony that overlooked the beautiful garden. Christine unconsciously found herself placing two rockers on the balcony. What better way to spend a quiet evening than rocking with a glass of juice and barbecue snail!

Other rooms were sparsely furnished a sign they had probably never been occupied. The sitting area was large with simple but exquisite furniture. Christine discovered another room she assumed was designed for either a guest parlour or living room. Whatever it was created for, was not clear because it was bare.

She walked through and found a door opened to the beautiful garden. She opened it and leaned into sunshine. Oh, lovely. She breathed. She looked round for signs of other houses. There were none. What a loner Chico was. She limped into the kitchen and realised she was very hungry. There was left over food which Chico had stacked away in the freezer. She brought them out and microwaved some rice and fish.

Chico's kitchen looked like one which belonged to a professional cook. It was large and organised, and with a lot of gadgets Christine had never seen before. There were knives everywhere, scary. The cooker had ten burners.

She made a cup of tea for herself, despite the warmth of the day she was a tea addict, and then limped back into the room. The air conditioning dammed the effect of the tea, and she settled to think about her life and what all the drama was about.

Absently, she rubbed the swollen parts of her thighs and winced. She needed to get to people who could help her. Her pastor would be scared and upset but she wasn't sure he would come looking for her. He was a man of faith and wouldn't panic. Though Christine wished he would now. She was completely cut off from everyone except Chico and whoever else in the ranch, working with him. She felt so lonely and afraid.

A part of her dismissed her fears while the other part magnified it. She didn't have her handbag and cell phone any more. And she hadn't the opportunity to report this to the police. She hoped her pastor would have done that on her behalf. She hoped all the drama would get a head soon and she could get back to her normal life.

There was no television in the house but Christine found an amazing wealth of books on butchery and farming, and surprisingly, theology and religion in Chico's wardrobe. He didn't have much in clothing most of his clothes were white and brown and black. More than half of the walk-in wardrobe housed his books. Christine looked at them, hoping to find something of interest.

She picked out a book on Christian health and settled down to it. She had never seen herself as having health problems but apart from holiness books, there was little else that held her interest. She was really impressed he had so many books though. Aa butcher?

Chico found her cuddled with three books on his bed, fast asleep. Her foetal position made her look like a small child. He pulled the books gently away from her and looked at them. What was she doing with butchering tools catalogues? Curious. He put the books away and returned to the bed. He wanted to tickle her toes—

"Will you wake her up?"

He nodded and tapped her shoulder. She came awake at once. She must have been asleep for long. In a lady-like manner, she unfolded her body and stretched before looking at her visitors.

The woman with Chico was pregnant. Her fat, round body carried the status remarkably well. She wasn't pretty in the face but she had a great body, despite the bulging stomach. She waited on Chico who was mesmerised by Christine and gawked as the latter rearranged herself on the bed, into a sitting position.

"This is Omasan, Ejiro's wife," he said, as though she was supposed to know Ejiro. The woman looked at her and nodded. She smiled in return. "Oloye said you sprained your leg so Omasan would look at it for you."

Christine's gaze questioned him. She was in pain alright but she wanted to be sure of who was treating her and with what. Chico got her message.

"Omasan is a trado-therapy nurse. She's good too. She's brought some herbs in addition to Oloye's, to rub into your leg and to relieve the pain," Chico said.

"Let me just take a look. It may be nothing serious," Omasan said and stepped around Chico.

She sat beside Christine and without permission, began to examine Christine's legs. Chico stood back and watched as she skilfully touched both legs. She moved up to Christine's thighs beneath the flared skirt of her floral dress, and began to press oblivious of the heat transpiring between the other two.

At some time during Omasan's examination, Chico began to imagine the hands on Christine were not the woman's but his. Their gazes were locked neither breathing nor moving till Omasan touched some part and Christine screamed, jolting all three of them.

"Ha, thank God it's not serious." Omasan straightened and looked at Chico's dark eyes. "I'll pull it, and in a few days, if she keeps massaging it, it would be fine."

"Pulling is painful—" Christine began to protest.

"It'll help you," Chico said quietly. He leaned against the wall as though he was not ready to leave soon.

Omasan pressed her lips. "You may need to remove your clothes." She turned to Christine. "The hip bone needs to be massaged and then I'll pull it."

"Okay," Christine said slowly.

She refused to look at him again. She lifted herself slightly off the bed, enough to shift her dress, and then gave Chico a pointed look.

"I'll prepare something for dinner," he said gruffly and stomped out of the room.

Both women paused to watch his exit but neither commented.

Chico walked into the kitchen and pulled raw food out of the cupboards and freezer. He'd seen she had eaten a small portion of the leftover food and tried to clear the dishes away. He wondered how a woman would not be able to cook but seeing her family home, he had half of the answer.

Born with a golden spoon, she probably never had to lift a finger. Well, he had been lifting every bit of his body parts from birth and not ashamed of his heritage. She ought to be ashamed of hers, he thought angrily as he put together a delicious pot of fresh vegetable soup. He wasn't a fan of main dishes and enjoyed proteins and vegetables. Left to him, he would eat lots of the soup he cooked with fish and go to sleep.

As he put water on the fire to make some wheat flour he heard her scream. Omasan's soft soothing words followed and he froze. Another air-rending scream rent the air. He dropped the spoon in his hand and stomped through the house to the bedroom. He didn't care if she was naked or not—he stopped short just at the entrance. She was moaning pathetically as Omasan tried to encourage her to release herself for the therapy.

"—just one more time. Once it snaps, you hear that kraun sound, you'll be fine," Omasan said softly.

Christine sobbed. Chico leaned against the wall just outside the door, concealing himself from them. He'd known her injury wasn't good the way it was swollen the day before. He listened to the two women till there was a loud shrill and scream and then Omasan's soothing words. Chico wondered how someone so small could make such a shrill sound.

"It's over. There. Rest easy," Omasan cooed.

Chico returned to the kitchen, sweating, and finished the cooking. Omasan came over to look for him.

"She'll be fine. Can you massage it for her in the night before she sleeps and in the morning?" Omasan asked and got a searing glare from Chico.

They all feared him and treated him like a god but she wanted to know if he could take care of Christine, and of course, have something to gossip about in the village.

"Or I could come in the morning to do it for her again," she said and he nodded. She took her leave then and Chico dished some food for both of them.

Christine was hugging a pillow and sitting up, propped against a pillow with another two under her thighs. Her face was serene after the pain she had experienced.

He placed the tray of food beside her. "How do you feel?"

She closed her eyes and he noticed her breathing was not normal.

"Oh God," he muttered and rushed out of the house. He'd taken the inhaler when they left for the hill but forgotten to remove it when they returned. He rushed back with it and found her eating.

"Why did you do that?" he snapped.

"Do what? I want to go home," she said softly.

"Why did you act like you are having an attack?"

She cut a morsel of semovita and touched it to the soup before swallowing.

"I wasn't acting. I was trying to hold my anger."

He exclaimed. "Anger?"

"Why did you bring that woman to hurt me? I want to go home," she snapped, cutting another morsel to eat. He noticed with humour her anger and pain had not dissipated her appetite. "My pastor would be mad. I'm sure he has called the police."

"What about your family? Would they not be worried?"

He sat beside her and dished a small portion of the meal with a huge helping of vegetables and fish.

"My pastor will come here tomorrow I'm sure—"

Chico cut in. "He already came. With a battalion."

Her face lit up. "Good. What was the outcome?"

"Half of the men had a share in the Easter cows I sent to police headquarters. They were anxious to go back and do their investigations."

She gasped. "You bribe the police?"

He arched an eyebrow. "Bribe? No. I never give bribe but I have a faultless reward system. The police is my friend. And you know how I treat my friends." He arched his eyebrow. "Tolani got a taste."

The pleasant look on her face disappeared. "Pastor must have been upset with them. The commissioner of police is—"

He shrugged. "I couldn't be bothered." He took a moment and studied her mouth. "Is your pastor married? I have reason to believe his intentions toward you are not totally pure."

She cried. "Of course, he is married. Didn't you see his wife in church? She left town after service."

"A single lady should not be his personal assistant."

"He's not like that."

"He looks it."

"You don't even know him."

"I don't need to."

"I'm not really his P.A. anyway." She shrugged. He dished more meat and soup for her and she picked a piece. "And he has men who are even closer to him. I'm just his daughter in ministry," she said and he scoffed. "You can believe whatever you like."

"Tell me about your family."

"Why are you so curious about my family?"

"Because it's strange for a young student like you, from a rich home to be abandoned."

"I'm an adult and I wasn't abandoned. They know I take care of myself," she said defensively.

"Hmm." He picked the tray of leftovers. He was in and out of the room within seconds with a bowl of water and napkin. When she was alright with it, he returned the bowl and came back. He didn't sit again but leaned against the wall as he had done several other times.

"You cook very well, and you serve well too," she said. "Thank you." He continued to stare at her. "Did you work in a restaurant before coming into abattoir business?"

"No," he said gruffly. "I have always been a butcher."

He thought she was uncomfortable under his gaze and to worsen matters, she couldn't move. Even a slight shift would cause her pain.

"Hmm, I see all your books."

"I told you I schooled myself."

"You've done a fine job, Mr. Ode," she said.

"Thank you."

"You have taste too. Your house is lovely."

He didn't budge. His face remained expressionless. "I built it myself. I like to work with my hands."

"You've done well for yourself." She sighed. "Your parents must be very proud."

At the mention of his parents, he lifted himself off the wall so sharply she winced. He took one long stride and stood before her, his gaze murderous.

CHAPTER
TWENTY-TWO

"I'M NOT AFRAID TO talk about my family, you know," he said with ironic softness. "My father murdered my mum when I was fifteen. He died a few years later. He was trampled by a mad cow," he said, daring her with his hard glare. "I'm alone. No family exists anywhere except my crazy grandfather. When he heard his daughter had been killed, he went mad temporarily and climbed up the hills to hide. You've met him."

"I'm sorry," she whispered.

"What are you sorry about?" He lowered himself to the bed and raised her chin with strong fingers. "I've made something out of my life," he whispered. She returned his angry gaze. "I'm not running from my shadow."

She moved her chin away from his grip and hissed. "I don't want you to know about me does not mean I'm running or afraid."

"I believe you are not a very confident young woman," he said, searching her face.

She sighed. "Are you a mind-reader now?"

"It's not one of my talents."

"Then you have no right—"

His forefinger traced her lips, stopping her mid-sentence.

"What are you hiding?" he said softly and involuntarily, her hand came to remove his.

He caught her hand in a play of love. His was calloused, the hand of a hard worker. The more she tried to free hers, the more he entangled it. Her hand was as soft as his was rough but she couldn't deny the tingling at the bottom of her belly.

"If you were not an environment student, I'd say you are a good detective. You know everything about me yet, I'm not sure I even remember your name," he said lightly.

Their gazes locked. She was trained to hide her feelings. This time, she hid the truth well, but she wasn't sure of the same about her emotions. He still had her fingers trapped in his, and her stomach continued to burn.

"You are not talented to read people," she concurred and he surprised her with a shy smile. A rare one.

"I'm so curious to know more about you," he said pathetically. He locked their fingers together and brought the hands up between them. "We are so different," he mumbled.

"What do you want to know about me?" she asked. Tell him and let him leave you alone before you try to kiss him again, her heart thudded with anticipation.

"Everything."

"Why?"

"Curiosity?"

She insisted. "Why?"

"Because you're here in my house."

"I'm leaving tomorrow," she said with certainty. "Then it wouldn't matter what you learn or know about me."

"Oh, that's what you think?" He released her hand and caught it just before she tucked it safely away, and laughed. His reflex was superb. "You want to escape. I see."

"You'll never see me again once I leave this place." She breathed. "Did my pastor really come here?"

He stopped playing with her hand and held it, locked. "Yeah."

"And?"

"He came with some police officers. He was so concerned for you."

"Why didn't you let him come and see me?"

His eyes widened as though she had asked for the impossible. "I didn't think about it," he mumbled. She tried to unlock her fingers but he held on. "My nails are clean, ma'am," he mocked.

"Obsessively so."

"Haven't I heard you say that before?"

"What did the police say?"

"You know what?" He stood releasing her hand. She promptly tucked both behind her. "We've caught the culprits, okay? My man, Bala is the problem and someone from the ministry of environment who believes you helped me catch Bala from ripping me bare. The idea was just to punish you. It flopped. They wanted to leave you in the bush for a few days—probably rape and flog you, starve you as well." He shrugged. "So definitely, you're leaving tomorrow."

She sat up. "How did you catch them?"

"We set a trap. Everyone left as though we'd closed. Lucy had hinted someone may try to stop those caught men from speaking. She was right. We ambushed the traitors."

"Just like that?" She snapped her fingers. "It's over just like that?" She gazed ahead, lost in thought for a moment. "Really, Lucy?"

He headed for the door. "She's a good woman."

"My mother likes to say that about people. She's a good woman, he's a good man. Everybody's good to her," she said, stopping him short of the entrance. He turned, a slight upward tip of his lips foreshadowed a smile. "My father would say just the opposite—everyone's either a moron or a bastard," she said.

He shoved his hands in his pockets. "Your parents sound like mine," he said softly. He didn't press about her family anymore but she wanted to talk.

"We all avoided my dad, except my sister, Janella," Christine said.

She didn't want him to leave her yet. She wanted company. Tomorrow, she would be back to her lonely life. Till date, he was the only one who ever took thought and care of her. She would never forget him.

"She's the favourite?" he asked.

"Yes. My mum and the rest of us were forced to worship her. Till my dad died three years ago, and even now some habits just stay," she said.

He prompted. "The rest of us?"

"I'm the first, then Janella, and then Saffron. The last is Pebble. We're four girls."

He sniffed. "Hmm. Are the others as pretty as you are?"

She smiled involuntarily. "Prettier. My mum is a very beautiful woman. My dad always said it's the only reason he married her. She's mixed, French mum Nigerian dad. My dad is mixed too but a quarter."

He remained at the door, his hands in his pockets much as she wanted his to return to sit with her.

"Really? No wonder your colour is—like this. Unique," he said, looking her over. "I would marry you but you're too young for me."

His words sent a tingling through her nerve endings. She would marry him even if he was a hundred years old. She'd never felt this attracted to a man in her life. A strong desire to move close, touch him, tell him the truth got her sweating.

"Your names are all lovely too," he said. "Exceptional names. Never heard any before, except yours."

"Dad liked to be exceptional in everything he did. I must give it to him for being so brilliant," she said.

"His daughter is also very brilliant."

She shrugged. "My sisters are more like him. Except Pebble."

"Pebu. I was wondering what the name means."

"It's not Pebu. Pebble."

"Pebble." He rolled the name. "Stone pebble? What a name?"

"There's a story behind it," she said.

He walked back to her and stood over her. "You don't want me to know it?"

She brought her hands out of hiding and twisted her fingers. "She has down's syndrome." He didn't comment and she thought he didn't know what it was. She took a steadying breath. "Down's syndrome is—"

"I know what it is," he cut in. "What I don't know is how the name applies."

"Dad said she was like stone in his meal. Pebble. He never called her anything else. Right from the first day he saw her." Christine looked at him, feeling so sad, tears pooled in her eyes. "She's the most adorable human being on earth."

"And you all called her Pebble, including your mum?" he asked, aghast.

"You said our parents were alike? What was your dad like?"

"I see what you mean," he said gruffly. "I'll call her Precious."

She opened her mouth to speak but swallowed with emotion. A tear dropped and he moved away from the bed.

"You need to sleep. I'll take you home in the morning," he said. "I'll take a look around the abattoir."

Her eyes pleaded with him to stay but he left all the same. He went for a long time and she was fast asleep by the time he returned.

Omasan was early the following day to check on Christine's thigh. The swelling had improved but Christine found it hard to walk without help.

"It's worse," she sulked. "I walked round the house yesterday."

"It's because you didn't walk round with it for so long. Once you move around a little now, it would feel better," Omasan said. "Here, I'll bind it."

After massaging and causing Christine to scream some more, she wrapped the thigh with bandage.

"Make sure you walk around with it," Omasan said as Christine daintily sat down on the bed after the painful exercise. "Oga Chico can help you to walk round in the afternoon then we can do it again when I come in the evening," Omasan said, packing her medicine bag.

"I'm leaving as soon as he gets back from work," Christine said.

"He comes back in the evening so you can do the exercise—"

"He just went to do some work, he'll be back soon to take me home," Christine cut in.

"Okay. Then you have to do the exercise on your own. Don't remove the bandage for another two days. Then come back and I'll check it. And try and always walk on it very well," Omasan said, looking at her sceptically.

Christine saluted in mockery. "Yes ma!"

"I think he likes you though, and would want you to stay," Omasan said.

In her estimation, they would be age-mates. Christine shook her head. "I don't think so." She knew the other woman was searching for a gossip column and she couldn't care less. "He thinks I'm too young for him," Christine said tartly.

Omasan burst into laughter. "That is very funny. Can a woman ever be too young for a man? I was fifteen when Ejiro came to marry me. Why? Too young ke?" She laughed.

Christine smiled. "But that's what he said."

Chico didn't even know her age. He would be shocked he was closer than he could ever imagine. But his assumptions were fine by her. She would leave and put an end to the short but memorable encounter they'd had.

"You know men like Oga Chico are very active men. Just like my husband," Omasan said. "When they come home they want to do that thing to unwind and because they are used to using their energy for everything, it is also the same in that area."

Christine held her breathe. What was the woman talking about?

"You know, even in this my condition." She looked at her bulge. "My husband does not spare me o. Sometimes five six rounds," she said and laughed shyly. "So maybe that is what Oga Chico is thinking about. You know, you look like oyinbo. Maybe you're not giving him enough action."

Christine burst into laughter despite herself. Can you imagine? She thought.

"Hmm. It sounds funny but that may be the reason o. Even my husband, when he comes home like this, he'll have his bath and then eat. Some days he won't even eat first. He wants that thing. Then after he can eat, play and sleep. Any day I don't perform he would say it's because I'm a small girl," Omasan said.

Oh I see your point, Christine thought.

"How old are you?" Christine asked curiously.

"Twenty-four. And I married at fifteen. Still he would say I'm too young."

"Anyway, I see your point but Chico and I are not lovers. We did not have sex at all and won't because we are not lovers," Christine said.

"Tah." Omasan snapped her fingers. "Don't talk like that. Don't you see the way he looks at you? Even Lucy has been very unhappy. You just come from nowhere and steal her man—"

Christine lifted her hands up in surrender. "Not me. I didn't steal any man, please."

"Now, I see it clearly. He's using your age as excuse. Men are very proud. When you behaved as if you were not interested, he changed it on your age." Omasan put another twist.

Christine gave up. Let the woman think whatever she felt good about. "I guess that must be it."

"But me, I have never seen a woman who is not attracted to Oga Chico before. Tah." she hissed and snapped her fingers again.

Christine liked her anyway, and smiled. Are you? She thought mischievously.

"Or is it because you read book, you think maybe Oga Chico does not have education?" she asked.

"Of course not."

"Hm. He's a good man. You'll enjoy him. But if you don't want him, even better for Lucy."

"Better for her."

Omasan finished packing up and sat on the bed. "Oga Chico, hmm." Omasan rolled her eyes dreamily. "I can marry that kind of man o. And he is very rich. He owns the whole of this land." She threw her arms wide in a large circle. "Have you seen our side? We call it the village," she said. Christine shook her head.

Christine had thought the other woman was preparing to leave. She didn't feel like entertaining a visitor. Chico had nudged her awake sometime between three and four and told her he was off. Of course, she had been drowsy but not too sleepy to think he was insane to be off to work at that time of the day. He'd assured her once the sales begin to wind down, he would come back for her. She had slept off only to be woken again by Omasan at about six. Now she just wanted the woman to leave so she could sleep another hour or two.

"The village is not even supposed to be the name for that place because it is like a small city. That our village side." Omasan chuckled. "Everything is there. School o, clinic o, even market, apart from the small market at the slaughter side. Oga Chico makes sure the place is very okay for us. He is like the king of this community."

"That's wonderful," Christine said dryly.

"And he protects us. You know he got this place by force but after all the trouble, there is peace now."

"Really?"

"If he wants you, he would get you, you know," she said. "He's like that. Anything he wants, he gets."

Christine was tired of it. "Sorry, but I'm having headache, I want to sleep," she said.

Omasan stood. She obviously had not realised her welcome had over-stayed.

"Remember to step on that leg and walk around," she said. At the door, she turned and winked mischievously. "And remember that Oga Chico has power!" She clenched her fists and brought them up to gesticulate and laughed before she left.

Christine thought she was a silly woman though nice.

CHAPTER TWENTY-THREE

CHICO DROPPED HER OFF at home. Contrary to Omasan's orders she couldn't step on the leg and he had to practically carry her into the house. As she had hoped, there was no one around to know she'd come in. Her mum usually stayed in her rooms upstairs with Pebble. She'd learnt to stay out of people's way with her special daughter. Pebble attended a school for retarded children and also had learnt to keep out of the way whenever she came back home. Christine did not encourage him to hang around but begged him to contact Tolani to visit her.

Tolani got her to go to the hospital and she saw her doctor who prescribed a walking stick amongst other medication. She'd been lucky to have Omasan according to the doctor but the local therapy had not been enough. Her abduction made news as it was discovered the conspiracy was not only from Bala but also Mr. Agoro who was nursing the hurt of the disciplinary action taken against him.

As soon as the police stepped in, everything blew open. Though the culprits were caught, her personal items were not recovered. Her car had been dismantled and sold in parts. Yet, Christine pulled herself together and recovered her normal life. She was at work on Thursday and got to relate her ordeal to her boss and friends in the office.

The weeks rolled by without hearing a word from Chico. Not that she planned to anyway. She had dismissed whatever happened at the ranch between them as mere weakness in the face of turmoil. She was a strong woman and she had been through a lot.

As the months passed, she was faced with even more tests of her inner strength. Janella announced her engagement to Ayo. The more she tried to stay away from their presence, the more she had to deal with it. It was tough on her, with Saffron flaunting her attitude in every one's face especially after the announcement. No one had bothered to empathize with her on her ordeal. Her mother mumbled something about being strong, and that was the end of any acknowledgement of the treachery.

She missed Chico. She loved his company though it could be she had been starved of male companionship. She couldn't get him out of her mind. But she did nothing about it. And wouldn't have.

Her director had been working on some projects in the office which she wasn't involved in and then he got the opportunity to attend a short-term course overseas. Christine was asked to act in his place. She was elated. It meant more work for her, but then, she wasn't complaining. The opportunity for promotion was enormous and she had come to terms that her job was the only thing worth the while in her life.

Christine was summoned to a meeting in the director's office as a start of what was to be a series of meetings. She knew the meeting was to be held with some of the stakeholders on current projects but she hadn't been briefed.

Her director stood when she entered the office. "Hm, Ms. Bello you have a huge task on your hands right now. We're meeting with prospective beneficiaries of the new mechanization project I am handling. They need to know you are now the officer in charge. The representatives of the united nations and charity foundation would also be here," he said rapidly.

She took the seat he offered. "What area of mechanization, sir?"

"Storage. Food storage. We would learn more about that in the meeting. We have some farmers and cold room operators attending."

Some farmers turned out to be a hall full of rough-looking peasants and workmen. The director, seeing the number, voted the meeting moved to the main conference hall within the premises, which could sit at least a hundred people. The foreign officials and their local counterparts sat in front of the hall, where chairs had been hurriedly arranged for them. With Christine and her boss.

The idea was a great and laudable one and the funds for it already released. The monitoring committees were then set out to interview beneficiaries. Forms were given out to be filled and the beneficiaries encouraged to wait for the shortlisted candidates to be contacted.

Back in the director's office, he handed over all the forms to Christine.

"We'll work on this before I leave," he said. "What I want you to do is sort them out. The criteria for qualification are in this folder. You need to also read it before you shortlist. We would convey a meeting in two days to review your list."

"Okay, sir."

Christine took the rest of the day to read through the dossier of the project and understood huge project was worth millions of American dollars. In all, the project would benefit ten producers of foods and drinks across three states in the region. The storage facilities were state-of-the-art and the mere thought excited Christine to be a part of it. She proceeded to work on the forms.

A few were unreadable, and she discarded them. At the end of the exercise, Christine had twenty names. She had been thorough and professional. There were farmers, cold room operators, entrepreneurs and abattoir owners.

Abattoir owners.

After screening all applications by abattoir owners in the state, she discovered Chico's was not among. She didn't have his cell phone number and this was the opportunity of a lifetime for his business. Most unlike the other qualified abattoirs, Chico had the land and the drive for success.

Quite unprofessionally, Christine screened one of the four qualifying abattoirs out and decided to visit Chico. She had worked all night to make sure she did a thorough job. But she had reserved a slot for Ode Abattoir.

During what should be her break time, and when she was sure Chico would be in his office, she drove out with her new driver and truck. She had gotten a clean form from her director with the hope that Chico would fill it out and she could present it along with the others at the meeting the following day.

The abattoir was usually not very busy at that time of the day. Chico was on one of the slabs, butchering a huge cow. The common crowd had disintegrated to a few people. Christine assumed the order may have been exclusive. She stood at the end of the slab close to where he worked and tried to catch his attention. He continued focused as though he had not noticed her. Two men waited on him while two other cows were being dismantled on the slab. She waited patiently. When he straightened, he looked at her and wiped sweat away from his face. He then threw stern orders at the men on packaging of the meat. Refusing to acknowledge her, he jumped down and brushed past her. She followed, wondering what the matter with him was. Had he forgotten who she was?

She half-ran after him. "Hey Chico, hi."

"Hi yourself," he said, not slowing his pace.

"Hmm, are you angry I didn't contact you? You're just as guilty," she teased. He continued without a word. "Would you just slow a bit?" Men could be so petty. He did, stopping so abruptly he almost knocked her down.

"What do you want?" He turned on her and snapped, shocking the life out of her.

"To discuss something with you. Are you in such a bad mood or what? Can't we go to your office at least?" she cried, unable to understand why he was like this.

He was so angry the muscles on his jaw twitched. She had never seen him so livid, and she wondered why.

"Yeah, my office," he said between his teeth.

He continued toward the office but opened a door to the side instead, when they reached there. He was so abrupt, slamming the door after himself. She would have jerked the door open but she heard the shower—oh so? Was that the reason he was so edgy? He was bloody and sweaty coming down the slab but it was expected. She didn't mind.

She walked to his office and opened the door. To preoccupy herself, she looked through the window to the slab area. The men were packing the meat into tall sacks branded with the Ode Abattoir logo. She observed with a tinge of affection, as though she was a part of what was going on. From Chico's office, there was a clear view of all the slabs but of nothing else. No one would ever know the wealth buried in this abattoir. She would come back one day and demand from Chico a complete tour of—

He yanked the door open and she turned to look at him. He was washed clean from head to toe and smelt of perfumed soap. You couldn't imagine he had been drenched in blood and sweat a few minutes earlier. Though still dressed like a butcher, his white shirt and brown jeans was crisp. Christine smiled at him but it wasn't reciprocated.

"Now you're all clean, at least you can relax," she said softly.

"Say what you want and leave," he snapped, his jaws set, his eyes cold, his teeth clamped, his fists clenched.

What was the matter with him? She took a seat and opened her bag. Maybe he had a bad day.

"I brought a form for you from the ministry. They are empowering people in your line of business to have storage facilities and it is a huge project—" she said. She tried to keep the excitement from her voice. She hoped this would soften him and put him in a better mood. "I happened by and saw the people picking the forms and when I didn't see you—"

"You happened by." He exploded. "You happened by?"

"At the ministry, I mean."

He pointed to the door. "Get out of my office, Ms. Bello."

"What's the matter with you?" she screamed. "Why are you being so nasty?"

"What's the matter with me?" He bared his teeth. "This is the matter with me."

He pulled a drawer out of his desk almost breaking the hinges, and bunched some sheets of paper together before flinging them at her. She stood and only just missed the hit. The bunch fell to the floor and she slowly picked it up.

She knew what it was even before she opened it. The beneficiaries had been given brochures with the form. Chico had been amongst the throng at her office, and being so overwhelmed by the crowd, she hadn't noticed him. He'd seen her introduced as the chief research officer in charge of the project. Her director had been out to impress the expatriates, going to great lengths to present her and her qualifications, her master's degree her many courses at home and abroad—

"When were you going to tell me?" he lowered his voice, without reducing the intensity.

She picked the documents and placed them on his desk and then straightened with resolve. She breathed in and looked at him. "I guess I you'd not want to hear my explanation but—"

"You spent how many nights in my house. You lied to me about everything you are—your dysfunctional family, your supposed research project, even your assumed abduction. If you have any dignity or self-respect, you'll not be flouncing around like a worthless lout full of lies. Lies lies lies," he yelled right into her face.

"I don't need any insult from you—"

He looked round and threw his hands up. "Insult? Have I insulted you? Take this as an insult," he snapped.

She hadn't known he was so close to her till his lips captured hers in a vicious kiss. His hand shot out and held the back of her head in place as he ravaged her lips. It was meant to be a punishing kiss. There was nothing loving about it. It was blatant and defiant. Yet, she had never felt so passionate in her life. Her body shook from head to toe and she thought she was being lifted off her feet. Her hand came up to touch the one holding her head in place, to steady herself, and she moaned as he changed his direction to kiss her more deeply.

The kiss must have lasted only a minute. She felt it went on forever. He staggered back, his breathing, loud and hoarse. His hand trembled as it dropped back to his side, and despite herself, she summoned every will to look at him.

"I think you just insulted yourself, Mr. Ode" she said, trembling.

She didn't have anything else to say to him. She picked her file and bag from his table and marched out of his office, willing her legs to take her just as far as her official vehicle. Here and now, all she wanted to do was cry.

But she held herself till she was within the safe confines of her rooms later in the evening and then her dam broke. Her greatest and worst fear was he had been so angry with her. He had never shown so much emotion before. He was so angry he couldn't even articulate his feelings. She hated herself for lying to him, but when could have been so appropriate? She thought she wouldn't have anything to do with him again but fate thrust her back into his life.

With the form in her hand, she had planned to tell him the truth. She'd thought he would find it funny. She had never imagined he would be so upset about it. And that hurt her the most. His kiss had been to humiliate her but she was sure it did more than that for both of them. For her it unleashed her reserves. For him, she guessed it released his pent-up emotions. Perhaps she should have apologised and overlooked his anger and insult instead of walking away. But why was he so angry?

So angry he threw away the opportunity of a lifetime.

CHAPTER TWENTY-FOUR

CHRISTINE FELT RESPONSIBLE. SHE had always been that way. Growing up, her sisters took advantage of her, making her feel guilty and accountable for their mistakes or carelessness. She knew Chico was supposed to be more professional and sensible than he'd been but she couldn't shake off the fact his loss was as a result of her deceit. So, when the team sat to evaluate her short-list, twenty businesses, as she returned the one she dropped, she brought up the Ode Abattoir.

Initially, the expatriates discarded the thought of bringing someone who'd not applied but after some persuasion from her, Chico's business was pencilled down for an interview with the condition that he sent in his filled form ahead. Hence, twenty-one prospects were to be contacted and when they arrived, interviewed.

In her heart of hearts, she knew she wasn't seeing him on a personal level again. She would send the forms to him through her driver and if he still refused to show, that was his business.

Through the day, she busied herself with handover notes and invitation letters. With her acting role, she would have a secretary, and as much as that sounded cool, she was scared she would not have enough to do to occupy her day, and night.

As her director was left with only a week before his departure, the interview was fixed for the following two days. At the close of work, she gave her driver the letters with instructions to dispatch them first thing the following morning. She'd spent the day to prepare for the meeting. It would be hectic but Christine loved it.

When she got home in the evening, she was exhausted. She took up a meal to her apartment, and had a bath. She would study the brochures and draw up her own strategy of running the project and then sleep. After a sumptuous meal of local rice and pepper stew which she discovered she could hardly eat, she cuddled up around the brochure and began to read through it for the umpteenth time. She knew she had to get a full grasp of the workings before she could form her own strategy.

There was a knock on her door.

"Yes?" she answered. The housekeeper came in. "Mammy," she said, as the elderly lady was fondly called.

"You have a visitor downstairs. Mr. Ode," she said.

Christine's heart skipped a beat. What did he want? Could she afford to entertain him downstairs? Where was everybody? Would it not be better to bring him up to her apartment and hide whatever shame he'd come to subject her to? Or meet him outside? She was so confused she just glared at Mammy, her lips trembling.

"Are you alright?" Mammy said. "He brought a gift too."

"A gift?" Well. "Please show him the way up," she said.

She didn't want anyone to walk into a display of any sort. She had succeeded so far in keeping her private life isolated from her nose-snooping sister, she didn't want any more assault on her raw emotions.

Chico walked into her sitting area with a huge white triangular box wrapped with a lovely lilac, patterned transparent sheet. It was so huge he held it away from his face so he could walk properly. She stood in the middle of the room in anticipation, dressed in what she was most comfortable in her, work jeans and a t-shirt.

"Hi." His face was straight, relaying nothing. He looked beyond the parcel at the room, and placed it on her small dining table. "I don't have your number or I should have told you I was coming." He took a seat on the couch.

She stared at him, her arms defensively folded across her chest. Her lips still tingled from his kiss, which she just couldn't get off her mind, and seeing him made it worse. For a brief moment, neither said anything.

He spoke first. "Sit down please."

She couldn't recognise her own voice. "I'm alright here."

"I caught the biggest fish in my pond, and dressed it for you," he said, pointing at the gift he wrapped.

"Oh." She swallowed. "Thanks."

He walked to the table. "Let's unwrap it together."

She was reluctant but obliged him. Quietly, they opened the box and she couldn't have suppressed her surprised gasp. The fish was huge.

He leaned in. "I've been keeping it for over a year. It grew so big I had to keep it separate so it won't eat the smaller ones."

"Wow. I've never seen catfish this massive."

The aroma from the fish filled the room. Though she'd had dinner, she was so tempted to taste it. She touched it gingerly and he nodded.

"Go on. I hope you like it," he said.

The fish was still hot. He must have taken it straight off the grill.

"I put it on low-roast so that it would be well done. It had been on the spit since yesterday," he said using his fingers to cut off a small piece.

"Since after I left?" she mumbled and cut some too. She didn't look at him but put the fish in her mouth and groaned. "This is heaven."

"Since after you left." He turned her to him, and wrapped her in his arms. He put the piece in his hand on her lips and ate it off before she could. It was a most intimate gesture. "I'm sorry for treating you like that yesterday," he whispered.

She swallowed. "I should have told you the truth too."

"You should have," he concurred. "Now come on, I'm famished. I can't wait to devour this fish," he said abruptly letting go of her. His reflex was sharp. While she tried to recover from his audacious behaviour, he sat at the table and delved into the succulent fish.

"Would you like some rice with it?" She moved over to her fridge and brought out a bowl of Mammy's leftover rice and stew. She had the habit of storing food to warm later without having to call the kitchen, and now it paid off.

"Very little," he said. "You cooked?"

"No. Mammy does," she said. She set a plate in front of him. "I'll heat this up in the microwave."

"I see."

He tore out a healthy portion of fish and put it on the plate and she exclaimed. "You can't finish that."

"We'll eat together," he said.

She placed the rice and stew on the table and they dug in.

"I'm so tempted not to share this fish with anyone in the house. But Mammy would be so grateful if I give her some." She moaned. "Hmm."

"The elderly lady?"

"Yes. She was our nanny when we were kids. Now she's housekeeper and cook." she said. "You need to eat energy-giving foods more. Your job needs power—"

"How old are you?"

"I turned twenty-eight last time I checked. About a month ago."

The day had come and gone without event. She hadn't even remembered until bedtime. She expected him to say something, he didn't.

"I need protein more." He changed the topic back. "I eat a bit of carbohydrates just for strength. I am a very healthy man, though," he said proudly.

"I see it. Virile too," she said before she could stop herself then she laughed, hoping he would not pick up on such an indecent comment. She had no such luck.

"Really? How virile am I?" he asked teasingly. She remembered what Omasan said and laughed more. "Yes? I'm waiting."

She needed to make it look like she wasn't embarrassed by this conversation. "Quite macho. And it's proven too that you're a stud."

"Now you're treading on dangerous waters. How would you know?"

She shrugged, tongue in cheek. "Omasan told me."

His eyes smouldered. "How did she know?"

"You tell me," she laughed. "How did she know?"

He bit his lower lip just as her front door opened and Saffron waltzed in.

"Well well well." She raised her hands wide in the air. "Who's visiting miss lonely?" she kept her gaze on Chico. "I was passing and heard laughter—thought it was the TV."

"Chico, this is Saffron, my sister," Christine said, her voice taking on a strain she had tried over the years to remove.

It was hopeless. Whenever Saffron came round her, she tensed. She'd tried to keep to the rules to never introduce Saffron as a younger sister, and never with her married name. Still, her sister took great delight in putting her down.

"Chico Ode." Chico stood. "Pleased to meet you."

Saffron gave him a once over. "Are you my sister's new catch?"

Christine heaved. "Saffron, please—"

"A friend."

"Oh, sister. He denies you right on. Smart guy," she batted her eyelids. "What do you do for a living, Chico?" Saffron clasped her hands and assessed him with a "not bad looking," expression on her face.

Christine gasped. "Saffron, this is not—"

"I'm a butcher."

Saffron's eyes bulged and she crinkled her nose. "A what?" She looked on the open triangular box on the table between them, took in the fact that they had been eating from one plate and then looked at Christine before dragging her gaze back to Chico. "A butcher as in, butcher. Kill cows, dirty nails, bloody clothes, smelly, poor butcher—"

Christine marched to the door. "Saffron please can you leave my—"

"Smart girl," Chico cut in once more. "Yeah, pretty much. A butcher."

Saffron snapped. "Excuse me. Who's asking you? I was talking to my sister."

Chico shrugged and sat back at the table. He took off eating where he stopped.

"Saffron, you have thoroughly embarrassed me today in front of my guest," Christine said in a low voice.

"I? Guest? Did you say guest? A butcher? You have embarrassed our family by bringing a butcher—" she paused and swallowed on the word as though saying it drained her of energy, "into the house. Dad would be livid in his grave."

"Well, Dad is not here and I thank God for that."

Saffron gasped in horror. "Mr. Chico, if my sister is not bold enough to tell you the truth, I will. You don't belong here in her class. For God's sake, she has to buy this giant fish to feed you. Probably it's your first decent meal today."

Christine opened her mouth to scream but Chico's words stopped her.

"I'm sorry, madam. I'll leave," he said and turned to Christine with a small nod.

"No, please, Chico. You can't leave just yet. Saffron, please go. We'll talk later. Please." Saffron hesitated. "Please, Saffron."

"Shit happens." Saffron hissed and swaggered out just as she came.

Christine was close to tears as the door closed behind her sister. "I'm so sorry about that—"

"You shouldn't be. You should stand up to her. How old is she?"

"Twenty-four." Christine sat opposite him. She wanted to cry.

"Younger, hmm." He pressed his lips together. "You know, despite the fact that I was angry at you, you were very confident at that gathering in your office. I was proud of you," he said. "You're a different person here. Why do you allow her to intimidate you?"

She sighed. "It's a long story." Saffron had totally messed up her mood.

"I'd like to hear it," he said. She stopped eating and when she refused to talk he gestured for her to eat. She shook her head. "Maybe I should really leave then."

She covered her mouth to curb the tears threatening to burst free. "No, I'm sorry."

"Okay. I'll change the subject." He swatted the air between them. "You know, when I was young, much younger, and my mother was still alive, I'd follow her to visit my grandpa. And in those hay days, Oloye would bring me here for deliveries."

"You mean that?" She gasped. "You're just pulling my legs."

"I'm not. You won't believe it. Twice, we came here, I can't forget. Oloye delivered meat to this mansion." He rolled his eyes up and down. "I never came inside. But merely being outside the gate in his rickety truck, dressed in my Sunday best, thrilled me beyond anything else."

She giggled. "And you never mentioned it."

"I'm mentioning it now."

"I've never known another home." She sighed heavily and smiled. "It's a family compound. My great-grandfather built it as a two-storey mansion but Dad decided to change the design. So now the ground floor is a massive six-room apartment. Dad stayed there in his sick months. The last floor is the same but this floor was divided into four. For each of the girls. We each have similar two-room apartments." She sighed. "Sometime later Saffron broke down the wall to Pebble's because she—"

"Precious."

"Precious. Saffron uses hers too." She heaved a sigh. "She stays with Mum on the last floor now. Dad stayed there before he got sick. Then Peb—Precious stayed here with me."

He smiled. "I'd like to meet her."

"She'll love you. She loves people."

"Now."

"Now?"

"I want to see the house too. I'm fascinated." He took a long drink from the juice Christine had poured for him. "Oh yeah, Saffron would be loitering around the corridor."

"Part of the problem," she mumbled, trying not to laugh. He obviously was trying to make light of the issue but she knew it wasn't funny. Yet she wanted to laugh. In fact, she wanted to laugh so hard and never stop.

"I want to meet Precious and I want to see the house. And your mum, would she care for left-over fish?"

She burst into laughter. "She really wouldn't mind." She moaned. "I'll keep some for myself," she said snugly. "The head definitely. That should be my dinner tomorrow."

He smirked. "If I don't come and take you out. That is."

She stiffened and shook her head. She didn't really know this guy and hadn't seen him for half of the year and he just walked into her house and acted as though they'd been going on for years. How was she to react to him? She enjoyed his company more than she had any other person in her life. But was she ready for a relationship now? And his assumption she would go on a date with him? No. She disliked presumptuous men.

"Talking about family, I'm curious about something. Your name. It doesn't state where you're from. Chico sounds eastern and you adopt the name of the town as your surname."

"I'm a northerner."

"What? You're full of surprises." Her eyes widened. "What are you doing here, deep down west?"

"Generations of my family came down as cattle-rearers and settled. You should know I identify with my mother's family."

"Oh. I would too." She gesticulated. "But how come Chico?"

"When I left home, I moved to Ode Abattoir where my grandpa was a master." He paused and she nodded with rapt attention. He continued. "A little boy called Chinedu followed me around. We called him Chico. He later died of sickle cell anaemia. He was six. I changed my name to remember him. My surname changed to Ode when I took ownership."

"So sorry. Poor boy. So what—"

"Don't ask me what my name was." He laughed but then his eyes softened to the one she'd become so familiar with.

She picked up the used plate and items she could, and stood. "Excuse me."

He carried other items from the table and waited to follow her. She reluctantly led the way to her small and kitchenette.

"How's Omasan?" she asked nervously. "She ought to have delivered by now?"

His breath fanned the back if her neck. "She has a daughter."

She jumped. He was so close behind her. She had thought her kitchenette was small now it felt like a hole with Chico standing in it.

She turned to face him. "What?"

"Omasan."

"Oh yes. That's great. Is it her first?"

He dropped the bottle and glass in his hand on the kitchen top and pulled her into his arms. She whimpered even before he touched her. His lips trailed the side of her face before he found her lips and took them in a romantic embrace. He had a minty sweet in his mouth, and he passed it into hers and back again. She tried to wriggle out of his embrace but it was too consuming. He was gentle, most unlike yesterday, bordering on loving. His kiss was intoxicating, engaging and she gave herself to it.

She dragged in a deep breath when he released her. "No, Chico, please we can't."

He breathed and took the tip of her earlobe between his teeth. "Why?"

Christine grabbed the front of his shirt afraid she would fall off somewhere. She summoned all the energy within her and wanted to step back but she was wedged between him and the sink. He stepped back instead and rubbed his eyes, visibly shaken.

"Huh?" he gasped. And then laughed a short, shaky laugh. "I'm sorry." He leaned back against the doorpost. "I'm sorry."

"I'm just not this kind of person—I don't—"

How would she tell him she was a Christian who would not kiss or touch before marriage? And she wasn't even in a relationship with him. Yet he had kissed her once too many. And she'd responded. She knew he knew she'd reciprocated.

"Are you a virgin?" he asked bluntly.

"No. I mean—no but—"

"You have repented of all that?" He still wanted her, it was obvious in the way he breathed.

"I think I should put the fish away," she said. She moved past him long enough for his hand to pull her back. And into his arms.

"You won't kiss me. You won't talk to me?"

"We should go and see Mum and Precious—"

"Why do I want you this much?" he whispered into her face. "Do you want me?"

"Chico—let's help ourselves and stop this—"

"I can't help myself."

He took her lips again and kissed her hungrily. After the kiss, he clung to her for a while, just holding her. She didn't struggle against him as she contended with her own inner turmoil.

"Those nights you spent in my house were hell for me. I couldn't sleep. I was on heat like a female dog," he said softly. "Every day after that I battled with my feelings, with finding you. I wanted to come here."

He pulled back and cupped her face. "Did you miss me?" She closed her eyes and nodded. "I missed you too," he whispered. "I wanted to marry you then but I thought of your age, your family, of your fears—I still want to now." He willed her to look at him.

CHAPTER TWENTY-FIVE

Tolani gasped. "He asked you to marry him?"

She was perched on Christine's desk at the close of work the following day. It had been hectic all day but as soon as she had the time, she had called on her friend to come over. Though she had kept her composure most of the day, she couldn't any longer. She needed to unburden. Never in her life had she been so pressurized.

"Did you accept? You don't even know this man."

"He didn't ask like that. He was just talking about himself and how he wanted me so much and he couldn't almost control himself. And he kept touching my body and kissing my face and neck—" Christine moaned. "I feel so much like a sinner. I can't believe this is happening to me again, Tolani. I am so weak. So weak."

"Did you let him know how bad you felt?"

"I think he got the message because I was just accepting everything he was saying and doing—"

"You were just accepting everything?"

"I was not—coordinated. He was talking and touching me." Christine sighed. "He wasn't so together himself."

"Wow, you are in love?" Tolani laughed. "I always knew you'd be very dramatic when you do fall in love."

"He didn't mention love at all. He wants me he wants me—that was all he was saying." Christine breathed in. "I was shameless. I think he was too—" She massaged her temple. "He kept rubbing his eyes and shaking his head and moaning that he couldn't seem to control himself—afterward he stepped back from me and told me to take him to see Mum."

"Really, he met Mum?"

"And Pebble," Christine said. "He named her Precious and kept telling me she was the prettiest of all of us." She smiled, remembering. "And he was so taken with Mum—and Mum with him. I've never seen her chat for so long. As though they'd known themselves before. He left well after midnight and there was Mum insisting he must come back."

"I've never seen you this disoriented." Tolani smoothed back Christine's hair. She was sweating. "You're warm."

"You know Jon was a bit different—but this is how I couldn't control my emotions with him—"

"Jon was different," Tolani snapped. "Jon controlled you."

"Yes, I know but I couldn't say no to him. I couldn't think. I wasn't myself." Christine struggled with words. "Just like now."

"You said he stopped when he noticed you were not okay with it. And you said he was also confused?" Tolani tried to reason. Christine nodded. "Don't compare him with Jon. Jon was an opportunist. He took full advantage of you every chance he got."

Christine sighed. "He came for the interview today."

"Jon?"

"No. Chico. He came for the project interview today. I told him about it yesterday, before he left."

"Did he say anything to you?"

"He sent a note to me that he wanted my cell number," Christine mumbled and Tolani chuckled.

"You mean after all the necking he doesn't have your number?" Tolani gasped, and they both burst into laughter.

"I didn't have his too. He sent me a text that he was coming over this evening."

"You have evening service."

"I told him to pick me up in the church."

"And?"

"And nothing. He'll pick me up there." Christine shrugged. They both kept quiet for a while, both pondering their own personal analysis of the situation.

Tolani bit her nails. "Do you think he means the proposal?"

"Is it really a proposal? I don't know. He wasn't himself." Christine dragged a hand over her face." He's usually very composed. He wasn't yesterday."

She felt ill. Jon never ever mentioned marriage and they were together for over three years before he realised Janella had more appeal. Three years of breaking every moral rule of Christian courtship. No one knew they did anything together, in that Jon at least respected her. No one knew she was sleeping with him all the while, and getting rid of babies in the bid.

"Let's see if he would come up with it again," Tolani advised. "But you need to stop being physical with him!"

Christine nodded. "I know." She covered her face. "I know."

"It's the past." Tolani rubbed the back of her hand. "God has forgiven but we can't repeat the mistakes."

Christine nodded, then swallowed as a new thought occurred to her. "Do you think he'll be taken by Janella?" Christine voiced her worst fear. Her sister had taken two of her men already.

In the family, Christine was the least pretty. Even her mother was prettier than she was and that had been one of the issues her father had with her. Dad loved the prettier people. Janella was the prettiest. No man had seen her and not been overwhelmed. "The earlier they meet the better," she mumbled.

"You'd better squelch that line of thought," Tolani scolded. "I thought he said Pebble was the prettiest. So who did he see yesterday?"

"He saw everyone except Janella."

"If he's yours, he won't notice Janella."

"You only say that to console me—"

"Besides," her friend continued, "you told me Janella is married now to Ayo, is it not true?"

"They did some form of thing I think they went to the registry or something secret. The church and traditional hasn't yet been done but then Janella just came home and announced she was married." Christine shrugged. "Janella still lives at home and Ayo is not moving in so I don't really know their arrangement. We don't talk," she said with a strained voice.

Her relationship with her sister was a huge concern to her. She still battled the bitterness of not one but two major betrayals not to talk of the many minor ones. She had really wanted Ayo.

"Do you see yourself with this Chico? I mean, you won't want to move to live in the slaughter?" Tolani said, voicing her own major concern.

"He won't move into our house either. I know that for sure. To live on the farm? I really don't know. What is here for me, Tolani? My father left nothing. Even that apartment is on loan." She felt like crying.

"I thought you were contesting his will."

"Saffron has the money. She controls everything. Even Mum's allowance. What chances do I have of winning? They keep adjourning the case." She swallowed hard.

Tolani straightened and clenched her jaw. "This is strange. You never told me before."

"When Dad was diagnosed with the liver condition, he started planning his death. You know what Dad was like." Christine took in a deep breath. "A stickler for bureaucracy he reviewed his will. One of the things he wanted was a successor for his business so, he called me. We were never friendly we never really agreed. He wanted me to follow in his steps as his first child but I didn't want the things he wanted. I wasn't a good business person, it meant I would leave my job, and I hated politics so when he called me, he wanted me to marry Hassan Hassan—"

Tolani jumped to her feet in shock. "Saffron's husband?"

"Yes. In fact, he tied my inheritance to that," Christine said softly.

"My God." Tolani exclaimed. "Why? What does the good-for-nothing man have?"

"His father had a business relationship with mine." Christine could not stop as silent tears slid past her eyelids. "He mentioned it several times—the heir to both empires having a sort of merger through marriage. Hassan irritates me. I never could stand his guts even when we were children." She swatted the tears away.

"But he's so lazy for crying out loud. Saffron dominates and he's just her puppet."

"When I told Dad I would never marry Hassan, he called Janella and made the offer. Janella shouted him down and he called Saffron."

"I can't believe your Dad—"

"He always was like that. Saffron asked him to lay down the terms. He told her plainly she swaps my place if she takes the man. Only that she gets her inheritance along with mine. Dad gave me nothing. Where I live now is at Saffron's mercy. Mum begged her to let me keep my flat and for Mum's sake I agreed to stay," Christine said. Her tears refused to stop.

"This is incredible. Now I understand why Saffron is so proud. What kind of marriage do they have? I mean, does Hassan live in that house?"

"He does. But he is so reckless—his father was glad to be rid of him to that marriage. Before Dad died, he made sure they got married and Hassan moved in. The alternative was for them to move into one of the other properties owned by either father. Best option was for them to live at the manor with Dad keeping an eye.

"Tolani, can I ever forgive my father?" Christine looked at her friend with teary eyes. "He was so rich. He left everything to Janella and Saffron.

I didn't even get a kobo. He left Peb—Precious and I high and dry at the mercy of the others."

"You know, when you told me your car was taken back by your Dad, I didn't understand. I thought he was going to change it. Then you went and accepted that car loan—and I just didn't want to poke you know—Huh?" Tolani sighed. "What about Mum?"

"Mum should be sustained by Saffron till her death."

"God forbid—"

Christine's phone began to ring. "It's Chico," she mumbled and picked the call. "Hello?"

He hesitated. "Hello. Where are you? I'm in your church," he said softly.

"Wow. I'm still at work but I'll leave just now," she said and sniffed again.

"You're crying," he said. "Where are you?"

"I'm in my office—I—"

"Why are you crying?"

Involuntarily, she sniffed again. "It's nothing. I'm—I'm fine."

"I'll come and pick you then."

"No don't worry—"

"Are you alone?"

"I'm with Tolani."

"Let me talk with her," he demanded. She hesitated but handed over the handset to Tolani.

Tolani grimaced. "What?"

"He wants to talk to you," Christine said. She stood and began to pack up as Tolani exchanged pleasantries with Chico.

"She's fine—just a bit emotional—yes. Just wait, yeah. Okay. Bye," Tolani said and hung up. "Hm, Ee chuuu!" she exclaimed and laughed. "This love is killing me o."

"Tolani!"

CHAPTER
TWENTY-SIX

CHICO ARRIVED EARLY TO see Christine's pastor. He hadn't seen the man of God since that day he walked out on him. He knew quite clearly despite his aversions to the style of worship in Christine's church, and the pastor's personal beliefs, he needed the holy man. Christine was obviously important to her church and her pastor and he had seen it from the way police was dispatched to the abattoir in search of her. He knew it was the proper thing to do. Already he had jumped too many steps and he wasn't one who liked to break protocols.

The air was hot and humid contrasting sharply with the cool of Pastor's office. Chico had never even bothered to find out his name, he realised. Well, this would indeed be an interesting meeting. The holy man sat behind his huge desk and waved Chico to a leather seat. His big bible was open before him and he seemed in a meditative mood. The service would not start until another hour and a half. Chico had chosen the time hopeful he'd have the pastor's full attention.

He wasn't easily intimidated by anything least of all a mere man but he found himself eager to impress Christine's pastor. His pastor didn't know him personally but he'd been around the church long enough. He just didn't believe the pastor needed to know him despite who he was and how he'd been a huge contributor to the finances of the church.

Regularly for the last five years he had donated at least one cow in every event in the church. More than one if it was the annual convention. It had become a norm in his church that cooking accompanied every small event. Yet, he'd done all anonymously—what your right hand is doing, let not the left know—being his philosophy. He was sure his pastor would faint if they discovered he was the nameless giver because he had never stood out in any way in the church. Several times there had been insinuations and attempts to discover the donor. He couldn't let them know.

Pastor did not offer him a seat, and didn't show much interest in his presence either. Who could blame him? Chico drew up a seat and took it, relaxing and pasting a subtle smile to hide his discomfort. He had never done this before in his life.

"Mr. Ode," Pastor said, folding his hands on his huge bible. "How may I help you?"

Chico stretched his hand across the table. "Good evening, Pastor—?"

The pastor looked at the hand and then at him. He withdrew his hand and met the pastor's gaze. He had never been able to patronize anyone and he hated it too. If pastor wasn't in the mood to be friendly, neither was he.

"I wanted to see you about Christine," he said, matter-of-fact.

"What about her?"

"I'm going into a relationship with her," Chico said, and picked up a small, unique crystal ball on the table.

Pastor snapped. "Mr. Ode, is this supposed to be a joke or something?"

"Well, Pastor, you seem not interested in what I have to say so I might as well say it and leave. I believe you must be very busy, and I would not want to waste your time." He put down the crystal and looked at the pastor. "Or mine."

"The last time you came into my office you were rude, impatient, and angry and you ended up walking off. Now you come into my office, all arrogant and just say you are going into a relationship with Christine.

My daughter? I should ask you to get out of my office right now," the pastor said so softly the ironic tone hit Chico harder than yelling would have.

"I'm sorry—"

The pastor's face relaxed. "Tell me about yourself, Mr. Ode."

Though he seemed more receptive, his body language had not changed. He sat rigidly in his chair as though poised to explode. "I am a butcher. I've been all my life," Chico said, and sat up. He had expected to be interviewed any way. "I work at the Ode Abattoir, and I live there too." He shrugged. "I'm thirty-three years old. My parents are both dead. I'm an only child."

Pastor sneered. "Are you born again?"

"Yes, sir. I took the decision about fifteen years ago."

"Tell me what prompted you to take this decision."

"Well, I had a very violent upbringing. My father abused my mother—I left home at fifteen and when I was eighteen my father died. He killed my mother shortly after I left. When he died I refused to attend his burial. A customer at the slaughter preached to me to forgive him and attend. And also preached Christ. That's when I gave my life to Christ," he said.

Pastor leaned forward. "Did you forgive him?"

Chico arched his eyebrows. "I don't know. I don't think or talk about it," he said.

"That doesn't—"

"Sir, I have diverted my energy into more positive and impactful ventures. If I think about my father or my life before now, I'll go crazy. My grandfather is crazy—he allowed himself to be affected."

"You must deal with it," Pastor insisted.

"And I will. Someday."

Pastor changed the subject. "How did you meet Christine?"

"She came to the slaughter to do a research. I didn't think I wanted her then because she seemed too young." He smiled. "But when I got to know her better, I just could not resist."

"What do you do at the slaughter?"

"I supervise mainly. I have masters and butchers. I also have a farm and some animal rearing. I run the place," Chico said.

"You own it?" Pastor said.

"I do."

"How much is your income?"

"I make money daily, and I pay my tithes," Chico said cheekily.

"You didn't answer my question."

"I make an average of—wow. I make a lot of money daily. I can't put my figures together but on a bad day, I cash in up to a quarter of a million," he said and leaned back on his seat. He hated stating his worth but this was Christine's pastor. He wondered if the man was materialistic like a lot of pastors he'd met. If he joked about getting a cow—

Pastor interrupted his thoughts. "Tell me about your education."

"I schooled myself."

"Means you didn't go to any school?"

Chico straightened. "That's what I mean."

He always tried not to be defensive about his education. The truth? In this society, people accepted people with formal education more. Anyone else is illiterate. Despite his wealth, he hadn't been able to penetrate that social circle. The question always came up which school—It had become a wall for him. Yet he could not bring himself to go back. How would he do that?

Several times he'd thought of it but it was a fear he hadn't been able to overcome. It was part of why he studied manners, carriage, dressing, and class. And he was attracted only to educated women. Now he wanted a woman with a masters' degree. It may salvage his ego, he thought warily.

"Christine has a post-graduate degree and—"

"I know," Chico said edgily.

"Does she know you 'schooled' yourself?"

"I told her." He picked at his meticulously manicured nails.

"She comes from a very class-conscious elite family. Her father was a minister of the federal government and an ambassador to a foreign country before he retired and came home to focus on his business. Before he got sick. She is not in your class, at all," Pastor said.

Chico looked up at him, feeling uncharacteristically small. "Her father died," he said bluntly.

"Still."

"I guess she should be allowed to decide if she wants a relationship with a bloody butcher after all. I have no family class. My father was a bloody butcher and his father before him. And his father before him for that matter." Chico shrugged. He was trying his best not to get upset.

The pastor netted his fingers and placed them on his lips. "What do you want with her exactly?"

"A relationship."

"What does that mean?"

"I don't know the answer to that question. You don't know what a relationship means?" Chico breathed in. He had to give it to this man. He knew all the right annoying questions to ask. But then how many men would have come to him for this same reason.

"You want to date her, marry her or just mess around with her?" Pastor said stiffly.

"I want to get to know her better. I want her to know me better as well. Marriage, yeah. That should be the ultimate for us."

"Does she know how you feel?"

"I wanted to tell you first." Chico crossed and uncrossed his legs. It was a high score with the pastor. His face softened into what almost became a smile.

"Tell me about your church," Pastor said. "Does your pastor know you?"

"My church is the Evangelical Missile. My pastor would not know me personally. He knows I'm a butcher though but he wouldn't know where I work."

"I know your pastor very well. If I ask you to bring a letter from him, can you?"

Chico narrowed his eyes, and shrugged.

"How long have you been there?"

"All my Christian life."

Pastor frowned. "That's incredible. And your pastor does not know who you are?"

"I prefer it that way. I don't have a social church life. I don't want one."

"How did you come to be the owner of the abattoir?"

"My mother's father owned it with a few other butchers. It was a very small and unsuccessful venture. When my mother died, her father went lunatic. The other butchers managed the place till it practically folded up. I took it over when no one was interested. Most of the days I killed the cows alone. Sometimes ten in a day."

Pastor looked at him as though he was the lunatic.

"You don't expect I believe all this?"

"You don't believe it?" Chico smiled. "My grandfather thought I was mad when I decided to take up the ranch for goodness' sake, I was just a youth. I thought he was mad to go and live in the deep alone. But I took advice from him whenever he was in the mood to talk. He told me to buy the abattoir from the other owners. There was just bush everywhere so I took all of it and started expanding and getting authorisation as I went along," Chico explained. "But you really don't need to believe me anyway. It has nothing to do with what I came for."

Pastor leaned forward and glared at him. "Make me believe you."

"You don't think I can take care of Christine, do you?" Chico arched his eyebrow. He was irritated but tried to conceal it. "You don't think I make a quarter of a million a day?"

"Convince me."

"I find that a very difficult thing to do," he said, returning the pastor's glare this time around.

CHAPTER TWENTY-SEVEN

C HURCH WAS ALMOST CLOSED when they arrived. Chico stood at the entrance like an usher on duty. His expression was grim and for a moment Christine wondered why he looked angry. But when they got into his truck and he gazed at her, his countenance softened.

"You were crying when we talked. Why?"

"How did you know?"

He snickered. "You sniffed. And your voice was husky."

She had to explain the real reason she was sad and it was only then he consoled her.

"My father was mean too," he said. "I watched him brutally abuse us and had to leave home so I would not kill him." He shook his head. "Live above it. Don't let it hurt you."

Then he took her out in the night and treated her to a beautiful dinner in a continental restaurant. There were no sexual innuendos, he was in complete control and a perfect gentleman. Chico treated her like a close friend, laughing freely and sharing personal jokes. She couldn't bring herself to fault him.

Their relationship followed the pattern. Neither discussed his visit to her pastor. She knew about it because her pastor warned her off him but since he didn't bring the meeting up, she decided to be quiet on it as well, and simply learn to know him better.

A month later, he invited her to his church for Ejiro and Omasan's baby daughter's "coming to church" service. He wasn't a steward in his church and didn't have to be there as early as she was used to.

She took her time preparing and settled for a simple but chic rose-beaded georgette dress. Since going out for dates again, she had become a little more careful with her dressing. She assessed herself in the mirror, and liked her appearance. She flat-tonged her long curly hair and allowed the long wisps fall to her shoulder. She was re-examining herself when she heard his truck drive in. She peeped through the window and saw him pull up at the side of the mansion.

He always kept to time which she loved about him. Ever since her car got stolen, she hadn't been able to get the insurance company to do much for her. She regretted her foolish decision not to do a comprehensive insurance. The tracking company recovered her engine but that was all. She couldn't argue because she hadn't reported the car missing till she got back from her incarceration. The car had been dismantled and sold in parts.

But Chico drove her anywhere she wished. She only had to ask.

⟫⟫ ⟪⟪

Chico got out of his truck and walked to the front of the house as he usually did. He was a bit excited about this date. For the full month, he hadn't yet reached a conclusion and definition of his relationship with Christine. On his part, he knew what he wanted but for her, he wasn't sure she knew what she wanted with him. She wasn't the "play hard to get" type, but she was so into herself he found it hard to penetrate that shell, get her to be free to pursue the relationship with him. She was holding back. He hadn't gotten to her core yet though she agreed to his dates and seemed to enjoy his company.

The door was opened by Mammy. She greeted him pleasantly and ushered him into the lobby.

"She's still in her rooms. Would you want me to tell her you're here or you'd meet her there?" she asked.

Chico smiled and pondered. "I'll wait for her. You need not worry yourself, Mammy." He patted her back fondly. "She would have seen my truck by now. I make sure I park under her window."

Mammy laughed. She had so much enjoyed his courting of Christine. Her pantry had not lacked a variety of meats since he started visiting.

"And thank you so much for the snails you sent last time. I've never seen them so big." Mammy said cheerfully.

"I rear them myself. I could plant a farm for you if you wish," he offered. "There's plenty of land here for it."

"Saf would never agree," she whispered. Mammy excused herself and left him.

The lobby was a beautiful formal space with rich leather upholstery. He stood and admired the oil painting of an island on the wall. It was one of those artworks you admire over and over again, a classic.

Someone walked in and he turned, expecting to see Christine. It wasn't. He stood stock-still unable to move, or greet. His reflexes failed him. He had never seen anything so beautiful in his life. She wore a white sultry, silk gown that stopped just above her knees. Her colour was almost translucent cream, her long black hair must reach her waist line if he wasn't misjudging. Her eyes were dark, her mouth full, lips deep pink. She looked like a goddess if ever he had seen one. She was tall, and slender, and buxom, and hippy—everything just flowed in the right proportion. She wore high heels that drew attention to her long, beautiful legs. Chico was reckless in his peruse. She smiled tentatively and entered the room fully.

"You must be Christine's butcher," she said in a low, breathless voice.

Chico took in a deep breath.

Christine walked in. She was smiling but paled at the sight before her. He couldn't even make himself steal her a glance. She stopped short, the smile on her face frozen. Chico had no eyes for anyone but the beauty goddess in the room. He stood glued to one spot, stupefied. Christine looked from him to her and back to him, and cleared her throat noisily.

"Oh Christine." Janella turned to look at her and smiled. "I was just meeting your—friend,"

"I'll wait outside," Christine said to Chico, who finally gave her his attention.

"Hi," he said as though he had an egg in his throat. He turned back to Janella. "You must be Janella?"

"Yes. And you are?"

Christine moved toward the front door resolutely. This was the big moment for her, and she didn't want to be shamed in front of Chico.

"Chico," he said and followed Christine. "We'll meet again," he nodded before his exit.

Christine felt like exploding. He had blatantly admired her sister. Till they got into the truck, he didn't even comment on her looks. Not that he usually did anyway but to be so enchanted by another woman meant he had the ability. She got to her door before him and opened it for herself. He normally got the door for her but she didn't want anything to spoil her Sunday morning and if he forgot to open the door and she'd have to tell him, she would be too upset about it.

He turned to his side of the truck and got in. "Wow. Now I see what you mean," he said breathlessly before starting the ignition. She didn't say a word.

"Do you still think Pebble is the prettiest?" she snapped after a stiff period of silence.

Hs voice hardened. "What's gotten you so angry?"

"I asked you a question. Can't you answer it?"

They pulled up into the church premises.

"Don't upset me. Her name is Precious." He got down and turned to open her door but she pushed it open, hitting him in the process. He stepped aside for her to pass.

"Her father named her Pebble!" She stomped by. He followed her.

The programme was elaborate. Christine enjoyed herself thoroughly despite her upset over Chico's behaviour. She did all her possible best to ignore him and avoided saying anything to him.

The church was not as flashy as hers. The pastor and his wife were modestly dressed, and sat on the first row with the rest of the congregation. Christine understood Chico's irritation with her church and style of worship. On the other hand, his holier-than-thou church, much as she liked them, didn't look too accommodating.

"There's a party at the ranch. Would you like to come?" he asked as the service closed.

She swallowed. She wasn't used to being angry for so long. She wanted them to talk about it but couldn't bring herself to tell him she was offended by his actions earlier in the house. In her characteristic way, she swallowed her anger and her feelings and nodded.

It was her first time in the village too. She was quite impressed by it and Omasan was very happy to see her. Chico didn't say a word to her and she tried her best to ignore him as well. At least he hadn't told her in front of Janella how he felt about her. In that, he had spared her the dreaded embarrassment and defeat.

The party was a huge one, beating Christine's imagination. The village square was prepared for the party with canopies, tables and chairs. There was lots of food and drink. Chico was treated like a king when he walked into the party with her. Several people walked over to greet him—and her.

At the end of the party, he drove over to his house and without inviting her in, got out and went in. When he showed up fifteen minutes later, he had changed from the grey linen kaftan he wore to church into casual clothes, jeans, t-shirt and brown boots. It seemed he'd also taken his bath.

She sat fuming beside him as he got back in. He asked a couple of questions and when she refused to speak, he followed suit. They drove back to her house in stilted silence. At the villa, he parked and she got out by herself again.

When he got out of the truck, she turned on him. "You're not welcome in my house unless you're coming to see someone else."

"What's wrong with you, Christine? Since morning."

"Nothing is wrong with me."

He moved toward the front door. She blocked his advance. "I mean what I said."

"Who else do I know to visit in your house?"

"You just met Janella this morning. You've met the others—"

"You brought me here. Now let's go in and stop this show."

"You're not welcome."

"Since when?" He faced her for the first time. His jaw twitched in controlled temper. "Because I was shocked by your sister's beauty? Am I not permitted to acknowledge her?"

"No, you're not." she yelled. "Listen, you have every right to do as you please but not at my expense."

"Just wait a second, Christine. Just so you know, I don't find this funny. You've been a grouch all day depriving me of your company—"

"Who caused it? Who started it?"

"What did I start? I met your sister—"

"And you think she's beautiful. Don't you think she's beautiful?"

"She's very beautiful, I am not blind."

"More beautiful than I am?" she asked with a voice close to tears.

"We both know that but—"

"Just go away, okay? She's all yours if you want." Christine screamed and stomped into the house.

Christine ran through the house, tears blurring her eyes. She just wanted to go to her room and cry. He hadn't said he was in love with Janella yet but wasn't that how they usually start? The first two years with Jon had been the best time of her life. On hindsight, Jon had only been interested in her family's wealth.

After her father cut her out of his will, Jon started taking an interest in Janella. She had thought nothing of it at first. She foolishly thought her fiancé was just being nice until he started spending the night with her sister, and purposely got caught. The relationship later soured and Janella called it off. Jon wanted a part of their father's dynasty but lost out in the end. Then Ayo. Now Chico.

She couldn't believe he would even admit it to her face. In her room, she stood at the window and stared out at where she'd left him. He liked to park in her area of view where she would see him clearly.

He remained at the same spot, staring at his shoes, probably thinking whether to follow her in or not. Or go in search of Janella, she thought wearily. She let out her breath when he got back into his truck and did a hair-spin turn, raising dust and gravel.

A wave of sadness overwhelmed her. She didn't like to quarrel with him. The day would have been so much more fun if they'd not had this between them.

She was tempted to call him, and ask him back. Chico would return. He never played ego games with her, and it was one of his traits she admired. She slid to the floor, an empty hollow in her chest. The serenity around her was interrupted by a loud bang. Christine startled.

The noise came from down the hall like the sound of crashing glass. A mind-curling scream followed. She ran to Janella's door sure the sound was from within, and jerked it open. What she saw wrenched a shrill cry from her lungs.

Ayo was throwing a horrid tantrum. Janella was a picture freak—perhaps one of the bales of being so beautiful but half of her framed pictures were in shatters across the room. Janella cowered at one corner, screaming obscenities. Christine rushed to her to see if she was fine. She was, though her face was bruised. She ran to Ayo and tried to hold him.

"Stop this. Ayo please," she cried.

"You tell your rotten sister to stop," Ayo growled and flung her away from him. She landed on her side and endured sharp pain on impact. Janella stood from the corner and faced him.

"You bastard. You'll regret this. See what you did to my face." Janella shouted. Half of her face was swollen and she had black rims under her eyes.

Christine, half-sobbing begged her sister to be quiet. "You know what, you haven't seen anything, boy. I'll so deal with you, what makes you a man will wither in your very sight." Janella screamed.

Panting from the other side of the room, Ayo looked at her with fire in his eyes. "What did you say?" he soughed. "You'll what?" He started toward her. Christine stood in between them.

"She didn't say anything, Ayo. Please." He pushed her away. She spun backward and fell on her bottom. A soft cry escaped from her lips.

Ayo faced Janella, panting. "You'll what?"

"If you ever raise your hand to me again, I promise you, I'll sleep with every officer in your mess—" He cut her off with a slap that landed her flat on her back.

Christine scrambled to her feet and confused, ran back to her room. She had dropped her bag on the floor inside by the door when she came in. She found her phone and dialled the first number on her mind, and screamed for help. Chico.

Then she went to find Mammy. Mum and Precious would be upstairs but she'd rather not involve them. Mammy's room was locked. Probably she wasn't back from her church. It wasn't late just about six in the evening. She rushed to the gate house and called on the two security men, chatting.

She was running back to the main house when Chico drove into the compound like a mad man.

He jumped out of the truck, slamming the door shut. "Where are they?" he barked.

She was almost hysterical. "Upstairs in her room."

Ayo was found locked in a battle with Janella. The more he pummelled her, the more she clung to him, though her grip was now weak from the battering. Ayo hit her everywhere as though he fought with a man; her stomach, her face, her shoulders.

Chico flung the door open, grabbed Ayo by his collar and belt and threw him out the door and on the opposite wall of the corridor. Ayo hit his head hard and slid to the floor. Chico turned to Christine and hugged her tight. She was too shocked to react. Ayo was a six-footer at least two inches taller than Chico. And Chico was lankier, but he had lifted the officer as though he was just a kid.

"Did he hurt you?" he asked gently. She nodded and sobbed into his shoulder. "Where?" he inspected her face. The two security men arrived and gasped at the chaos.

"My back. Hurts."

"You need a pain-reliever. Do you have in your room?" he asked.

Janella moaned and Christine pulled back a little. "She needs a doctor."

"You need to rest your back. Where's everyone in the house?" He ushered her to her rooms. Ayo remained unmoving on the corridor and Christine shuddered.

"I'll call our family doctor to come." She made the call on her cell phone.

Chico opened her door and led her to her bedroom. He made her lie down and removed her shoes. "I think Ayo has passed out completely," she murmured.

"Don't worry about him."

Her face tightened. "I hope he will be alright."

She still could remember the man Chico slapped at the slaughter. Though he'd said the man didn't die, she hadn't met him yet and wasn't sure he had survived the slap. Now Ayo. How could he have thrown a man as huge as Ayo so easily as though he was just a child?

"He doesn't deserve to be," he said. "Touch your hurt point." He rolled her to her side. She turned to look at him, ignoring his instructions.

"He has to be alright, Chico. He's a naval officer and—"

"I'm more concerned about your sister—and you should be too. A woman doesn't take the kind of hit he was subjecting her to—did you see her face?"

His comment upset her. "The face you wanted to die for this morning," she snapped.

He pursed his lips. "It gives you some satisfaction the face is battered?"

"How can you say that?" She sat up sharply and winced. He tried to make her rest but she hit his hands off. "You think I hate my sister?"

"I think you are consumed by your fears. She intimidates you so badly by her presence you can't even think straight."

"How dare you—?"

There was noise in the corridor and resisting him, she limped out of her apartment. He followed her. To her relief, Ayo sat propped up against the wall, holding his head. As Chico had predicted, Janella seemed in a bad condition. The doctor kept her flattened out on her rug, insisting she should not move. He called for an ambulance and told them she had to be taken to the casualty ward.

Saffron came in with her husband in tow and started making a fuss about Janella's condition.

"My God." Saffron exclaimed, pushing Hassan aside. "Christine, where did you get such an animal from? I think brutish men generally gravitate toward you?" Then turned angrily on Ayo. "The FOC must hear about this. Wife-battery is a criminal offence in the military. I'll make the report myself. You'd be lucky if you're not out of your career by the time I'm done with you." She carried on.

The medical assistants came in and lifted Janella off on a gurney. Ayo pushed himself to his feet and staggered after them.

Mammy, who had come back from her outing and seen the commotion, walked through Janella's rooms, gasping. "I'll call in the maids to come and clean this mess."

Christine hugged the elder woman. "I'm so sorry, Mammy. Thank God we came in on time."

Saffron waltzed round the rooms and made dirty sounds and remarks. Chico stood in the corridor outside the apartment, leaning against the wall with his arms folded across his chest, fuming at Christine's comments. Hassan lit a cigarette and smoked recklessly, not making a single comment.

From his blind sight, Chico saw Mum and straightened up. Wendy Bello walked toward the front door of Janella's flat but Saffron stopped her.

"No, Mum," she cried. "Just go back upstairs. You can't see this. You can't see this," she said hysterically.

"Is Janella alright?" Mum asked trembling.

"She's fine, Mum. Go on up, I'll come see you," Christine said.

"Is my baby okay?" Mum covered her mouth with trembling fingers. Pebble walked up behind her and looked at everyone.

"Is Janella going to have a party again? She makes such noise," Pebble said.

"Mum, take Precious up. We'll come see you," Chico said and turned her round. She looked at him inquiringly and he nodded. Mum did not argue. She walked back the way she came with her last daughter. Chico turned to Christine. "We should make sure she's alright."

"And who are you?" Saffron came out of the lobby where she'd been giving orders to no one in particular. "Giving instructions—oh oh, are you not the butcher? What are you doing here?" She stood right in front of Chico.

Christine's mouth dropped open. "Saffron."

"If you want to flaunt this person around why don't you keep it within your four walls and not roaming around my house," Saffron snapped.

Chico went back to Christine's flat.

"That is not a fair thing to say," Christine said and marched after Chico.

Now she had to apologise to him when she really didn't feel like talking to him.

He was just inside the door when she walked in. She wanted to speak but he dragged her to his chest and spun her around against the wall. His body pinned hers back in a captivating mode.

"Sshhh," he said, putting a finger to her lips. "Just listen very carefully to me. I'm leaving now, and when I do, I want you to go and sit with Mum and explain things to her in detail. I'm sure Janella would be fine, just assure her of that." He paused and then stared into her eyes.

"I haven't touched you all this while, not because I didn't feel like, and definitely not because I thought I would not be able to control myself, or stop before we fall into sin—no. But because I saw it made you feel uncomfortable. I respected your views—" She wanted to talk but he returned his index finger to seal her lips.

"I respect you and your views and I'll do what pleases you. Now, about your sister, Janella. She is stunning and very very beautiful. More beautiful than you are. But I don't want her. She doesn't move me. And I don't want you to think about it anymore. Let this be the end of that. I don't want us to talk about it anymore," he said stiffly. "Do you understand me?"

She opened her mouth to speak but he bent his head and took her lips with his. It was a demanding kiss that drew a response from her instantly.

His ten fingers went into her hair holding her head in place. She clung to him at the waist, giving him full access to her body.

"Don't talk about it again," he moaned into her hair. "It's you I want. You."

CHAPTER
TWENTY-EIGHT

PASTOR REUBENS HAD JUST finished the morning prayer session when Christine walked into his office. His face lit up and she curtsied pleasantly. He ushered her to a seat and called out to his secretary to keep visitors away unless it was an emergency.

"Ha, Christine. How are you?"

"I'm very fine, pastor. I got your message."

"Yes, I wanted to see you before my six-week trip to the United States but it was just too tight."

"I understand, sir," Christine said. "It's just that you sounded like it was so urgent I was worried. I had to leave from work to come."

Pastor Reubens clasped his hands. "It was crucial. And I was worried. I needed to ask, how well do you know the man, Chico Ode?"

Christine's smile froze on her face. She hadn't expected the question. She shifted forward and cleared her throat.

"Huhm, Pastor—he is—a friend. We met and we've been—friends," she stammered.

"How well do you know him?"

Extremely well, she thought. They were together almost every night. Chico was fun to be with. He was funny, generous, respectful—

Christine shrugged. "A bit, sir. We talk. We're friends."

"Did he tell you what he does for a living?"

Christine nodded.

"And what he wants with you?"

"We're friends, sir—"

"Just friends?" he asked. Christine nodded again. "Christine, why are you not telling me the truth?"

"Sir, I'm sorry. He—he hasn't said anything. But he's making the moves."

"He even gave you a car, not so?"

She scratched her scalp. "Sir, I was going to tell you—he thought it wasn't good that I didn't have access to mobility on weekends—since I was using the official car during the week."

"Did he tell you how much he earns?"

"No, sir."

"Ha, Christine, daughter." Pastor Reubens stood and dipped his hands in his trouser pockets. "And he gave you a car—you're not worried he may have stolen the money for it."

"It's a small golf car, sir. He can afford it."

"But you don't know how much he earns!" Pastor snapped. "He is a butcher, Christine. What kind of money can he have?" Christine looked at her fingers, feeling so embarrassed. Pastor pulled up a chair beside her and sat down. "Look at me and let me be sincere with you. He came here to see me."

Christine's head jolted. Chico had not told her he came to see her pastor.

"He didn't tell you?"

"No, Pastor."

"Well, he called my number just before I flew out, and said he wanted to see me. He came and we talked. Like he has been to you, he didn't mention his intention, just that he came to see me because he was your friend—I need that word to be defined. Friend. And Christine, we talked. We really talked. I drilled him. Because I cannot risk you to just any man. And Christine," he leaned forward, "not you of all people. And not to him."

"Pastor, I respect you very much and you are like my father. I would take your advice." Christine could weep.

"I know how you feel but see this man—he's going to exploit you. He does not have an education and has refused to say which school he attended at all. He attends a church where no one knows him, his pastor does not know him. He tells me he pays his tithe—in millions yet the pastor does not know him?" Pastor Reubens walked back to his seat.

Christine exclaimed. "In millions?"

"Your friend says he earns about five hundred thousand naira a day."

"A day?" Christine gasped and laughed. "He doesn't have that kind of money."

"Oh ohho," Pastor said. "Why would he lie to me? Even his name has no meaning."

"He told me about his name."

"How are you sure the name he told you is really the real one? And look at him very arrogant, no name, no money, no background, no education. Have nothing to do with him, Christine. Whatever he is looking for with you, let him go elsewhere to find it. You don't need someone like him."

"Yes sir," Christine said with a small voice. Her stomach churned.

He settled back on his swivel chair. "Tell me what you plan to do"

"I'll go and return his car to him and stop contact with him."

"That's good."

Christine stood. "Thank you, Pastor. I really appreciate your concern." She walked dejectedly to the door.

Pastor raised his voice. "Christine."

"Yes Pastor?" Christine turned to look at him.

"All will be well, okay? God will answer you. Come here, I want to pray for you."

She trudged back to kneel before him. He prayed a short prayer and allowed her to leave.

Christine had come with her official car. She asked the driver to take her to her house and go back to the office from there. She took the car Chico had given her just the previous week, wondering how pastor had gotten to know about it, and drove straight to the abattoir. She had decided to use the car only on weekends to avoid questions in the office—just because she was shy about it.

She had never had a friend who gave her anything so expensive, one who gave her anything. Yet Chico had told her pastor he earned half a million a day. Why would he say that? Why would he go and see her pastor without telling her? She was upset with him.

At that time of the day, just after noon, the slabs were clear and clean. The one closest to Chico's office however was not. He was on it, cutting a cow in pieces. Three men stood around, assisting. All were working packing the beef, collecting, stacking. Two bodiless heads sat on the slab, waiting to be disposed of. Chico was covered in sweat and blood. Christine marched to the edge of the slab and stood rigidly. His face lit up when he saw her.

"Wow. Hello. What brings you here?" He stood, blood-stained, and beaming, Christine almost could not speak.

"I want to talk to you," she said. Chico took a step toward her. "No, you don't need to stop your work, I won't take long."

He drew his brows together. "Is everything alright?"

"Yes. I'm through with you and whatever we've been doing. I parked your car in your house," she said stiffly. "That's all."

"Ajani. Finish up," he barked and jumped off the slab.

A stocky man moved in the direction of the unfinished job. Christine began to walk away toward the exit. He followed her. "Let's go to my office," he said under his breath.

"It's not necessary. I've said all I came to say."

The butchers continued to work as though they were deaf though everyone within earshot could hear Christine.

"Well, I have a say, don't I? After all, the relationship is with me."

"What relationship? Do I have a relationship with you?" she asked. He started walking toward his office. She followed him angrily.

"Well, don't you?" he snapped, stealing a glance to be sure she was behind him.

"What sort of relationship? Is it a friendship? Are we—are you my fiancé?" she yelled. His strides were long and she had to half-run to catch up with him.

He turned eyes flashing with anger. "Are we? What are we to you? Are we lovers?" They glared at each other for a long second. He broke the stare and turned toward his bathroom.

Her words stopped him. "I won't be here by the time you come out of there."

He sighed. "Will you let me clean up and we can talk about whatever is eating at you."

"I won't be here when you step out."

"Christine."

She took a small step backward. "What are we doing together?"

"Is that the reason for all this display? This embarrassment in front of—everyone." he hissed. "You want to know what we're doing. You tell me."

"You know what? I don't need to have this nonsense talk with you. You're used to playing games. It's what you do. And I'm done with it. Forget you ever met me, and that's all. That's all." She turned back and started to march away.

"We're lovers," he called to her and she stopped. "We are lovers," he repeated slowly.

"We're not," she replied not turning to him. "Lovers define their relationship, not just mess around."

"Our relationship is defined, is it not?" he asked softly.

"No. You never asked me what I wanted—"

"What do you want?"

She swung round to look at him, eyes blazing. "What do you think? Every woman wants to be treated like a lady. To be asked for marriage."

"I see." He smirked. "You should have said that nicely, instead of flaunting and charging like a caged beast."

Her eyes widened at his words. Too annoyed to say anything, she held her head in her hands and stomped away.

⟫ ⟪

"What's wrong with you?" he called after her, following at a slower pace. She didn't respond. "Wait," he shouted.

"Marry me. Marry me then and rest," he said on top of his voice.

The butchers stopped what they were doing and turned to look at him. Christine continued to walk away, her steps so fast and unstable he feared she would fall or sprain her ankles.

He turned toward the butchers, and they all turned back to their work like robots. He flung the bathroom door open and within minutes burst out, clean. He stomped into his office and out. Got into his truck and drove crazily in the direction of his house.

⟫ ⟪

Tears blinded Christine as she walked away from him. She had never been so angry and humiliated in her life. She wanted him to follow her and beg her not shout at her or fling a proposal at her in front of the whole of Ode Abattoir. She felt ashamed at herself but more infuriated at him. Why would he call them lovers when he'd never asked her for a relationship? At the end of the day if he chose to do it, he could walk away without any bad feeling.

She got into the tricycle at the bus stop and rode to the junction where she got a taxi to her office. She wanted to cry but held herself till she got to the privacy of her office. Then let the dam break. She had to move on without Chico Ode.

But it was easier said than done. She told her secretary she didn't feel well but instead of going home, she rushed back to church.

Pastor Reubens was on his way out. She fell at his feet and wept like a baby. He helped her up and led her back to his office. He didn't say a word until her tears had subsided.

"You told him?"

She sniffed. "Yes, pastor."

"See, my daughter. This is the best thing. Chico Ode says he owns the abattoir, and makes half a million a day. His pastor does not know him. How can that be? What kind of man is he? You don't need him, Christine."

"He owns the abattoir—"

"He doesn't. He's a mere butcher. A hired hand. He lives big in a fancy house, owned by the real owner. Christine, don't be deceived. The car he gave you belonged to the owner's wife who lives abroad. I've met him through Chico's pastor. He gives a cow to the pastor every quarter and during festivities and special occasions."

Pastor Reubens raised her chin. "I know the owner."

CHAPTER TWENTY-NINE

CHICO FOUND HIMSELF MORE involved with the slabs as the festive period drew near. December had always been the busiest time of the year for his business. There were weddings, burials and many ceremonies strategically fixed for the month.

Orders by private personnel were becoming frequent as well, and he had a small slab constructed so he could work alongside the other butchers. The slab was situated close to the goat farm on the other side of his office, where he usually parked his truck. Many of the butchers could handle nothing more than one cow a day. Some took on two. Chico worked five cows on busy days from morning till night.

It was another day with several cows to be slaughtered for private orders. The local government chairman was burying his mother and Chico had an order for four cows. He'd had Ejiro prepare the cows well before dawn. As the butchers climbed their slabs, he did his. Three new butchers assisted him. Before noon, he was through over six hours non-stop work.

But that was the way he wanted it.

Since Christine left, his life had been empty. It was like there had never been a time when she wasn't a part of him. He still could not believe what had happened at the abattoir that day two weeks earlier.

In the previous month, Christine had thrown tantrums. She'd even called off their "relationship" several times. She'd questioned him. He'd told her things no one else knew about him. He reasoned her inquisition was to give her all the reasons she needed to bridge the gap between them even though he didn't see any need for it still he respected her, and her need for explanations.

She'd gone to spend time with his grandfather, miraculously succeeding in bringing the old man out, more often. He had fallen in love with her beyond reason. Why would she just snap and call everything off? Why would she ask if they had a relationship? Didn't she know they had a relationship?

He knew he had not done the right thing, talking to her that way in public, and worse still, let her leave the way she did. But he had been caught unawares. He couldn't imagine himself handle a knife talk to her. He wanted her to be calm first, but then he'd lost his patience.

But as the days passed, Christine refused to talk.

She didn't pick his calls and when he visited her at home, he was refused entry. He was in her office the following morning and after spending an hour of enduring her cold shoulder, left. She didn't want him and though unacceptable to him, her refusal to provide a reason for the break-up bothered him.

Chico entered the bathroom he'd insisted on adding to his office building. All his life, he'd seen the way butchers were treated. His father and grandfathers. They stank, and he would never live like them. In those days when he didn't have an office or a chance to clean up at his whim, he would come to the slabs with a keg of water which he hid till he was through with his work, then he'd do a quick wash oh his hands and face.

The bathroom had been designed to taste. Two stalls both with blue and white tiles on the floor and walls, had a shower in one and a bath in the other. Two toilet shanks and bidets were installed in two separate units. Chico had had the mind he may have to share his bathroom at some time he may not predict, and decided on having two components instead of one. The tap ran cold and hot water. Two dressing rooms were equipped with cupboards which contained clean towels and other toiletries.

Chico liked to use liquid soap and he had a brand. He stepped into the shower and rinsed off the dirt. When he was clean, he pressed out soap from the tube into a sponge and scrubbed. He stepped out and turned off the shower. He picked a clean towel from the rack and dried off. He strolled to one of the dressing rooms and removed a fresh pair of clothing. The work clothes had been dropped in a bin close to the entrance. The young butchers cleaned the bathroom and washed all the dirty linen daily.

Chico stepped out of the bathroom, preoccupied. He noticed just on time, lifting his head, the two ladies who stood out like sore thumbs in the abattoir. He was almost sure they had never come near here before. Or anywhere like this. They were not facing him yet. They must have been contemplating their decision.

The taller of the two wore a red dress that stopped just below mid-thigh. Her wedge heels were red as well. The dress clung temptingly to her attractive figure. Her long dark hair was left flowing in shiny curls all the way down her back to her waist. The other woman wore a green flowing gown. She was slightly shorter. Her hair was heaped on her head just as dark and curly but not as long.

He knew who they were before he got to them, but was just as surprised.

"The Bello sisters on my land?" He gave both a searing once-over. "To what do I owe this privilege?"

He knew who would speak. She didn't disappoint him. She gave him a return-look as searing as his had been. He wore a white shirt over brown corduroy trousers tucked into black knee-length rain boots.

"You should feel privileged," Saffron said.

Both women looked as beautiful as he knew them to be with light but appropriate make-up.

Janella's neckline was insanely low, revealing so much of flawless skin, the desired effect appalled Chico. Her face bore no sign of the assault it had been subjected to weeks earlier.

"I wanted to see you. To thank you," Janella said softly.

"Is there an office here to sit or something?" Saffron looked round. A fly accosted her and she swatted it with steam.

Chico followed her gaze. "No. I don't have an office for you to sit."

"Butchers don't have offices, do they?" She turned to her sister. "Well, you needed to see him, though we could have sent the driver or Mammy."

"You saved my life—"

"I did it for Christine."

Saffron rolled her eyes. "Oh, there we go."

"I want to return the favour." She took a step closer. She wasn't too close but the gesture spoken volumes. "Ayo has apologised, of course—"

Saffron frowned. "I should have had him court-martialled."

"I want to invite you to dinner, sometime."

Chico's gaze remained steady. "Thanks, but no thanks."

Janella licked her lips and downturned her shapely mouth. "It's the least I could do."

"I don't appreciate it. Thank you."

"We should be on our way back, Janella. I'm done with—this place."

Janella placed her hand on Chico's chest and Saffron snickered. "I need to be alone with you just for a while. I need to talk to you—"

"You could book a hotel or something and give him details." Saffron tented her eyes with bejewelled fingers. "This place stinks."

Janella took another step closer. "That sounds good."

Chico moved her hand away from his chest and dropped it by her side. "People see perfection. I see the soul." He walked toward the entrance of the abattoir. They followed as he knew they would.

At a Porsche car parked not far away, Chico stopped. He assumed it was their car, and he was right. The driver behind the wheels sat up and started the ignition on their approach.

"You have a perfect body, Janella. But no soul." His dirty look was as demeaning as his words. He opened the back door and held it for her. "Have a good day."

Janella hesitated. Saffron walked past her and entered the car instead.

"Let's go, Jan. I told you I had no time for trash."

⸎ ⸎

They visited Mum every day. Sometimes, they would spend half an hour sometimes more or less. But Chico never left without seeing her. He would sit with Precious and read with her. It had become such a ritual they all were accustomed to.

The first night without Chico in her life, she had not been able to visit but the following day, Mum called to find out if all was well. Precious had thrown a tantrum, asking for him. Since he started visiting, she had improved with her communicating habits. He'd proceeded to teach her how to cook, which Precious found extremely entertaining.

After the first night, she resumed the routine. Precious whined but gradually accepted the absence of her new friend. It was hard however, to discount the impact Chico had in the few months he was with them. He discussed daily with Mum something no one had done with her in years. Even Christine was surprised at the wealth of knowledge her mother possessed about different fields of learning. She had thought Wendy was a quiet, unassuming, bordering-on-retarded, wife and mother. Instead she discovered her mother could haggle intellectually about foreign policies and economies, politics, and parenting.

Precious on the other hand, despite all the challenges attached to her physical and mental condition, was a survivor. But with Chico, she was a winner. Once when Chico analysed her condition to Mum and Christine, both were stunned at the extent of his knowledge.

Wendy Bello gasped. "How do you know so much about it? You had someone in your family?"

"I studied the condition after meeting Precious," he said, stunning them even more.

He had gone ahead to bring some literature on down's syndrome, joined a foundation called Friends of Down's that helped in caring for and counselling parents and guardians, teachers and care-givers of children with the condition, and taken Precious out of the private deaf and dumb school she was in.

Once a month, Chico travelled to Ibadan, 200 kilometres away, to attend the meeting of the foundation. What improvement Precious had in those months with Chico was nothing compared to what her family had given her in her eighteen years of existence.

Christine knocked softly and opened the door without invitation. As was usual for that time of the day, Precious and Wendy were watching her favourite programme, Fuji House of Commotion. She joined in on the programme and laughed with them till it ended.

"Cooking time." Precious announced as she had done every single night the past two weeks.

Mum called to her and brought out her colouring book, another passion. "We still have many pages left. Bring your crayons."

Precious promptly capitulated. "Colouring time."

Mum set the colouring book on the dining table and when Precious was well-engrossed in what she was doing, she joined Christine at the sitting area.

"How was your day?"

"Chico!"

Both women jumped at the call of the name and looked toward the door before looking at Precious who was jumping up and down, and clapping in excitement.

Mum strolled over to her. "Where's Chico?"

"In the colouring book."

She looked at what Precious was pointing at and smiled. "He coloured that for you?"

"Chico."

Mum flipped to a page not yet coloured and smiled at Precious. "This is Pebble. Colour here."

Her face was distorted when she returned to sit with Christine. "She misses him so badly."

"I know, Mum."

"He won't come around again, I guess?"

"I don't think he would." Christine sighed and swallowed a lump. It couldn't get any tougher, she thought wearily.

"He seemed good enough. He could talk to anyone."

"He wasn't what he told me he was. He wasn't what he seemed."

"Hmm. Men are generally like that. No use." There was a strained silence. "Do you love him?"

Christine straightened ready to throw a missile of her own. "Why ever did you marry, Dad? Did you love him?"

"It was a family arrangement." Mum's voice had never sounded so strained to Christine. "Apparently, I was his type of woman, my beauty and all. My father owed his family some money." She laughed shakily. "It was converted, you know, to my bride price." She swallowed, and shook her head. "I was nineteen."

Christine sat forward and looked at her mother closely. The woman was ageless. At forty-nine, the lines on her face were faint, almost invisible. Her skin was fair and smooth, milky, silky. Much of her hair was from her mother, who was a French brunette. The hair was long, and thick, rich. All the girls had their mother's hair except Pebble. It wasn't possible to know anyway, because Dad had insisted the hair was kept low-cut. Christine always thought their mum was the prettiest woman on earth, in the family. Janella looked just like her, though.

She studied the sad lines etched around her mother's almond eyes, and thin lips. Dad always made everyone believe it was love at first sight for Wendy. He would tell them how he married her just because of her heritage, and beauty, and nothing more but how she was 'crazy' about him. Dad was of mixed race as well. His father, half-English, half-Nigerian had married his mother, who was a full African woman, making Dad a quarter-caste.

"I don't understand." Christine reached out and touched her mother's hand. The older woman gripped it and held on. "Dad said you met—in a neutral place—and you fell madly—"

"Your dad believed a lot of things that did not exist, my dear. I'm sorry."

"You don't have to be sorry."

"I am sorry for the kind of life we gave you."

The door opened and Saffron characteristically waltzed in. She took in the scene with a sweep of her eyes, and snickered. "Getting all cosy now or what?"

Pebble started, packed her colouring book and ran into the room. Saffron laughed. Christine released her mother's hands and sat back.

"You just came in?" Mum asked pleasantly.

"Yes. And it was a very busy day." She slumped into a seat. "A good day too."

Wendy smiled but they didn't reach her eyes. "Great, Saffron. Would you share it with us?"

"Yeah. That's why I came." A smug look settled on her face. "I was at Christine's butcher's place today." Christine winced. Saffron laughed again. "With Janella." She winked at Christine knowingly.

"Janella keeps looking for trouble." Mum breathed. "She's had too many men."

"She only meant to thank him for throwing that brute off the other day." Saffron stood to her feet daintily. "He didn't even ask for you—after all these weeks?" She headed for the door and then turned just before reaching it. "I nearly forgot. I was at my lawyer's as well." She opened her bag and flung an envelope at Christine. Mum gasped. Christine dodged just in time. The fat envelope hit the tiled floor.

"Your case was flung out due to a technicality." She frowned. "I was waiting for this case to be wrapped up, you know."

Her drama was repulsive. She walked slowly back to the seat she just vacated and sat down. "I now have my full right over this house, as Dad stated in his will." She divided her gaze between their stunned faces, and said, "Ayo has agreed to move in so I'm breaking the walls." She stayed her cold eyes on Christine. "I need your rooms to add to Janella's. You have two days to move up here."

She walked to the door, and out.

CHAPTER THIRTY

Pastor Reubens sat back in his fancy leather chair and assessed the man seated opposite him. The man was extremely handsome, if there was any such thing. He was a smooth talker as well. And a huge giver. Reubens got gifts during Christmas but nothing like what this man brought. A live turkey, an assortment of drinks, and a hamper. And his request was a simple one.

He'd sent for the request to be attended to promptly, and was only waiting for it to materialise. In the meanwhile, he'd asked a lot of questions. And gotten all the answers he needed.

Jon Osi had dated Christine years earlier and then broken up abruptly with her. At the time, Reubens had not approved of the relationship because Jon had not been a believer. Though Christine was convinced he would change, her pastor had refused to approve. So, when she came crying to him that he'd called it off, his advice had been straightforward. Move on. But that was more than three years ago, and Jon was back.

During the years, Jon had found God. He had several testimonies up his sleeves about his conversion, which Reubens found quite thrilling. He had spoken to his pastor about his desire to find Christine and marry her, and as a proof of his conversion and his pastor's approval, gotten a letter of recommendation from his man of God to back up his claim.

Jon Osi was an electrical engineer who worked with the state power department. His job was a good one, heading the metering unit and had good career prospects. He lived in a three-bedroom house he built by himself, and at his age, was ready to settle down. He had all going for him. Just the kind of person Reubens wanted for his faithful member. And a giver. He'd almost forgotten the thick envelope the young man had respectfully placed on his table.

Christine was on the way to Ibadan for the last-Saturday-of-the-month meeting of the Friends of Down's Foundation, when she got a call from Pastor Reubens. For a moment, she refrained from picking up. She didn't want to miss this meeting. It was the first she would be attending alone, without Chico. And it was the last for the year. For her, it represented so much. She did not want to pick her pastor's call only to find out she would miss the meeting. But when the call rang out, she felt a pang of guilt and called back.

Pastor picked after the first ring. "Hello, Christine. Where are you?"

"Hello, pastor." She stifled a curse. "I'm on the road, sir—on my way out of town." It wasn't entirely false. She had picked the taxi from her house to the car park where she would board a cab to Ibadan.

"Are you in a taxi or something? Have you gone far? Because I need you here in my office."

"Hope all is well, sir."

"It would be, when you arrive."

She was conflicted. "I'm going to Ibadan—for the down's syndrome support group meeting."

"I can't wait till you return. Where is your exact location?"

"I can turn back, sir." She couldn't tell him her taxi just passed the front of the church.

"You do that, dear. I'm waiting for you."

She would be in his office in five minutes if she stopped, so she followed the taxi all the way to the car park, and then got another taxi back. She felt foolish, and sad that she would be late for the meeting in Ibadan.

She was ushered into Pastor Reubens office the moment she arrived.

She met with a huge surprise and stopped short right inside the office. Jon stood, but pastor merely ushered her to a seat. Christine walked slowly to the seat, and sat on the edge.

"Good morning, pastor," she said quietly, refusing to acknowledge the other man.

"Good morning, Christine," Jon said softly.

"Christine, thanks for coming." Reubens beamed. "You see how important it was for you to come now."

Christine did not see it but she nodded all the same.

"Jon wanted to see you, and with my approval too."

"Yes, pastor."

"Jon, tell her what you told me." Reubens waved at the younger man. He opened his big bible and leaned back in his seat, reading.

Jon cleared his throat, and reached out for her hand. She snatched it away even before contact was made. He sat forward and folded his hands on the table.

"You remember the first day I saw you at Ode mall. We were both working. You," he faltered, cleared his throat and sighed. "You came to inspect the waste managers with your boss, I came to check power." He smiled at her.

She flinched and looked away. He always knew how to catch her attention.

He continued. "I can never forget that day. You introduced yourself thinking I was the waste manager. Then you smiled." He reached for her hand again. She dropped them at her side, keeping them out of his reach. "You smiled, and that was when I knew I had to have you, Christine." He lowered his gaze. "I had to have you."

Christine cleared her throat and sat up. "Please get to your point."

"I was lost in your beautiful eyes. Your smile. Everything about you got me. Before I had the chance to back off, you had me." He leaned toward her and lowered his voice to that pitch she always responded to. "And it was mutual. We were taken by each other, Christine."

She jerked to her feet, vibrating with rage. "Pastor, I am sorry. I have to leave."

Pastor Reubens arched an eyebrow. "Christine, sit down."

She did not hesitate, but dropped back into her seat.

"What is the matter?" Reubens asked.

They chorused. "Nothing, pastor."

Reubens grinned. "A true sign common to lovers." He looked at Jon who smiled, and Christine, who frowned.

"I am not his lover, pastor, I can never be. Again."

"I do not agree with you, Christine." Reubens narrowed his eyes. "He is a changed man. He has told me all the wrong he did to you and he wishes to make changes, turn a new leaf. And he is convinced God wants you to be together."

"Pastor—"

"Pastor—"

He looked at both and laughed. "You know what, Jon, you go on home. I'll talk to her."

"I just want her to know that I am different now. I have completely repented of all my former ways."

"Did you tell pastor you are a chronic liar?"

"I was. I'm no more, Christine, please—"

"Old things are passed away. All things have become new. The days of ignorance, even God winked at, how much more you, daughter." Reubens entwined his fingers and bunched them under his chin.

"He had sex with me as well—Has he purged himself of that ugly and insatiable urge?"

"Christine?"

She jerked to her feet much as she had done earlier, as though a spring was released under her. "And when I was cut from my father's will he decided to switch to my sister, who was more favoured in the will."

Reubens leaned back in his seat. "Are you even listening?"

"I'm sorry, pastor. But all that was long ago. I'm different now."

Reubens gesticulated. "Christine, sit down."

"No, pastor. I cannot." She marched to the door, and turned. There were tears in her eyes. "I'm sorry, pastor. I have to go." She yanked the door open and ran out.

⟫⟫ ⟪⟪

Christine arrived at the hall of the Kakanfo Inn in Ibadan, breathless. She had missed the first and second cabs at the park and had had to endure the slow-filling of the bus loading to Ibadan. By the time she arrived, the meeting had been on for over an hour.

She found a seat at the back and sat beside a young mother who carried a baby in her arms. Christine subtly noticed the child had down's syndrome. The mother looked wearied. Christine offered a kind smile and looked at the baby's face. A boy. He slept peacefully.

"Can I hold him?" she whispered. The mother looked grateful but declined. "My sister is eighteen. We have lived with down's for eighteen years," Christine said softly. "How old is he?"

"Would be six months in a few days."

"He's beautiful."

Christine settled in after this. There were about a hundred people in the large hall. It was more than she had ever witnessed. The campaign had been on for months and many parents were responding.

"Let's make welcome our guests, Tobe and Yemi," the moderator said, clapping excitedly.

She was a gaunt-looking woman who had lost her daughter to a heart-disease complication a few years earlier. The girl had down's syndrome, and the woman had grieved so terribly until she met another woman who was in a similar situation. Together they had found FODS (Friends of Down's Syndrome).

When Christine and Chico joined the group newly, they had been introduced to the leaders and asked to tell their story. The first hour which Christine missed was usually dedicated to introducing new people, which would be done at the end of the meeting as well. Then testimonies were taken of challenges overcome and miracle stories. There would be a special talk followed by personal comments, and questions. At the end of roughly two hours, refreshments would be served and people would interact, and the meeting closed.

Two children with down's syndrome climbed the stage and everyone began to clap for them. Christine discarded her thoughts and paid attention. They would be in their late teens or early twenties, though with their condition, it was hard to tell.

They faced the audience and curtseyed. Classic music began to play and they held each other and performed a near-perfect tango. When the music came to an end, not a single person remained on their seat. Christine, through her tears, noticed tears in the eyes of the mother beside her.

The moderator climbed the stage, clapping and weeping. She hugged the two, who were breathing very hard. The applause continued on and on and on, till the dancers were ushered out of the stage.

When everyone was settled, and tears wiped, the moderator thanked the dancers. "I'm glad to announce to you that with this performance, Tobe and Yemi have launched their dance career." A loud applause went up. "We are privileged they honoured our invitation today. If you would want them to attend your occasion, please contact me.

"For the next five minutes, I'll like to invite Professor Kabiri of the University College Hospital, to give a brief lecture on 'Your chances of having a child with down's syndrome.' Professor Kabiri is a consultant gynaecologist who has done extensive research on pregnancy and child-bearing, with over forty years of experience in the medical profession. He is also the acting chief medical director of the university college hospital. Please rise, as we make welcome the professor Kabiri."

Professor Kabiri couldn't have been any other thing but a professor. He wore spectacles low on his crooked nose, and looked down on every-one through it. But he smiled a great deal, which helped to soften his hard and unattractive features.

The professor thanked the foundation profusely, and went on to wel-come everyone, by which time, his five minutes was up.

"I am going to be brief," he said in the seventh minute. "To under-stand what T21 condition is like, you have to understand what causes the condition. Trisomy-21, T21, or what you call down's syndrome is caused when an extra chromosome develops in the system of the baby. Chromosomes are responsible for everything in the make-up of human beings. They are thread-like structures within each cell, and are made up of genes. Genes as you may know, determine your hair colour, sex, and every other thing about you.

"Most people have 23 pairs of chromosomes, that is, 46. A baby with T21, has 23 and a half pairs which sums up to 47. The extra one is the reason for the challenges attached to this condition.

"Why me? Many mothers have asked. Why us? We had a healthy son, a healthy daughter before this one, why? May I rest your mind that it is nothing you did? Though studies have shown women who are thirty-five years or above are more likely to have babies with the down's syndrome. No health issues have been established in the parents of the baby as cause."

The lady beside Christine leaned toward her. "He's my first. I am twenty-five."

Christine stared, not knowing what to say. Mum was about thirty when she had Pebble.

"Indeed, after the age of thirty-five years, a woman's chances do increase. But let's look at the figures. It is interesting." Without looking at his notes, he continued. "Research shows that at age twenty, you have .08% chance. Age thirty: .15% thirty-five: .36% forty: 1%.

"We also discovered 80% of babies born with T21, are born to mothers thirty-five years or under, though we have less women aged thirty-five and above having so many babies. And this show the older aged women may not have much to fear."

"My time is far gone. Thank you for having me." The professor walked off the stage, waving the microphone left and right.

The moderator climbed up and collected it from him, joining the audience to applaud. "Thank you, prof. That is very educating. We have a few questions." She looked round and saw several hands go up. She picked a hand at random. A middle-aged woman stood.

"Please introduce yourself and your relationship with FODS," the moderator said.

"My name is Bola Abba. I am forty-one years old and I have a daughter who is three years old. My fear is that it is believed these children die young—Is it true?"

"Professor Kabiri, please?"

The professor stood and without waiting to be given a microphone, began to speak in a voice surprisingly strong for a man who probably was in his late sixties or early seventies.

"It is not true. Care. Care is the answer." The usher with the mic gestured to give him but he ignored him and continued to speak without. "Thanks to medical technology, the UCH now has a fully equipped facility built to cater to all the complications associated with Trisomy-21

Come to the clinic on Wednesday. We attend to children with special needs and educate parents on how to care for them." He took the mic from the persistent usher. "Your child can live up to fifty years. He will bury you."

An applause went up.

Another hand was signalled to and another middle-aged woman stood. "My name is Mary Jonas. I am fifty-two years old and my daughter is twenty. She can do nothing. She hardly falls sick and we give all the medical attention necessary but—" Her voice became husky and she paused to swallow tears. "I was really touched by those young, beautiful dancers today." She paused again, and this time someone handed her a handkerchief. When she could speak, her voice came out strong. "My daughter can do nothing. She hardly speaks and is not interested in any activity—"

Professor Kabiri stood and shouted. "What kind of education do you give her?"

"We have spent fortunes on her education from one private tutor to another one special school to another. She behaves like a two-year-old instead of the twenty that she is—"

"Take her off all the special needs schools. Put her in a normal school, let her mix."

The woman was aghast. "What about the stigma?"

"What stigma, madam?" It was the sober voice of the moderator. "Yours or your child's?"

Mary Jonas began to visibly tremble. "Twenty years of shame."

"Please, keep quiet, please—" the moderator said as the hall went up in heated murmurings.

"Can I blame her?" the lady beside Christine said. "I can't even attend family occasions with my boy."

Christine made to reply but her words hung in the air when Chico stood up rows ahead. He was seated right in front, where they'd both sat the last two times they attended together. He looked pretty much the same in blue jeans and multi-coloured shirt. She couldn't see his feet but guessed he would be wearing his cowboy boots.

He didn't pass through the aisle close to her so he probably didn't see her. He must think she didn't come. Must be disappointed in her. She felt a strong urge to follow him. His strides were longer than usual, like he was in a hurry, his face set, though it usually was.

"Excuse me, please." Christine stood abruptly, surprising the baby's mother, who was still talking about the stigma.

Chico's truck had just swerved dangerously to join the traffic when she reached the parking lot. She fought tears.

CHAPTER THIRTY-ONE

Basi Lejoka looked ten years younger than his forty-three years. When he moved to the Ode ranch, and bought a piece of land, many had been intrigued by him. He had come with money, lots of it. Rumours had run wild he was into blood money. Very few knew him from before. Some said he had been a soldier in his youth and had gone to war. Some claimed they knew his father, who had been a butcher in Ode. No one was sure of what information they had.

Why the ranch? This question had run through the minds of everyone. Surely such a rich man would not just decide to come live up the abattoir with a bunch of uncouth butchers. Within weeks of his first entry into the ranch village, he had moved into his house, a magnificent duplex which stood out like a sore thumb.

For years, the people living on this side of the ranch were just roughnecks, settlers and outcasts from the main Ode Abattoir. Many of them scavenged on the other side of the village. Chico Ode was king of the other side. Some doubted he even knew this side existed, though many believed he only chose to ignore them till he was ready to take possession. It was a possession the villagers not only yearned for they'd tried to lobby for it. Chico took well-care for his side.

When Basi moved in, the villagers thought their messiah had come. They would no longer need to trek for kilometres to get to Ode Abattoir. Probably he would build a school for them like Chico had done. Right now their children paid school fees and they had to register with money to make use of the health centre on the abattoir village. Stubbornly, they'd refused to be called anything else apart from Ode ranch village.

But Basi Lejoka made it clear he was also a survivor. Though he lived in the biggest and the best house, he would disappear for weeks and whenever he showed up, he had nothing to display. Soon the villagers concluded he was just a forerunner of the messiah they expected. He didn't have a wife, and showed no interest in the local women neither did he ever bring any woman to the duplex. When he interacted with the local men, he did not taste wine or the local ogogoro which almost all the men indulged in.

Soon, Basi Lejoka was a riddle. They would form an adage and reflect it in the light of Basi's reappearing and appearing acts. One thing though, Basi Lejoka had charisma, and he endeared himself to the villagers. He would bring bush meat to the village square and while he sipped water, share the meat with the men. When coming into the village with his big car, he would pick villagers from the way and allow them a feel of his air-conditioned comfort. He never said much about himself. He never gave the prospect a chance.

Basi pulled his 2011 BMW M3 into the garage of the duplex and left the motor running while he fiddled with his blackberry phone. Several pings were answered before he switched off the ignition and got out. He stretched before opening the back door to bring out his rucksack from the back seat. Locking the car with the remote, he walked out to the front of the house and looked round. All well. He strolled back into the garage and shut it with the electronic lock. The garage was thrown into darkness.

He found his way to the door and let himself into the house using his card key. The house was just as he left it. A short corridor from the garage door led to the rest of the house. To the left was the large sitting room, the bar, lobby, and the first guest room. Basi turned right. The dining room, kitchen and store rooms were situated behind the staircase.

He took the stairs two at a time and headed for the master bedroom. Up the stairs, there were five bedrooms, all en-suite, a library, and a living room. The master bedroom was designed for a king.

Basi threw his rucksack on the dressing table and strolled into the bathroom. He had a cold-water shower and dried off. Inside the walk-in wardrobe, he picked a pair of slacks and trainers, and a t-shirt. In front of the full-length mirror, he assessed himself, rubbed hair cream on his clean-shaven scalp and picked a pimple on his nose. He opened the rucksack and took out his laptop, dropping it on the bed. He removed his blackberry and wallet from the top of the bed where he'd dropped it, looked round the room one more time and headed out.

Downstairs, he walked to the kitchen and got a can of coke from the refrigerator. He opened it absently and took a long drink. Looking out in the yard, at nothing in particular, he realised his dog house was ajar. Strange. He had employed one of the village boys to keep the Alsatian for him. Whenever he came, he left enough money to feed the dog he saw more as a pet than a watchdog. His instructions were very strict about the dog. He should be let out only in the night. It wasn't even six o'clock yet.

He opened the back door and walked out to the dog house. His dog was feeding on a large piece of raw meat, its eyes wild. Basi hissed elaborately and locked the door. Maybe the boy was around. How careless he could be. He strode back into the kitchen, with plans to relieve the boy of the duty. What if he wasn't here? Is this how the boy treated the dog in his absence?

Basi finished his coke and threw the can in the trash, putting it right inside from an impressive distance. He stepped through the threshold and stopped short. A mad man was opening his refrigerator with a remarkably clean hand.

The man's hair was tangled and thick, dropping in dirty dreads all the way to his back. His clothing was just a long-tattered robe. He was barefooted.

Basi tip-toed in but the man turned just in time. "Too careless, Basi. I say it all the time. You're too sloppy."

He was old, though the wrinkles on his face were gracious, and his eyes were bright with knowing. His tangled beard had a lot of greys in it, grey hairs that were lost in the thick tangle on his head. His lips were lost in the bushy moustache, his ears almost all covered with sprouting hair. He was by all means a hairy man.

"What are you doing here? Giving my dog trash and drinking from my fridge."

The mad man snickered. "Your dog, your fridge. Your house, Basi."

"That's life. All mine." Basi brushed past him and headed for the sitting room, knowing he would follow him. "Your choice too." He called out. "You wanted this. Have you seen my new car? You said you love white cars so I bought a white." Basi laughed. He entered his exotic oriental sitting room and flopped into the settee.

The mad man came in with a glass of clean water.

Basi sat straight. "You didn't get that from my fridge. I don't have water—"

"I was just looking at what you had in the fridge." He looked round the room. "How come I never entered this room before?"

"You never entered this house before."

The mad man winked, discounting Basi's statement with a mere shrug.

Basi looked at him blankly. "What do you want? Why did you come here?"

"I need a shave."

He was so angry, he was shaking. And he wondered why it bothered him so much. He was no longer a part of her family. He had questioned his justification for leaving the ranch on a Saturday morning at the end of the year to attend a support group that had absolutely nothing to do with him. There was no justification. At some point, he would need to purge himself of her, of her family, of her sister. Her sisters.

Chico drove into the premises of Ode Abattoir at dusk. He'd got a call which took him out of the FODS meeting and headed straight to government house to pick up additional order for the New Year's thanksgiving party.

So many personal and corporate orders had been made in the last few days no single butcher had had a day of rest. Sundays were not excluded, neither were Fridays. All hands were on deck. Chico had barely had time to barge in and out of his work suit to do any other thing. Some nights they stayed awake to meet up with morning orders.

Men were working on the slabs and he drove to his office. He was out to join them within minutes. The men worked for hours till well after dark before they retired. Chico went to his office and caught up on his paperwork. And slept off in the office.

When he woke the following morning, he had cramps but there was work to be done. The butchers mostly attended the church in the village but he went to town. But not today. He was too tired to drive. He walked to the village, worshipped with the others and went to the abattoir to make up orders. Two days to New Year. And he had never had so much work in all his years as a butcher.

The governor had plans to feed the state. And Ode was to supply fifty cows to the effect. Chico had no idea how he was going to do it. Two local government areas were allocated to him and he decided to call on the chairmen to arrange for logistics. He would send his men to butcher the cows at the desired locations so the abattoir could be free for other businesses.

Succeeding to dispatch the cows by evening time, and making up for a backlog of orders, and paperwork, Chico staggered into his house at about 8pm on Sunday night with only one thing in mind. Sleep. He would sleep till 3a.m. when his normal day started.

He noticed the BMW parked right out in front of his house as he entered the compound. He didn't recognise it. The sleek white car was a beauty to behold. He'd always had a thing for luxury cars and had dreamed of buying his wife a real beautiful machine. The small car he'd given Christine was still parked where she left it.

He dragged Christine out of his mind and parked his truck beside the BM. He noticed there were four people in the car, and the ignition was on. He walked to the driver's side without locking up, or closing his door.

Chico's eyes popped in recognition. "Basi."

Basi got out of the car. "Usmani. It's been long."

"Wow. Come in. Sorry for keeping you outside. It's been a devil of a season."

"I have—people with me." Basi bent and signalled for the others to join him, switching off the ignition.

Chico looked beyond his shoulders. The three came out from both sides of the car almost simultaneously. Chico's heart stopped. He was sure he had died and gone to heaven.

CHAPTER THIRTY-TWO

CHRISTINE SAT QUIETLY AND listened to the stiffest chastening she had ever had in her life. Pastor Reubens was livid. After the service, he had summoned her into his office and given her more than a piece of his tongue. When the storm was over, she went on her knees and cried for forgiveness. Initially he ignored her, allowing others who needed to see him, come in and out. He let her remain on her knees until his wife came into the office.

Mrs. Reubens looked at her, amazed. "Christine, Papa, what is the matter?"

Reubens looked up as though he was ignorant of her question. "Hm? Oh. It's your daughter." He waved at her. "She wants to ruin her own life and marry a liar and a thief. So be it."

Reubens wife was portrait-perfect. The only kind of woman the flashy man of God could marry. She looked almost twenty years younger than him and though no one ever got to know her real age, many suspected she was almost as young. Some were waiting for her fortieth birthday, which they were sure would close roads in Ode. She would have been a very beautiful woman but for her shocking fair-complexion and loud make-up. She had her hair, nails and eyelids fixed perpetually many didn't know what the natural looked like.

Mrs. Reubens beckoned on Christine to stand up. "Come and sit with me. Come on."

Christine stood and weeping like a child, sat beside the woman of God. Without any provocation, Reubens launched into a tirade.

"Honey, can you imagine? The ruffian came here the week she was kidnapped, and like a true hooligan without respect or regard, stomped out of my office and dragged her along. Upon all our effort to get to the root of the matter, he bribed his way out of the whole thing." He swallowed and continued promptly. "I expected your daughter would learn her lesson and steer clear, next thing, the thug comes here and tells me he wants to marry her. Marry. Instead for your daughter to find a way to lock him up for abducting her, she comes to me and starts defending him."

Mrs. Reubens gasped and stared at Christine. "Ha, Christine."

"I'm sorry, Mama."

"Did he bring wine along?"

"Wine? Mama, wine? He didn't bring good manners it is wine he would bring? Long and short, I commanded her to end the madness, and I think she did." He turned to her and snapped, "Did you?"

Christine cried. "Yes, pastor, I did."

Reubens hissed and turned to his wife. "The tout did not show up again after that. To God be glory." He picked up his bible and began to read.

His wife looked from him to Christine and back to him. "Is she begging you to go back to the gangster?"

Reubens laughed and closed the bible with a snap. "What's my own? If she wants to mess up her life, she can go ahead. But I would not," his voice rose, "let her make a mockery of me in the presence of respectable members."

"Papa, tell me what happened, please."

"Just yesterday, this man walks into my office, well-dressed, well-spoken, and respectable man. Says he came to me for a favour because he knows I can help. Brings a fat envelope, some gifts as well." Reubens waves to a seat. "I ask him to sit. He introduces himself as Jon Osi—do you remember him? I didn't till he explained."

His wife shook her head. "I can't remember him."

"He used to date Christine. Then I was against the relationship because he was not a believer. But now he is changed. He has a fantastic testimony. And guess what, he wants to marry Christine."

"Hey, that's great."

"Listen." He hissed. "I summoned your daughter to come at once. She does so reluctantly. When she sees him, she disregards my presence, lashes out at the man and walks off. Christine walked out of my office and slammed the door."

Mrs. Reubens clasped her hand over her mouth. "Ha, Christine? Abomination."

"What hurts is that she did not even give him a chance to explain. You saw the brother who testified in church this morning? The one who wore the white lace?"

"Yes, Papa."

"Can you believe that is the man who came to marry your daughter and she was busy talking rubbish?"

"Christine? He donated some money—fifty thousand naira to the building fund."

"Of course. He paid tithe yesterday before he left." Reubens shrugged. "Your daughter likes delinquents." He raised his chin. "A good-for-nothing ragamuffin. The bloody butcher appeals to your daughter. Mama." He clapped. "Can you believe the thief told her he owns Ode Abattoir? A good-for-nothing common butcher. Took her to a fancy house that does not belong to him. Gave her a car that belongs to his boss's wife. Told me he makes half a million naira a day. Common wine, he can't bring for her pastor."

Mrs. Reubens' eyes widened. "Ha, Christine, you have disappointed Papa and me."

"I'm so sorry." She sniffed. She looked at Mrs. Reubens for support but got none.

"As a woman, let me advise you, Christine. And this is what I tell all you single ladies all the time, to shine your eyes. Love is no longer blind. Without my praying about it, it is so obvious that Jon Osi is God's choice for you. Ha, please o."

"Please, Mama, I—Chico said he owned the abattoir."

"He doesn't. I told you he doesn't. One unschooled, uncouth vagabond that is so arrogant and full of himself?" Reubens looked at his wife. "I know the owner through his pastor. I told you this much." He turned back to Christine. "But you are bent on loving a fool and making a bigger fool of yourself. The impostor doesn't even use his real name. The owner of Ode Abattoir lives in Lagos with his beautiful wife and children, and invests in other businesses. His name is not Chico Ode." Reubens clicked his tongue. "Chico Ode, my foot. Common Usmani Victor, useless butcher running from his shadow and using a fake name."

His wife scowled. "Who is the owner of the abattoir? I've always been curious."

"Ode Abattoir is owned by Basi Lejoka, Lagos business man."

Tolani sat across from Christine and allowed her to cry all she wanted after she narrated her ordeal in her pastor's office. When she was through, she took a deep breath and looked straight into Tolani's eyes.

"They just waved me off like a piece of nonsense afterward."

"If pastor has a name to the owner of the abattoir, don't you think you should just leave well alone?" Tolani rationalised. "Chico hasn't come around has he? He probably thinks it's better to leave you alone and go after some other easier prey."

"There's no name they didn't call him—tout, criminal, thief, gang-ster."

"Have you ever had reason to doubt their judgement?" Christine shook her head. "Then don't you think you should take their advice?"

"And agree to marry Jon?" Christine shook her head profusely. "I'd be a nun first."

"That Jon's angle makes it very tricky, you know." Tolani shrugged. "God has power to change people, and He does every day."

"Not Jon. He can never change."

"How would you know?"

"You know Jon didn't reveal his true job to me till months after our dating. He continued to hide everything from me for so long and the final straw was Janella."

"But that was long ago. You must forgive that, Christine."

"I forgive, but I can't forget—" She squared her shoulders. "I may never forget."

Tolani began to pace. "You can't be a good Christian in that way."

"I can't marry Jon." Christine stood and gripped her friend's hand. "I told you everything. You know everything about Jon and me. How can I live with that perversion?"

Tolani frowned. "You haven't forgiven yourself?"

"The sex. The abortions—I'm sure he didn't tell Pastor the whole truth. No pastor who knows the truth would join us." She gave a shaky laugh and rubbed her temple as her headache increased. "Four abortions. I can't ever forget that." She looked at Tolani with teary eyes. "Could I ever even have a child?"

"Don't you see this is the more reason why you two should get mar-ried?"

Christine was laughing and shaking her head and going back to sit all at once, making Tolani to halt her speech. "Jon has the names of all his children. He wants six." She sobered. "If I can't give him, he'll get them elsewhere. He used to chant it."

"But they say that was then. He's a changed man." Tolani moved back to sit with her and took hold of her hands, rubbing them reassuringly. "You need to forgive yourself. Old things are passed away."

"I did. I had. But to marry Jon would be like a dog going back to her vomit. I'll be reneging on what I promised God." She looked at Tolani. "I told Chico everything. That was why he stopped um, touching me."

Tolani gasped. "You told him about the abortions?"

Christine nodded, and sighed. "He thought Jon and I were awful. He didn't speak to me for days." Christine looked heaven-ward, pulled her hands away and ran them through hair that must have experienced this gesture one time too many since the day began. "Then he came back and told me it was settled. We should put it behind us."

"He didn't question your fertility?"

"He did. Said he was scared I would never have a child for him." She laughed again but it turned to a sob before it ended. "Said my lovely face would never be replicated and all—all his money would go to strangers. But he was ready to live with it."

"But he had told so many lies, you know. At least, about the ownership of the ranch." Tolani drew in a long-ragged breath. "You said he's stayed away. Let him be."

"But can't you see, Tolani?" Christine's eyes widened pleadingly. "He was such a man—he he made me feel like a woman without making me feel worthless. He—he made me realise my worth as a woman. Jon never gave me that." She grabbed Tolani's hand and made her look at her face. "Jon preyed on my weakness Chico abhorred it and made me fight it. With Jon I was desperate to please but Chico sought to please me. Can't you see I can never go back to Jon?"

"Let Chico be, please." Tolani freed her hand from Christine's and dragged it over her face. "What a mess. Let him be, abeg. Maybe not Jon, but not Chico either."

"I saw him yesterday in Ibadan, at FODS."

"Why would he go for the meeting?"

Christine sniffed and shrugged. "He never hid his love for Pebble. Whereas Jon felt embarrassed I had a 'sick' sister, he used to say."

"Did he talk to you?"

"I got there late and sat at the back. He left early, that's how I saw him. He didn't see me."

Tolani's face twisted with the struggle to capitulate. "Let him be, Christine, jo, biko, mbok. For the sake of national unity, let him be."

"I love him, Tolani. The more Pastor talked against him, the more I realised it."

CHAPTER THIRTY-THREE

CHICO STEELED HIMSELF, TOOK one last breath, and knocked on the door. It had been so long since he came here. Memories accosted his mind, sending sharp jabs of pain through his flesh. He had not seen her for more than a month. And he'd not realised how much he missed her till now. He would not come. He probably should not have. Easily Ejiro could have delivered the message but he yearned to see her again. So badly, it shocked him.

Precious got the door and Chico's heart skipped a beat. She was beautiful. He pulled her into a tight hug as she screeched his name. How he had missed her. Mammy had wanted to announce his arrival but he pleaded with her not to. He wanted to be in and out as fast as possible. Though the festive season had passed and they had begun to experience the January lull, he wanted to get back to his territory. For him, Christine's house was war-zone.

He'd chosen his day and time carefully. Tuesday, second week in January, midday. He expected to find Precious and her mother at home. Precious, because he had been to her school, and was told she had been stopped by her family from attending. Christine would be in her office.

"Cooking time." Precious announced and pulled him into the house.

He laughed. "Cooking time, Precious. You're great." He took a seat though Precious was trying to drag him out. "This is school time, Precious."

"Mum." Precious ran into the inner part of the house calling to her mother.

Christine and Mum walked out, and Chico stood to greet them. What was she doing here? He experienced an emotional torture and thought he had lost his voice. Christine avoided his gaze and headed for the door without acknowledging him.

"Mum, I'll go and pay the fees right now that I have her passport photo. I'm sorry I delayed. Bye." She waved at Precious.

"Christine." His voice sounded like it belonged to the incredible hulk. She looked at him with dead eyes, flat, emotionless, like she had just sold her soul.

"I came about Precious's school fees as well." He turned to Mum and gave a curt nod. "I was told her family removed her from the school?"

"Yes, Chico." Mum sighed. Pleasantries were lost in the heat of the moment. "Please take a seat. What can I offer you?"

Chico sat in the same place he'd been. "Nothing, thank you."

"Christine?"

"I should be getting back, Mum."

Wendy clasped her hands to her chest. "Please."

Christine sat opposite Chico, putting distance between them. Mum and Precious naturally sat in between.

Chico sat forward. "I was at the school today. To pay the fees—"

Christine looked at him. "Why would you want to pay for Precious? She's not your responsibility."

He returned her glare. "She is my responsibility. In more ways than you can ever imagine."

"She's not. She's my sister—"

Mum held up her hands. "Christine, please. I believe Chico is just being helpful."

"But we don't need his help, Mum. We can cope."

Chico turned to Wendy. "What school is she in now?"

Christine sighed. "It's a good school as well."

"You want to destroy her, don't you?" His eyes burned. "You know very well changing her school is traumatic to her. Meeting new people, adapting, slows down her progress."

"We are doing what we think is best."

He growled. "Mum, you think this is best for Precious? Moving her up and down?"

Christine cut in heatedly. "We're not moving her up and down. She's going back to her former school."

"Back and forth then. You're taking her to that deaf and dumb school where they treat all the kids the same. No special attention, no trained teachers."

"It's the best Ode has."

"We put her in a good, private school, where she can be seen as a normal child and she can learn with normal children, and you saw the progress she made in just a term." He now sat so close to the edge of his seat if he shifted any further, he would land on the floor, but he didn't seem to notice. "Why would you take that away from her? Why?"

"Chico, please. Calm down. So many things have changed in the last few weeks," Wendy said.

Christine hissed. "It's none of his business, Mum. You don't have to explain anything to him."

Chico couldn't understand the coldness. This was not the Christine he knew, loved. He shook his head to visibly remove the thoughts. She was a tough nut. She was acting, playing a role to get rid of him. Their relationship may have ended for a reason she adamantly refused to disclose but he couldn't fathom where this hostility came from.

"Saffron is redesigning the whole house," Mum continued nonetheless. "She's displaced Christine and we may need to move from here soon. She's promised to pay for a place for Precious and I if we have to move but one can't quite depend on that so —"

Christine jerked to her feet. "Mum, I need to get back to my office."

"Christine found a house and paid. And she thinks the fee for Precious' new school is a bit high for her to combine with—"

"Mum!"

Chico snapped. "Christine, would you please sit down?"

"Well, what's your prob—?"

The front door opened and Saffron walked in with a workman in tow. Four pairs of eyes turned to her. She took in the scene all at once. Chico sitting on the edge of the couch, Christine on her feet, Mum sat up and clasping her hands, and Precious, dozing off beside Mum.

"Sorry to break up the party. We want to measure the room." Saffron waved the man into the room.

Chico's face hardened. "Excuse us, we're in a meeting."

Saffron glowered. "It's my house."

Chico lowered his voice. "Tell your man to leave or I'll throw him out."

Saffron yelled. "Excuse me? You should get out of my house, bloody butcher."

Christine stiffened. "Saffron? Why would you talk to him like that?"

Saffron waved the workman into the house again but the young man stood listlessly beside her, glaring at Chico.

Christine retorted. "He's a guest. Please give him that respect."

"He's a dirt butcher who happens to speak English. Mason, measure this room for me if they're not ready to excuse you."

"I will need to move chairs and so on," the mason said.

"Go ahead and do it."

"I will need an assistant if they refuse to leave."

"Go and call one of your boys downstairs." The mason hurried off. "This is my house."

Chico hardly blinked. "I'll give you three seconds to get out, Saffron."

"In my house? Are you mad?"

"Two."

"I'll see you out first. Thrown out—Do you think you're talking to your goats or cows? Christine, please stop bringing animals into my house."

He was so fast. Only Christine knew he could be that fast because she'd seen him in action. When he slew an animal, his reflex was accurate. His hit never missed.

"Three."

In a split second, he was on his feet. He took hold of the back of Saffron's head in a steely grip, his fingers pressed into the sides of her head so that she couldn't wriggle out of his grip. "Apologise to your big sister for being rude to her guest."

Mum clasped her hands over her mouth. Precious sat up and stared.

Christine whimpered. "She's a lady."

Between his teeth, Chico said, "I know."

Saffron's face drained of colour. Her lips drooped and distended like she would cry. Chico agitated his hold and she cried out.

"Apologise," he said in a near-whisper.

"Sorry."

"Mean it."

"I'm sorry, Christine."

"And?"

Tears trickled down Saffron's face. "And—and Mum. And you too. I'm sorry."

Chico knew he was beginning to hurt her. Her face was turning pink. He walked with her to the door and opened it.

"Never ever try me again. And respect those who are older than you."

With that little admonition, he pushed her face against the wall as though to crash it in but stopped an inch before her face connected with the wall. She screamed out of fear just before he flung her out through the door. She staggered but didn't fall.

"You bastard. You won't get away with this," Saffron screamed and ran down the corridor.

Chico breathed in and wondered how he would face the ladies in the room. He had behaved like a real animal. Saffron had been so light in his hand when he grabbed her. He never laid his hand on a woman. Never.

He closed the door and leaned his head against it. "I'm sorry about that."

When no one replied, he turned and faced them. He loved these people. He meant well.

Mum's eyes were full of approval and compassion. "Thank you," she whispered.

"I just got tired of her. I shouldn't have held her like that."

Christine walked slowly to him. "Thank you."

He turned to look at her. "I guess I should leave now. But please, I will pay for Precious. Please. Don't take her out of her school."

She stood in front of him and touched his chest tentatively. He reacted. Stiffened. She traced a line up a path to his face and cupped his cheek. He fluttered, blinked but made no move to encourage or discourage her.

Mum cleared her throat and stood. She opened her mouth to speak, and then closed it, stretched her hand to Precious, who took it and stood too. They both exited quietly.

Christine watched them go, and then moved closer till her waist touched his hip. "I missed you so much." She laid her head on his chest. "Too much."

Chico's arms felt like lead beside him. He wanted to hold her. Her hair was brushed back and uncharacteristically loose, held with colourful pins, so that they stayed away from her face but hung down freely. He felt like burying his fingers in the forest resting on her shoulders.

Instead, he breathed in and found his voice. "Why were you so cold to me? And why are you doing this now?" He stared down at her. She looked up to his face, pleadingly. Her eyes seemed to suck him in. She blinked and then looked down, pressing her forehead on his chest. What was happening to him? "It can't work."

She spun her head up. "It can. I'm sorry. Forgive me. I was confused. Misled."

"By who? Your sisters?" His voice had become gruff and refused to go higher though he tried to raise it. The voice of its own accord remained in a whisper.

"I don't care what anyone think."

"I care."

"Please Chico. Darling."

"I care that you find it difficult to introduce me. I care that the people closest to you detest me. I care that I don't fit in. Fit into your class." He didn't know how or when but his fingers were in her hair, and he tortured himself with the softness and silkiness of it.

"I'm sorry. All that has changed. I want you. Chico—"

"I am a 'bloody butcher'. Your pastor thinks I'm a rogue."

She leaned back and looked at him resolutely. "I love you. I don't care what you are. I want you."

"No, Christine." He stepped away from her, feeling as though he was being torn into two. "No." He turned and walked through the door, without looking back, leaving her soft cries in his wake.

All the way back to the abattoir, he struggled. Go back and stop being a fool, the first voice said. She will get over you, and you will get over her, the second said. On and on, the voices spoke into his head. Yes. No. Yes. No. Yes. No.

He ran into his bathroom, and fully clothed, turned on the shower and stood under it. He didn't check which way it went and only noticed the hot water was scalding after several minutes.

Chico Ode turned off the shower and slid to the floor, his shoulders shook with the weight of his sobs. Only one word endured in his brain.

"Christine. Christine."

It was late before he let himself out of the bathroom. His corduroy and jacket were still damp. He walked to his office and switched on the light. Nothing had changed. But he felt "not right." He sat at his desk and looked at the paperwork he needed to do. Even in the middle of January, forty cows had been slaughtered today. Ten goats, four pigs. He did the summary of the accounts and filed them away. No chicken was sold but interestingly, ninety-eight fish. Four hundred snails. Hmm.

He filed the documents, locked up the cabinets and went back to his seat. There was only one thing to do, if Christine wanted him, then who was he to say no? Her wish was his command. He was in love with her, and that reality shook him to his foundation. He had never thought he could "be in love" with anyone. He pursued goals, and achieved purposes nothing else went into his equation. He would marry Christine because she fitted the speculation for his wife because that was what he wanted. But his theory seemed so wrong now. He had never cried for anything or anyone since the day his father beat him with a butcher's knife when he was eight. He didn't cry for his mother when she died. Nothing made him cry.

Almighty Chico had wept like a child in the bathroom. "I love her. I love Christine. I love Christine."

He picked up his keys and headed out. He had to find her.

CHAPTER THIRTY-FOUR

SAFFRON WAS LIKE A mad woman. Everyone who had seen her throw her tantrums had never seen it so bad. She had soldiers in the house, flinging things from the second-floor rooms Mum and Precious, and now Christine, used. The three huddled together in one corner and stared at her in awe. Nothing they had was valuable in the sight of the plunderers.

Christine had returned from work to find Mum pleading with Saffron to temper justice with mercy.

"Mercy? You sat looking at that animal while he touched me with his filthy hands, didn't you?" Saffron screeched. "Well, pay for it now. And he's not going to get away with it, either." She looked into her mother's eyes. "Go pick whatever you think is good, and leave my house. I don't care where you go."

"What's going on here?" Christine dropped her bag on the centre table and looked at both women.

Saffron lifted her hands up in the air. "Ha ah. Here comes. Go find your hero to save you from me now, will you?" She laughed. "I'll give you the privilege of picking whatever is valuable from here now. Three seconds he gave, right? Well, I'm not a brute. I'll make it ten, after which my men will throw your things out."

"What's wrong with you, Saffron? Why are you such a bitter woman?"

Her voice quaked. "He started from two. I'll start from four."

And there went the counting. After the encounter with Chico, and an emotional trauma, Christine didn't have much strength to argue. She'd cried half of the day, spending as much energy to cry as to hide she was crying. She walked into Precious's room without argument, and began to pack when two men threatened to throw her out through the window if she didn't leave.

That was how they ended up outside, watching their clothes and belongings flung out from the upstairs window.

"She has watched too many foreign films. She's detached from reality," Wendy said.

"Deranged, if you ask me," Christine muttered.

"I can talk to her after the men leave," Mum said quietly.

"We won't be here when the men leave." Christine looked resolved. "I want them to throw as much as they can then we can pack them and leave."

"She'll let us back in when I talk to her."

"Well, Mum, I don't want back in." She walked to the clothes being thrown and folded them neatly. "The house I paid for is being renovated. We can find a hotel tonight and tomorrow, I'll tell the landlord I want to move in right away."

Mum sighed. "I thought you were overreacting when you went for that house. You were right after all."

Christine looked up. Mum usually surrendered with no trouble but of late, she noticed her mother had had opinions about everything. She was a new person. "I told you she had a plan. Something has been eating her for long." Christine chuckled despite herself. "I think Hassan is having an affair."

"Christine!" Then Wendy also giggled. "I think you're right. For the life of her, she can't imagine her husband attracted to anyone else."

Both picked what they could and walked to the road. It was close to 7p.m.

"I think Dad is the reason for her behaviour. All her life, she fought to impress him. He never was. Till he died."

"I'm as much to blame. I was so uninterested in the life I had with your Dad, I just let him get away with whatever he wanted." Wendy patted her hand. "I'm sorry."

Mum hardly ever touched them. Christine knew she was right. She had never been interested in the family. Dad took all the decisions, and many were biased and laden with favouritism. Janella always was his favourite and they all suffered on that account.

"It's okay, Mum." She had fought her own bitterness, allowing the love of God to overshadow all forms of unforgiveness and anger she had toward her wealthy but detached parents.

"Christine?"

"Yes, Mum," she answered absently, looking out for a taxi.

"There's something I must tell you."

It was Wendy's tone that made Christine look at her.

"Yes?"

Mum hesitated for a while but just as Christine was about to prompt her, she spoke. "There's someone. I'm in a relationship." She licked her lips nervously. "Don't murder me, yet, please. I should have told you. He's been asking to be introduced."

"Of course not, Mum. You deserve to be happy." She laughed. "I am happy you're going out. Finally!" She threw her hands up in the air. "You know, I knew. I noticed you were different—laughing, talking, joking."

"No, Christine. You may not be so excited when you know who it is."

"Who cares? I fell in love with a butcher. As long as you're happy." Christine shook her lightly. "Come on, Mum. I'm happy for you."

"Can we go to his house tonight, instead?"

"To go sleep, you mean?" Christine's eyes widened. "You've gotten that intimate, Mum?" She laughed. "Won't he mind?"

Mum looked away, embarrassed. "No, he won't mind."

"Well." Christine shrugged. "Why not? I'd have loved to meet him under better circumstances though."

Chico had never felt so frustrated. He pulled the truck up in its usual spot and just sat in the cab, looking at nothing. It was almost 10p.m. From the ugly scene in Christine's house, he'd gone to the church, then to Tolani's house. And then to Pastor Reubens'.

Pastor Reubens had had the pleasure of telling him Christine could be with her new fiancé, Jon. He'd been directed to Jon's house and despite himself, had gone there. Her phone had ringed several times without answer. At least, she wasn't at Jon's.

Her house had been in a chaos when he got there. None of her sisters or her mother was around. The servants were packing, leaving. Mammy was hysterical and could not say what the matter was. His only option was her office which meant he had to wait till the following morning. What he had to say to her could not wait till the following morning.

He called one unlikely number. A number which still baffled him he could call. Basi Lejoka picked on the fifth ring.

"I need your help."

Ever since Basi showed up over two weeks earlier, everything in his life had turned upside down. Everything he'd invested all his life for was now on a fragile balance. Everything he believed he lived for was about to be taken away even before he could begin to enjoy it.

Basi had voices in the background. "I'm in your house, where are you?"

"I'm coming in."

There were three people in his sitting room. A couple cuddling in the love seat, and Basi. He nodded curtly at Basi, ignoring the couple totally.

"We thought it was better to come here knowing how angry you could be if and when you found out."

"Thanks." Chico dropped into the settee and acknowledged the couple wearily.

Oloye spoke up. His hands lying idly in the crook of Wendy Bello's neck, he raised his head away from hers. "Christine's in the guest room, trying to put Precious to sleep." He looked at the woman beside him. "Wendy couldn't bring herself to do it. She virtually broke down when they walked in." He pressed a gentle kiss on Wendy's forehead.

"How did she take it?" Chico started to massage his temple. This was not his plan at all. Christine wasn't meant to find this out till he'd sorted his thoughts.

"She didn't recognise me at first. They came to the duplex, and she seemed glad her mother was with me."

"Till I told her who he was."

⤜⤜⤜ ⤛⤛⤛

Christine heard voices. One voice she knew as well as hers, and walked toward it. Her head reeled at all she'd experienced since the day started with Chico's visit, Saffron revenge and Mum's—relationship.

"I think she was more shocked at the transformation." Oloye chuckled. "After all, she'd never seen me looking sane. All shaved up."

Chico snickered. "I guess it's proper to go and see her."

He turned toward the guest room but stopped short when he saw Christine standing in the connecting door, her arms dangling awkwardly beside her.

"My mum and your grandfather." She looked at him accusatorily. "You knew when you came this morning, didn't you?"

"I did." He shook his head. "But I was just as shocked. Especially because their relationship jeopardised ours. It's the main reason I thought we didn't have a chance together."

"She hasn't eaten since." Mum said weakly. "Chico please get something for her."

Oloye patted her hand with tenderness thick enough to cut. "Wendy. You worry too much. She's an adult and Chico is here to take care of her."

Christine walked fully into the room and found a seat, which she lowered herself into. "I would appreciate some explanations here." She turned to Wendy. "Mum?"

Chico cleared his throat. "It's a long story—"

Oloye cut in. "It started when Chico's grandmother got pregnant for me. I was only nineteen. She was sixteen. We were so much in love, it didn't matter that we were so young. I was a young butcher boy but I paid her dowry. She gave birth to Chico's mother but died having a second baby two years later. I was devastated.

"At twenty-one, I swore never to love again, and threw myself into raising my daughter. This abattoir did not exist then. The one we used became too small and we decided to get this place from government. There were three of us. Myself, Egun, and Laditi.

"Laditi is my father," Basi Lejoka said.

Christine looked at the flashy man. "I see." No one had thought to introduce him but at least, she now knew he was part of the abattoir family.

"But Egun was full of wine. He died not long after Laditi gave birth to Basi." Oloye waved at him.

Christine frowned. "Basi?"

"We were not introduced." He extended his hand. "I'm Basi Lejoka."

Christine flew to her feet. "You own Ode Abattoir?" She flushed. This was Chico's boss?

Chico wrinkled his nose. "Own? Basi?"

"But you told me you own this abattoir."

"I do." Chico smirked. "Why do you think Basi owns it."

She slumped into her seat. Wendy gesticulated with a wave of her hand. "Calm down. Let's hear the story."

"Anyway, we were two hardworking men. Laditi ends up having ten children from three wives. I remained alone. Then my sweet daughter, at the age of fifteen gets pregnant for Usmani, Chico's father. My heart broke a second time but I had no option than to allow her marry him. Everyone knew Usmani to be mean-spirited. And he was so much older than her."

Chico blanched. "He gave me his name which I swore would not follow me to adulthood."

"Several times my daughter lost pregnancy after pregnancy due to his brutality. He would beat her black and blue during pregnancy, she would lose the baby and then he would complain she was barren." Oloye sighed. "Several times, I was tempted to kill him."

"She suffered a great deal in his hands." Chico looked at Christine with so much hurt in his eyes. "One day she slept and never woke up. I think the doctors said she had a heart attack or something."

"That was when I vowed I didn't deserve to see the sun anymore. I ran into the bush and hid for years—"

Basi sat forward. "One day, my father, Chico and I came to look for him. You see, over the years, he had amassed a lot of wealth. Chico needed the money."

"Our bait was the news that my father had died. Run over by a mad cow in broad daylight. Oloye should be pleased to hear this and return to normalcy. He didn't," Chico said. "That was the day we entered our agreement."

"Before then, I had met Oloye. He supplied meat to us on several occasions," Wendy smiled at him.

Oloye looked at Christine. "I fell in love with your mother at first sight—but she was a no-go. She was married."

Wendy giggled. "We attended the same church, but we were not so acquainted. I didn't know about his crush on me."

Christine rolled her eyes. "I bet my father thought it was beneath him to be seen socialising with the man who sells him meat."

"You knew your father well," Oloye said. "I didn't want a relationship with him either because being close to the family, to Wendy would have been temptation too much to handle."

Christine looked at Chico. "And the agreement?"

"Yes," Chico said. "Laditi had messed himself up with the multiple wives. He was so broke he decided to sell his share of the property to Oloye."

"I allowed him to live on the ranch free though," Oloye said.

Basi smiled. "But Oloye loved me like a son. And when I told him I wanted to have a separate life outside the ranch, he sent me to Lagos to study. What a relief. My mother and father's wives had made life unbearable with their fights."

"I wanted to work the land. I wanted to succeed where my father had failed. That was the only passion I had," Chico said. "Oloye was ready to send me to school but I wanted to be here, so I home-schooled. I taught myself everything."

Oloye nodded. "He didn't want the lifestyle that arose from being wealthy. I didn't want a life at all. Basi was in Lagos, doing well. We decided to let him have the life. He was a shareholder anyway, though his father had sold his shares, I gave them back to him, half the value. I gave all of mine to Chico, and retained the same value as Basi."

Chico elaborated. "Ten percent each."

"The details are complex. I traded in stocks in Lagos so I was using the money from here to trade, and it's been so enriching," Basi said. "And I was paraded as the 'owner' of Ode Abattoir at several quarters to protect Chico. Yet, I took my orders from Chico."

"Even I took orders from Chico." Oloye winked, and everyone laughed.

Christine didn't find the roller-coaster her life seemed to have become funny. "So how did Mum come back in the picture?"

"You are the reason. The few times you visited I discovered you were Wendy's daughter. And that your dad had died. It took me so many months to build the courage but I had to. It meant coming back to a society I had shunned. Living like a normal human being again. But I had to try."

"Once he made up his mind, he tells no one, but sends for me. Then he sneaks up on me in my house which is his own, up on the other side of the ranch, and asks for a shave." Basi laughed. "Next thing I know, we're shopping for clothes and Papa is chasing a woman twenty years younger."

Oloye patted Wendy's cheek fondly. "She's not complaining, is she?"

"I have never been in love, never been courted. He came on to me very strongly. I didn't even think twice about it." She gave Oloye a sweet smile before turning to Christine. "Christine dear, you remember that Sunday I was away all day?"

"My goodness!" Christine smiled for the first time. "I feel so over-whelmed. All these stories."

"I should get you something to eat, and then you can rest." Chico stood up but she waved him down.

"I can't eat, thank you." Christine sighed heavily. "So, are you getting married or what?"

"Eventually."

There was an uneasy silence.

"I want to marry you, Christine. Since that Sunday when I got home and I saw Basi waiting for me, I haven't slept well." Chico stood and went to crouch in front of her. "Oloye was with him, all cleaned up, and looking randy." Chico arched his gaze toward the couple for a brief moment. "Your Mum and Precious were there as well." He reached out and held her hands in his. She let him. "I'd been thinking of coming to find you, beg you, coax you, do anything to make you accept me. And all that shot to hell. I kept thinking, Oloye would marry her, and then I would not be able to marry her daughter."

"That is old wives' fables." Oloye stood and stretched. "You have your life, I have mine. And don't go pulling you-are-your-own-grandpa on me."

He looked none of his sixty-eight years. Despite eighteen years in the wild, he had aged well. Apart from his eyebrow and eyelashes, there was no other facial hair, or head-hair, striking a strong resemblance with his grandson, though Chico started growing his hair again. He was an inch or so shorter, stockier, and slightly darker in complexion but he aged well, and his biceps were firm and well-toned. The rugged handsomeness was common to both kinsmen.

"Sweetheart, you need to rest." Oloye reached out and Wendy took his hand, lifting her weight up at his expense.

She naturally fell into his arms, slightly shorter than him. Christine had always been the shortest in the family a trait everyone attributed to her French grandmother.

Christine's gaze shot to them. "Are we leaving?"

Oloye and Mum exchanged a glance but it was Basi who spoke. "We are leaving."

"But I can't—"

Chico's voice was rough but low. "It won't be fair to wake Precious, and you can share her room.

He remembered the last time she stayed in his house.

Wendy looked at Basi. "You'll be fine and your things—?"

"I'll bring them right away. It's less than ten minutes' drive."

"That reminds me," Oloye said and headed for the door. "I need two cars. Basi, you'll do well to arrange that." Mum did a quick wave and blew the two a surprising kiss.

"Two cars?" Basi threw a salute to them and followed.

"Wendy and I." Oloye said. "You two, be good." He waved at Chico and Christine and promptly continued what he was saying. "You'll have to ask Wendy what brand she wants but I'll need a driver and a Volvo. Whatever Volvo they're driving these days and—" His voice faded as he exited the door.

There was a long silence.

"I thought they both took orders from you," Christine murmured. "Do you approve the cars?"

Chico laughed and sat on the floor facing her. "Oloye takes orders from no one. As for the cars, he has his own money."

"So, my pastor was right to say Basi owns the ranch."

"No." He snickered. "How many lies did your pastor tell you about me?"

"That you make half a million bucks a day?"

He grimaced. "Really? I told him I make half the amount."

"Do you?"

"A quarter, yeah. Approximately."

She exhaled. "Pastor wanted me to get back with Jon—"

He slapped his thigh. "No."

"Yes," she whispered. "He thought Jon will take better care of me. He hasn't spoken to me since I stood up to him." Christine closed her eyes. It hurt that her pastor treated her in this way. "He was the reason I broke up with you, returned the car you gave me."

"I couldn't have guessed."

Christine licked her lips. "He has told me he won't be at our wedding if I decide to marry you."

He tilted his head to one side. "I don't like your pastor." They both laughed. "But I guess he's protecting you the way he understands."

Christine didn't think so. "Picking Jon over you?"

Pastor Reubens didn't give Chico a chance and probably never would. She gazed at the man she loved. For him to give her pastor a benefit of the doubt was so sweet. It was one of the reasons she'd chosen him over anything anyone had to say.

"I work the ranch. I own the ranch." He cupped her cheeks. "I just don't like to be seen as the owner. Basi fronts for me. And he likes that job as well."

"I see. Hmm."

"I hope this settles the matter."

"It does. I believe you."

He took her hand in his. "I want Precious to live with us."

She gasped at his sudden switch. "Pebble? Why on earth would—"

"Precious. You must get used to her name."

"Sorry. Just shocked. Mum won't agree—"

"She agreed."

"She did?"

"Yes." He bent over her hand and planted a kiss. "Do you?"

"Of course. I'll love to care for her. She's my sister."

Another extended silence.

He moaned. "What are you thinking?"

"Everything. Mum, Oloye. Saffron, Basi, Pastor. Me, with you."

"A bloody butcher?"

She snickered.

And another long silence.

She idly scratched his scalp. "What are you thinking?"

He turned his back to her and leaned his head on her knee. Then he closed his eyes and drew in a deep breath. "Nothing. Just loving the peace around me. Loving you."

She slid her right hand down, brushing his scalp and ear. He caught the hand with his left and took it to his lips, planting a soft kiss in her palm before holding the hand to his chest.

"I love you, Christine. I'll marry you."

She leaned forward till her chin was on the crown of his head, and closed her eyes as well. "I love you, Usmani. I'll marry you," she whispered.

EPILOGUE

"T HAT'S THE CATTLE AND sheep preparation line. And over there is the cattle bleeding and preparation line. Here we have the splitting station. The other corridor leads to the tripe cleaning room. You see the lines and conveyors there. Those are twin rail tracks and the hooks. The saws, stunners, and splitters are still in storage. The offices are at the back.

"The poultry and pig sections are still being installed. Oh, and the fishery as well. We got a section for meat processing and the cutting machines have arrived. We're still expecting the mincers, mixers, and some other equipment for roasting—"

"Roasting?"

"Yes. We plan to make sausages, bacon, and other things. If a customer wants his meat prepared, we will be able to do it. We hope to serve the state at large. We also have packing machines, and trolleys, knife disinfection and other hygiene facility."

Tolani balanced her hand on her bulging stomach and pressed her face against the glass pane. "I am so impressed," she murmured.

The slab areas had been demolished and a modern slaughter house constructed in its place. The huge pieces of equipment were already installed but none had been used yet.

She turned away from the impressive stainless machines, and continued to walk down the passage way. The guide had refused to open the door to the areas where the machines were and they had to look through the glass from the straight passage way. After the slaughter area was the shop. The stalls were equipped with shelves and glass cabinets for display of wares. The guide, an Asian who spoke perfect English, gave a small bow at the end of the tour and excused the ladies.

Ever since the storage facility had been installed at the Ode Abattoir, many other things had followed. The abattoir had gone through an amazing transformation which attracted government and private investors.

Tolani stepped out into the bright sunshine and looked toward the only remaining slab. Chico had stubbornly insisted one stayed close to his office. In the days during the demolition and reconstruction of Ode Abattoir, that slab had been used for a lot of the work. With storage, it had been easy to work at all hours.

"It's amazing. I didn't expect anything like this," Tolani said.

Christine who was also heavily pregnant, smiled. They walked slowly back the way they'd come, toward Chico's office. "I told you to come round ever since."

"Half of the time I was sick, and so were you." They both laughed. "What happens to the butchers now?"

"Many of them left for other abattoirs but others were trained to use the equipment."

"So many! There's nothing like this anywhere in the country."

"No, nothing like it. Governor Rufus is getting the president to come for the commissioning in a month's time. I'm glad I'll still have a few weeks to delivery!"

"Oh, me too!" They looked at each other and shared a wink. "We may deliver the same day."

"I'm just so grateful to God to be a part of this." Christine drew in a satisfactory breath. "The first year of our marriage went into it."

"But it is worth the sacrifice."

"Every second of it." Christine nodded profusely. "Getting the approval was the first hurdle. And after that, the partnership that provided the funds."

"How much of it belongs to Chico?"

"He emptied his life savings for this. Of course, Basi and Oloye are shareholders and the state government crashed in at the end—"

"You don't seem too happy—"

"I'm quite pleased, on the contrary. Chico has controlling shares!"

"Wow! That's really great. I'm so happy for you, Christine. Look at you, so radiant." Tolani yanked her into a tight hug and they both laughed. "I can't wait to get Toke's daddy to come and see this place."

"Thanks. I'm happy for Chico. He's worked so hard. And I'm happy for me too!"

"How's your Mum now?" Tolani winked. "It's been so long, since that day of reckoning?!"

Christine shook her head. "Three whole years. Mum is fine. Oloye treats her like a queen. You know, they got married before Chico and me! And they've been travelling the world." Christine rubbed her stomach absently. "We even went to France to see her mum, you know. She'd not seen her in more than twenty years. Refused to attend her father's burial—"

"What? Twenty years?"

"Or more. She was upset with her mum for letting my dad marry her. It was a very emotional reunion."

"Wow. Her mum must be very old now."

"Not quite. I was shocked her mum was still so strong. She's seventy-seven now."

"Wow. So Mum and Oloye? Still unbelievable."

"Hmm. They cuddle like love struck teenagers. They couldn't wait to have each other." The two friends giggled.

"And your sisters? I saw Janella the other day—"

"I haven't seen them in forever. How was she?"

"Fat but still pretty as ever. I asked if she was pregnant and she said no. Maybe she just had a baby though she didn't say."

"You guys chatted?"

"Yeah for a while. We met at the market."

"Market? Or mall."

Tolani laughed. "Market. She said she wasn't staying with Saffron any more. Ayo fell out with Saffron and your little sister threw them out so now she lives in the navy barracks and goes to the market."

"That must be hard for Janella. She's never worked before, never done anything for herself. It's all been by one servant or the other, or dad, or mum, or me!" She sighed heavily. "Huh, Saffron! Mammy left as well, and now stays with Mum. All the servants left. She must be sad, alone with Hassan!" Christine frowned. "I feel bad. I didn't do enough—"

"There you go! You had little choice."

"I haven't seen either of them since that day we left the house!" Christine sighed. "Chico saw Saffron at the mall about seven months ago. I just took in and was craving for apples, and the mall was about to close. He was in a hurry. He didn't stop to say hi."

"I'm sure she didn't expect him to. You could check them out though. I'm sure Janella would feel grateful."

"The family is torn apart," Christine moaned.

"How's Precious?"

"Doing very well. Her cooking skill is so good now she could cater for a party!" Tolani gasped and Christine laughed. "Nah, just joking. But she's more self-dependent and confident."

"Thank God for that!"

They got to the office and went in. Tolani moved to stand at the reflexive window that overlooked the lone slab. Chico was on it, hitting with precision on the remains of what must have been a huge animal. He looked up briefly and smiled as though he sensed she was there. Sweat dropped from his head and slid into his thick eyebrows. He continued with his work, throwing some form of order at one of the boys waiting on him. The boy ran off to do his bidding.

"Would he ever get used to all this technology?"

Christine wobbled to stand beside her and watched her husband. "He can't wait to have all this. Technology." She turned to Tolani and smiled at her only friend. "He's been dreaming of a day when his profession would look more honourable. When his hands would touch less blood.

She waved her hands in the air. "When he would have all this."

The End

ACKNOWLEDGMENTS

Sincere thanks to Dr. Mrs. Imabong Mbre Inyang, Chima Ogbonna, Sub. Lt. Grace Somuyiwa (Mrs.), my dear husband, Afolarin Ogúnyin-ka, and daughter, Ifeoluwa Ogúnyinka for the editing, critic, and advice given on this book. God bless you all.

ARE YOU SAVED?

All that is written in this book may not be of much use to you if you haven't yet given your life to Christ. We cannot take difficult decisions unless we have the Righteous and Wise One that is greater than the devil to help and choose for us. The Bible says that greater is He that is in us, than He that is in the world I John 4:4. And we wrestle not against flesh and blood but against principalities, against powers, against the rulers of the darkness of this world, against spiritual wickedness in high places Ephesians 6:12.

This is why I want to encourage you to take this important decision if you haven't yet given your life to Christ. I took this decision over thirty years ago and I haven't regretted it even for one day. Please pray this prayer of faith if you are willing to surrender your life to God:

Lord Jesus, I honour you. I praise you and I acknowledge you that you are Lord. I know I am a sinner and I ask that you forgive me all my sins. I want you to be my Lord and personal Saviour. Wash me clean and give me grace to serve you wholly from now on. Come into my heart to reign supreme. In Jesus' name I pray. Amen.

Praise God, you are born again.

Now that you have prayed this prayer of faith, I admonish you to:

•   Get a Bible, and read it every day (Start from the first four books of the New testament to familiarize yourself more with your new Commander-in-Chief, Jesus Christ)

•   Pray every day.

•   Attend a Living Church

•   Introduce yourself to the Pastor and seek further teaching (you can join the foundation class and activity group in church – you are hence making yourself available to work for God)

•   Tell others about your salvation.

May God help you in Jesus' name. Amen.

THE NIGERIAN CHILD – MY VISION

Hab. 2:2 Then the LORD answered me and said: "Write the vision And make it plain on tablets, That he may run who reads it.

More than before, it's time for the well-to-do to cater to the less privileged. Over the past few years, the Lord has laid this burden for THE NIGERIAN CHILD on my heart and I believe it's time to spread the vision. I have the desire to help and to instigate help for THE NIGERIAN CHILD. There are currently five areas of help I have been able to identify.

1.   THE MARKET-SCHOOL PROJECT: this vision is aimed at eradicating street and market hawking in the long run. The strategy is to erect schools in market places where children hawking can take a few hours out to learn and then go back to their jobs. It is a long-term project and a highly capital-intensive one.

2.   THE BREAD AND MILK PROJECT: bread and milk will be given in the morning time to children trekking to school just before school resumes. It can be done once a month, once a week or every day. Or as rampantly as the provision is available. It is not very capital intensive and as little as N50 or $0.35 (US dollar) can feed a child with bread and warm milk

3.   THE UMBRELLA PROJECT: to help alleviate

the suffering of children who hawk on the streets (while we work towards eradicating hawking on our streets), by providing umbrellas, especially during the rainy season. The umbrellas can also be useful during scorching hot weather. Umbrellas of different sizes will be given depending on the size of the child. Prices of umbrellas range from N1 350.00 to N1500.00 or $2.50 to $3.50 (US dollar).

4.   THE SORT-A-CHILD PROJECT: This is aimed at helping at least one child in whatever capacity you can. It can be by paying a sick child's hospital bills, buying food and clothing for a child or paying a child's school fees. It can be as long as a lifetime commitment or a one-time affair.

5.   THE STUDENT CARE PROJECT: for secondary and tertiary students who can't afford their school fees. The idea is to help through the bob-a-job initiative.

THE NIGERIAN CHILD vision is not another non-governmental, money-spinning organisation. It is a service to God and provision for THE NIGERIAN CHILD. It can be done privately or corporately. The important thing is to help a NIGERIAN CHILD.

I beg to challenge EVERY CHURCH IN NIGERIA to adopt the SORT-A-CHILD PROJECT or as the Lord lay it on our hearts.

HELP!

Signed - THE NIGERIAN CHILD

Also by the Author

SISTER
MINISTER
STRENGTH OF CHARACTER (Devotional & Workbook for Sister Minister)
52 WAYS TO PROVOKE GOD (Devotional)
THE DEVIL LIED

TRUE DREAM SERIES:
DUMPED
YOUR WISH IS MINE
EVEN THE LAWFUL CAPTIVE
HE TAKETH THE FIRST
THE OTHER SISTER
WHAT'S GOOD FOR THE GOOSE
SHATTERED
SCATTERED
IYKE'S REVENGE
ÌKA
BATTERED

NOVELS:
SCENT OF WATER

PEPPER
FRAIL FLESH
THE DAYS AFTER THAT NIGHT

WISDOM SERIES:
WISDOM FOR MEN
WISDOM FOR PASTORS
WISDOM FOR WOMEN
WISDOM FOR STAYING MARRIED

ISSUES OF LIFE SERIES (CO-AUTHORED WITH AFOLARIN OGÚNYINKA):
SOMEBODY HELP! SHE LOVES MY HUSBAND
SOMEBODY HELP! HE LOVES MY WIFE
SOMEBODY HELP! I'M IN LOVE

REVELATION SERIES:
CHOICE

EIBA FAMILY SAGA:
TO WHERE THE WIND BLEW
PROMISE TOMORROW
TILL DAY BREAKS